"CHIEF BILI, BEWARE!"

The cat-brother's call came only moments before a creature of ultimate terror poked its huge snout into the vale, flicking a forked tongue as long as a lance shaft before it! The scales which covered every visible inch of its thick body shone the color of blued steel. The one eye Bili could see was as big as a lancer's targe. Thick as tree trunks were the legs thrusting out from that immense body.

Sighting the knot of horsemen, the beast began to move faster, and Bili, seeing that there was no way to retreat, urged his big black stallion forward to meet this nightmare threat. And just when it seemed to the breathless watchers that their leader would surely ride directly into those cruel, tooth-studded jaws, the black stallion came to a sudden halt. Whirling his thirteen-pound weapon round his head, Bili let go the steel shaft and sent the axe tumbling end over end, praying his aim was true—for at this distance there would be no second chance. . . .

The
DEATH
of a
Legend

A Horseclans Novel

by

Robert Adams

Ⓞ
A SIGNET BOOK
NEW AMERICAN LIBRARY

Copyright © 1981 by Robert Adams

SIGNET TRADEMARK REG. U.S. PAT. OFF. AND FOREIGN COUNTRIES
REGISTERED TRADEMARK—MARCA REGISTRADA
HECHO EN CHICAGO, U.S.A.

SIGNET, SIGNET CLASSIC, MENTOR, PLUME, MERIDIAN AND NAL
BOOKS are published by New American Library,
1633 Broadway, New York, New York 10019

FIRST PRINTING, NOVEMBER, 1981

6 7 8 9 10 11 12 13 14

PRINTED IN THE UNITED STATES OF AMERICA

This, the eighth book of THE HORSECLANS, is dedicated to:

Ramsay Campbell, past master of horror; Mildred Downey Broxon, a bubbly lady whose talents extend into far more than just writing;

Three of the few, extant dinosaurs—Nelson Slade Bond, Manly Wade Wellman and George O. Smith;

Jack Chalker, Eva and the Cheese Hound; and to The Frog, The Rabbit, The Beast, The Ferret and Mojo.

Prologue

The gray dawn had crept upon the stillness of the morning, its meager light reflected from the heavy, icy dew bedecking trees and leas and croplands of the Principate of Karaleenos. Slowly, grudgingly, the river mist—thick as bean soup and the unappealing color of dingy cotton bolls—began to clear from about the walls of the city which sprawled along the south bank of a swift-flowing river.

Over the last of the rolling, northerly hills, a dozen cloaked and hooded riders urged tired horses along the Traderoad toward the bridge that led to that city. Ease of movement for traders was the reason for the road's existence and maintenance, but the small, mounted party was not made up of traders.

A sharp-eyed sentry atop the stone watchtower guarding the northern end of the bridge easily spotted the telltale signs— erect lances, bowcases and quivers now covered with waxed leather against the wet and mist, the unmistakable posture of veteran cavalrymen—and a quick word from him to those in the room below brought a bugler up the ladder to hurriedly blare two staccato signal calls.

In the lower levels of the tower, the inner shutters were opened, letting in blasts of cold, damp air but giving the bowmen behind the slits a deadly and overlapping coverage of the approaches to and the passage past the stronghold.

From the south bank of the river, another bugle answered the first and, shortly, a distant but resounding clang told that the massive iron-sheathed oaken portcullis now most effectively barred easy entrance to the ancient city of Karaleenopolis. Once the winter capital of kings, it was now the seat of the Prince of Karaleenos, who ruled the former kingdom as the local satrap of the High Lord of the Confederation of Eastern Peoples.

As the small cavalcade neared the outer fortification, the lead rider threw back the hood of his travel cloak, unbuck-

1

led and then removed the helmet beneath it, baring his close-cropped, blondish hair and fair-skinned but weather-bronzed face.

The grizzled sentry turned to the bugler and the noncom who had come up to join them. "Best blow the 'Let Pass,' lad. That bareheaded one, he be the Undying Lord Tim Vawn, commander of the Army of the West. I sojered with him fer near thirty years, and he don't like waiting, as I r'call."

Within the massive fortress-palace, core of the citadel around which the city had been built, in a circular tower-chamber before a blazing fire of resinous pine logs, a man and two women sat at ease on low, padded couches. Atop a round table between them were small ewers of several wines, decanters of brandy and cordials, pipes and tobacco and a large bowl of unshelled nuts. They had been there throughout the night, and the wan light of the new day showed layer upon layer of bluish tobacco smoke filling those parts of the chamber where the hearthfire's draft could not pull it up the chimney.

Although the two women were very different—the one a very fair, blue-eyed blonde, the other of a light-olive skin tone, with eyes as sloe-black as her long, thick hair—they appeared to be about of an age, somewhere between twenty-five and thirty years. But appearance was, in their highly unusual case, deceiving in the extreme; the blonde, the Undying Lady Giliahna Vawn, was seventy-six, while the black-haired woman, Neeka Morai, was nearing eighty.

The man who sat with them differed only in degree of age-lessness. Where not darkened by sun and weather, his skin was darker than Giliahna's though lighter than Neeka's. So long as there had been a Confederation, the Undying High Lord Milo Morai had been its ruler—over three hundred years now.

Save for his rich attire, he could have—and often had—passed unnoticed on any street of any city in his domains. His glossy black hair was stippled here and there with errant strands of white and had gone a uniform silver at the temples, but his body seemed hale and fit, his movements strong and sure. He had appeared just so for nearly a thousand years.

Placing a sun-browned hand before her pale-pink lips, the blonde yawned cavernously, and the dark woman spoke. "Why don't you get some sleep, Gil. You know one of us will mindcall if . . . well, if you're needed. Our bodies need sleep just as much as any human one does, so go on up to bed."

"No, not alone." The fair woman shook her head decisively, picked up her small, bejeweled pipe and began to clean its bowl, leaning far to the side to tap the loosened residues into the ashes on the hearth. "Tim will arrive today. He may be on the bridge this very minute, and I mean to be up to greet him."

Milo said, his dark eyes narrowing, "Wishfulness, Gil . . . or another instance of *knowing?*"

She shrugged. "Frankly, Milo, I don't know. It's pure hell to have abilities you can't control. All I know is that last night I just suddenly realized that Tim *would* be here today, early."

She paused to blow through the stem of the pipe, then reiterated, "So I'll take my sleep when he has come . . . with him."

Milo chuckled and selected a brace of nuts from the bowl. "And scant sleep the two of you will have. You forget, I was at Theesispolis three years ago when he came back from the west. I just thank Sun and Wind that you two are what you are. The hearts of mortals would never have held out against such punishment. I've little doubt that a protracted session like that first two weeks or so would've put to shame a pair of minks."

The blond woman flushed but retained her small smile, which suddenly blossomed fully as, with a creaking of leather, a jingle of spurs and the clank and ring of fine steel armor, footsteps were heard upon the stairway which led up to this eyrie.

CHAPTER I

His name was Bili Morguhn. His place of birth had been The Duchy of Morguhn, and the time of that birthing was almost a century agone. His sire had been Hwahruhn, *Thoheeks* and Chief of Clan Morguhn, his mother Mahrnee of Zuhnburk, a daughter of the Duke of Zuhnburk. Bili, too, had held the lands and titles of his patrimony before he had been elevated to *ahrkeethoheeks* for a while and, finally, to his present rank and station—Prince of Karaleenos.

With his assumption of the exalted position and title, he had had to divest himself of the chieftaincy of his clan. His clansmen had then elected his younger brother, Djaik, to succeed him, and Chief Djaik's grandson was now Morguhn of Morguhn.

During his fifty years as Prince of Karaleenos, Bili had ruled wisely and well, and, as he had not finally been persuaded to quit his familiar and comfortable seat until his forty-ninth year, he had also outlived almost all his contemporaries.

But death comes, soon or late, to all mortal men and women, and in his great, canopied bed within his princely bedchamber, Bili lay dying—coming at last to the end of that long, long road on which he had taken his first, hesitant footsteps more than ninety-nine years now past in far-off Morguhn.

Yet as short a time as three months before, he had been healthier and more vital than many a man of far less advanced years. Disdaining litter or carriage and forking a big white saddle mule upon streets or roads and his coal-black hunter—Mahvros was the name that he and each of his predecessors had borne, all being direct descendants of the great black warhorse who had borne Bili down from his war training in the Middle Kingdoms to the north—in wood and field and lea.

Bili the Axe—as he had been known in his youth—had

been a man of action all his long life, and, with cares of state and weighty responsibilities so hampering him that he no longer had the time or leave to go a-warring, he had grudgingly forsaken warhorses and prairiecats for hounds and hawks, discharging his immense energies in the chase.

When more than four score and ten, Prince Bili had taken a four-hundred-pound boar upon his spear and had held the deadly creature thus impaled until the pack and other hunters had arrived to kill it. The singular feat had been the talk of all the principality for near a year and had added new luster to the legend that Bili had lived.

But Bili would ride and hunt no more, nor would he live much longer.

The bear had come down the river valley from the mountains to the west during last winter's extremely hard weather. He had lived well and avoided the proximity of man through spring and summer, but with the onset of autumn, he had somehow, somewhere, acquired a fondness for mutton, nor had he stuck at the killing or maiming of the dogs and men who guarded their beasts.

Bili had heard the complaints, organized and joyfully led out the hunt, behind a pack of specially imported Ahrmehnee bear hounds.

But the bear—all abristle with arrows, claws and jaws clotted with dusty gore, little eyes agleam with bloodlust, with those of the pack of hounds still able to hobble all snarling and snapping at his heels and flanks—had come in low, under Bili's spear, and had savaged the old man terribly before the hounds had pulled him down with Bili's hastily drawn hanger hilt-deep in his furry body.

With many a doleful lamentation, the hunt had borne the prince back to his city, none of them believing at the start of the journey that Bili would be alive at its end. But he was.

His Zahrtohgahn physician, Master Ahkmehd, had first hypnotized the prince, then he and his apprentice had worked long and skillfully on the horribly wounded nobleman. But their patient had never really recovered. Despite their best efforts, infections had set into the jagged wounds, the brittle, shattered bones had failed to mend properly, and, when last the physician had dosed the prince with drugs to ease his pain, he had had no choice but to inform all who asked that the legendary Bili the Axe would most likely be dead by nightfall.

Bili himself had had no need to be told. Poor old Master

Ahkmehd's obvious sorrow—for they two had been close friends of many years' standing—had been sufficient. As the waves of agony slowly ebbed in the face of the drugs, the Prince of Karaleenos wrinkled his canted nose at the stench of suppuration arising from the torn and deeply gouged muscles and flesh of his arms and shoulders and torso.

Despite the expected wave of sickeningly intense pain which overrode the strong drugs, Bili raised his left arm to where he could see the hand and wrist below the bandages. In the light of the candles, all the wrinkled flesh appeared to be as livid as the face of a corpse, and to the fingers of his questing right hand, those of his left felt ice-cold.

The old man bared his worn yellow teeth in a grimace. A warrior, he knew the signs; the fearsome black rot was well entrenched in his left arm. Amputation at the elbow or, better yet, the shoulder, might . . . *might* halt its insidious spread, but who could say for sure and who could say that the same deadly complication would not soon affect the other arm or one or both of the legs.

"No," he muttered to himself, "Sacred Sun has granted me almost twice as many years as most men live, and I'll not let them further butcher this body that has served me so well, simply to linger on a few more months or years as a cripple. If the pain gets too much for the drugs, I'll use my dirk, but I'll go to my pyre a whole man."

Slowly, as the drugs dulled not just the pain but his consciousness as well, he relaxed, and his half-dreaming mind journeyed far, far back, more than seventy years in time.

Taking a fresh grip on the haft of his mighty axe, Bili mindspoke his huge black warhorse, Mahvros, "Now, brother mine, now we fight."

With Bili and a knot of heavily armed nobles at the point, the squadron of mounted Freefighters crested the wooded hill and swept down the brushy, precipitous slope at a jarring gallop. Naturally a few horses fell, but only a few, and as they reached level ground, *Komees* Hari Daiviz of Morguhn's wing moved to the left to take the unruly mob of foemen in the rear.

Unconsciously, Bili tightened his thigh muscles, firming his seat and crowding his buttocks against the high cantle of his warkak, while bending over the armored neck of the thundering black and extending his axe in his strong right arm, the

sharp spike at the business end of the haft glinting evilly in
the pale light.

Then, they struck!

The big, heavy, war-trained destriers sent ponies tumbling
like ninepins, and the well-armed, steel-sheathed nobles and
Freefighters wreaked a fearful carnage among the unarmored
and all but defenseless horde of shaggy barbarians. The be-
leaguered lines of Ahrmehnee and Moon Maidens could only
stand in wide-eyed wonder at this eleventh-hour deliverance
from what would surely and shortly have been their last
battle.

A red-bearded headhunter heeled a tattoo on his pony's
ribs and directed the beast at Bili; he jabbed furiously with
his crude spear, but the soft-iron point bent against the
Pitzburk plate and Bili's massive axe severed the spear arm,
cleanly, at the shoulder.

Screaming a shrill equine challenge, Mahvros reared above
a pony and rider and came down upon them, steel-shod
hooves flailing. Gelatinous globs of bloody brain spurted
from the shattered skull of the man, and the pony collapsed
under the unbearable weight, whereupon Mahvros stove in its
ribs.

It was a battle wherein living men were ahorse; those not
mounted—noble, Freefighter or barbarian—were speedily
pounded into the bloodsoaked ground.

The shaggy men fell like ripe grain, most of their weapons
proving almost useless when pitted against fine modern
platearmor and only slightly more effective when employed
against the scale-armored Freefighters. To counter blows and
thrusts of broadsword and saber, axe and lance, mace and
warhammer, the primitive wickerwork targets offered little
more protection than did the furs and hides and ragged,
homespun clothing.

But though the shaggy men died in droves, it seemed to
Bili that there were always more and yet more appearing before him, behind him, to either side of him, jabbing spears,
beating on his plate with light axes, with crude blades and
with wooden clubs. He felt that he had been fighting, been
slaying, been swinging his ever heavier axe for centuries.

Then, abruptly, he was alone, with none before him or to
either side. At a flicker of movement from his right, he
twisted in his sweaty saddle, once more whirling up his gore-
clotted axe. But it was only a limping, riderless pony which

was hobbling as fast as it could go from that murderous melee, eyes rolling whitely and nostrils dilated.

Bili slowly lowered his axe and relaxed for a brief moment, slumped in his saddle, drawing long, gasping, shuddery breaths. Beneath his three-quarter armor, the padded-leather gambeson and his small clothes, his body seemed to be only a single long, dull ache, with here and there sharper pains that told the tale of strained muscles, while his head throbbed its resentment of so many clanging blows upon and against the protecting helm. Running his parched tongue over his lips, he could taste the sweat bathing his face and salt blood trickling from his nose, but he seemed to be unwounded.

Several more stampeding ponies passed by while he sat, and one or two troop horses, the last with a Freefighter reeling in the kak, rhythmically spurting bright blood from a left arm that ended just above the elbow. Exerting every ounce of his willpower, Bili straightened his weary body and reined Mahvros about, bringing up his ton-heavy axe to where he could rest its haft across the flaring pommel of his saddle.

Fifty yards distant, the battle still surged and raged. He had ridden and fought his way completely through the widest, densest part of the howling horde, which was a testament to the charger's weight and bulk and savage ferocity as much as to his own fighting skills.

So close that Bili could almost touch him stood a panting horse with his equally weary rider. There was no recognizing who might be within the plain, scarred, dented plate, but Bili knew the mare and urged Mahvros nearer.

When they were knee to knee, he leaned close and shouted, "Geros! Sir Geros! Are you hurt, man?" His voice was a painful thunder to his own ears within the closed helm. "Where did you get my eagle banner?"

But the other rider sat unmoving, unresponsive. His steel-plated shoulders rose and fell jerkily to his heavy, spasmodic breathing. One gauntleted fist gripped the hilt of his broadsword, its blade red-smeared from point to quillions; the other held a hacked and splintery ashwood shaft, from which the tattered and faded Red Eagle of Morguhn rippled silkily in the freshening breeze.

Sir Geros had once borne this very banner to glory and lasting fame while serving as a Freefighter with the troop of Captain Pawl Raikuh, but since his well-earned elevation to the ranks of the nobility, a common trooper had been chosen standardbearer, while the new knight took his expected place among the heavily armed nobles.

Bili tried mindspeak. "Did you piss your breeks, as usual, Sir Geros?"

Shame and contrition boiled up from the knight's soul and beamed out with the chagrined reply. "I *always* do, my lord. Always wet myself in battle."

Bili chuckled good-naturedly, and his mirth was silently transmitted, as well. "Geros, every man jack in this squadron knows that you've got at least a full league of guts. When are you going to stop being ashamed of the piddling fact that your bladder's not as brave as the rest of you? None of the rest of us give a damn about it, man. Why then should you?"

"But . . . but, my lord *thoheeks*, it's not . . ." he paused. "Not *manly!*"

Bili snorted his derision. "Horse turds, Sir Geros! You are acknowledged one of the ten best swordsmen in a dozen duchies and you fight like a scalded treecat. So why waste worry about a meaningless quirk of yours? I assure you, no one else is bothered by it."

"Yet I am the joke of the squadron, my lord," grated the young knight. "There is never any sort of alarm or fight but that someone mentions my weakness, my shame, and asks of it or openly lays hand to my saddle or my breeks. Then they all laugh at me."

Bili extended his bridle hand to firmly grip the knight's shoulder, chiding gently, "Oh, Geros, Geros, the laughter is not at you, man, it's at your evident embarrassment. And it's friendly, Geros, just well-meant joshing among peers. In truth, there are few men in all the host who are so deeply and widely respected as are you. Everyone knows you're a very brave man, Geros."

Geros just shook his helmeted head, tiredly, resignedly. "But I'm not really brave, my lord, and *I* know it, even if no one else does. I fight for the same base reason I strove to master the sword and other weapons: only to stay alive. And I'm frightened near to death in a fight, nearly all the time, my lord, and that's not valor."

"Not so!" snapped Bili firmly. "It's the highest degree of true valor that you recognize and accept your quite legitimate fears of death or maiming and then do your duty and more despite them. And don't forget what poor old Pawl Raikuh told you the day that we stormed the salients outside the city of Vawnpolis. Fear, consciously controlled fear, is what keeps a warrior alive in a press. Men who don't know fear seldom outlive their first, serious battle.

"And I'll add this, now, Geros: Self-doubt is a good thing in many ways, for it teaches a man humility; but you can't allow yourself to be carried too far by such doubts, else they'll unman you.

"But all that aside. Tell me, how'd you chance to be bearing my banner again? Can't keep your hands off it, eh?"

Geros was too exhausted and drained to rise to the joke. "My lord, I was riding at Klifud's side through most of that ghastly mess back there, and I thought me I had guarded him and the eagle well. Then, just at the fringes of the horde, a barbarian axeman crowded between us and lopped off poor Klifud's forearm. I ran the stinking savage through and barely caught the eagle ere it fell. Then I was in the open, here; I don't know what happened to Klifud, my lord."

Bili nodded brusquely. "Well, man, you have it now. How's your throat? Dry as mine, I doubt me not."

Feeling behind his saddle, he grunted his satisfaction at finding his canteen still in place and whole. With numb, twitching fingers, he unlatched and raised his visor. Lifting the quart bottle to his crusty lips, he filled his mouth once, spit the fluid out, then took several long drafts of the tepid brandy-and-water mixture. The first swallow burned his gullet ferociously, like a red-hot spearblade on an open wound, but those which followed it were as welcome and soothing as warm honey. Taking the bottle down at last, he proffered it to Sir Geros.

"Here, man, wash out your mouth and oil that remarkable set of vocal cords. If we're to really clobber those unwashed bastards, we must rally the squadron and hit them hard again."

For the impetus of that first smashing charge had been lost, as Bili could plainly see, and the majority of the lowland horsemen were fighting alone or, at best, in small groups, rising and falling from sight, almost lost in a roiling sea of shaggy, multitoned fur.

Bili realized that where mere skill at arms and superlative armor could not promise victory or even bare survival against such odds, the superior bulk and weighty force of the troop horses and destriers were his outnumbered squadron's single asset. To take full advantage of that sole asset, the horde must again be struck by an ordered, disciplined formation, charging and striking at the gallop. But before he could deliver another crushing charge, he must rally such of his scattered elements as he could.

On command, Sir Geros' clear tenor voice pealed like a trumpet above the uproar, while Bili himself, gripping the brass-shod ferrule in both his big hands, raised the eagle high above his head and waggled the shaft.

For a long, breathless moment, it seemed that none could or would respond to the imperative summons. But first a pair of blood-splashed Freefighters hacked their way from out of the near edge of the press, then a half-dozen more appeared behind a destrier-mounted nobleman, and slowly, by dribbles and drops, the squadron's ranks again filled out and formed up behind the Red Eagle of Morguhn. Not all who had made the first charge returned, of course; some were just too hard pressed to win free of the horde, and some would never return.

Bili took a position some two hundred yards off the left flank of the milling mob that was his target—the absolutely minimal distance cavalry needed to achieve the proper impetus in a charge. He had just gotten the understrength units into squadron front when the beat of hundreds of drumming hooves sounded from somewhere within the narrow, winding defile to his own left flank.

The veteran troopers were already preparing to wheel in order to face the self-announced menace when the riders swept down from out the mouth of that precipitous gap. In the lead rode Ehrbuhn Duhnkin, followed by the bowmasters of the Freefighter troops. But their bows were all unstrung and cased; their sabers were out and flashing in errant beams of sunlight.

While the archer-troopers took their accustomed places in the shrunken ranks, Ehrbuhn rode up to *Thoheeks* Bili, mind-speaking. "We had to miss first blood, Lord Bili, but I mean to be in at the kill. So too do some others, incidentally; they it was showed us the way down from up there atop the cliffs. So, in all courtesy, my lord, I think we should not begin this dance until the arrival of the ladies."

With the Maidens and the Ahrmehnee warriors riding in a place of honor—the exposed right flank of the formation—and with the grim-faced *brahbehrnuh* beside Bili in the knot of heavily armed nobles and officers at the center of the line, the reformed and reinforced squadron struck the confused, reeling barbarians almost as hard as had the first charge. And human flesh could endure no more; the savages broke, scattered before the big horses and armored warriors and streamed southwest in full flight.

Some few escaped, but not many. The destriers and troop horses were tired, true, but so too were the ponies, and superior breeding and careful nurturing told in the end at a cost of the ultimate price to the bulk of the mob of barbarians. To the very terminus of the long, narrow plateau were the shaggy men pursued, ridden down and slain. At length, Bili forced a halt, recalled and rallied his now heterogeneous force before commencing the slow, weary march back to the battlefield below the cliffs.

Bili trudged beside Mahvros at the head of his exhausted command, having allowed only the seriously wounded to remain mounted. The big black stallion was spent; he looked as tired as Bili felt, hardly able to place one hoof before the other, his proud head hung low and his glossy hide was befouled with drying lather and old sweat, with horse blood and man blood, all thickly overlaid with dust. Nor were the other horses of the much-battered squadron in better shape; many were, in fact, worse.

The *brahbehrnuh* helped a reeling Freefighter onto the back of her relatively fresh charger, saw him secure, then paced up to stride beside Bili. After a silent moment, she addressed the towering young man in accented but passable Trade Mehrikan. "What is the polite form of address for you, lowlander?"

"The Confederation Ehleenee say '*thoheeks*,'" replied Bili, "while my Freefighters say 'duke' . . . but my friends call me simply Bili. My lady may feel free to use whichever comes easiest to her lips."

With a brusque nod of her head, she asked bluntly, "You and your ilk are the born enemies of the Ahrmehnee and so, indirectly, of me and my sisters. So why then do you fight and bleed and die for us? Was there not enough loot in the vales for both you and the cursed Muhkohee? Think you that even this will earn you Ahrmehnee forgiveness for your many and most heinous crimes, Dook Bili?"

A woman of spirit, thought Bili with approval. No polite, meaningless words for her; she spits it all right out and be damned to you if you don't like it.

"Because, my lady, me and mine no longer are the enemies of the Ahrmehnee. Even now does the great chief—this *nahkhahrah*—treat with the High Lord. Soon all these

Ahrmehnee mountains and vales will be as one with our mighty federation of peoples; your folk too, probably."

"Never!" she spat, her dark eyes blazing. "Since the time of the Earth Gods have the Moon Maidens been sensibly ruled by wise women, rather than by stupid, clumsy men. Never will we submit to such utter debasement."

Then did Bili of Morguhn show an early spark of that genius which was to secure him a high place among the ruling caste of his homeland. "But, my lady . . . did my lady not know?"

"Know what, lowlander?"

"Why just this, my lady: the true rulers of the Confederation *are* women—the Undying High Ladies Mara Morai and Aldora Linszee Treeah-Pohtohmahs Pahpahs."

Her ebon brows rose and her jaw dropped, but her recovery was quick, and she demanded, "Then what of your infamous Undying Devil, this Milos?"

Bili answered glibly, constructing the tale as he went along. "Lord Milo commands the Confederation armies, especially in the field, on campaigns. You see, my lady, our armies are all of men."

Her olive forehead wrinkled. "But Dook Bili, how can your High Ladies trust this Milos to not bring this army of mere men against them, slay them both and usurp their rightful place? The men of my own folk foolishly tried such treachery many times over the centuries until, finally, in the time of my mother's mother's grandmother, men were forbidden to carry weapons or to know their uses. Since that time, the Wise Women have ruled us, unquestioned and unopposed."

Bili shook his helmeted head. "Such harsh measures have never yet been needed in the lands of the Confederation, my lady. For one thing, the Undying High Ladies cannot be slain with weapons, but, more important, the High Lord would never do aught which might harm or divide the Confederation. Moreover, it is said that he loves the High Lady Mara, to whom he is wed, and I have seen his great respect for the High Lady Aldora. Thus has it been for six generations and more."

They two walked on in silence for a quarter-hour. At last, the *brahbehrnuh* announced her decision by asking, "When and where can I meet with one or the both of these High Ladies, Dook Bili? With the Hold of the Maidens destroyed, we—my few remaining sisters and I—are cast adrift in a hostile world, owning naught save the little we bear and wear and the horses we ride.

"But I must be certain that we—this last, pitiful remnant of my race—will receive land in return for our allegiance and service to your lady rulers and that we will be allowed to practice our ancient rites and customs unmolested. These things must your lady rulers avow to us who serve Her, the Supreme Lady."

Bili mused, trying to guess the proper answer to give to this strange, handsome young woman. But, abruptly, the conversation was rendered of no importance.

Many a league to the north and west, in what once had been the Hold of the Moon Maidens, a defective timing device at last fulfilled its long-overdue function. A small charge exploded, hurling a barrel-sized charge over the lip of the smoking fissure which the Maidens had known as the Sacred Hoofprint.

Far and far it fell, bouncing from rock to hot rock, deeper and still deeper into the very bowels of the uneasy mountain. Within bare seconds, it fell from regions of hundreds of degress of heat to regions of thousands, and its steel casing began to melt, dripping away. Then the tight-packed insulation burst into brief flame and the immense explosive charge roared out, unheard by any living ear.

A sense of unbearable unease suddenly gripped Bili. His every nerve-ending seemed to be silently screaming, *"DANGER! DANGER! DANGER!"*

Even tired as they were, all the horses were uneasy, too. Weary equine heads came up to snort and nod, nostrils dilated and eyes rolled. Aching muscles forgotten, they danced with nervousness.

Beside Bili, Mahvros half reared and almost bolted when several deer and a pair of foxes broke cover, dashing out of a dark copse to rocket downslope and over the edge of the plateau. Hard on their heels came a living carpet of small, scuttling beasts, and up ahead of the men and horses a huge, gaunt gray wolf and a treecat raced in the same direction, almost side by side.

Recalling that the High Lord had once remarked that the prairiecats were closely related to treecats and that many of the latter could mindspeak, Bili attempted to range the fleeing feline, but he encountered only a jumble of inchoate terror.

Having long ago learned the folly of ignoring his instincts, Bili suddenly roared out, *"MOUNT!* Mount and form column!" Then, his weariness clean forgotten in the press of the moment, he obeyed his own order, flinging himself astride Mahvros and finding his stirrups.

He had but barely forked the black stallion when the very earth and rocks beneath the horse's hooves shuddered strongly. Horses along the column screamed in terror; so too did some of the men and women. The *brahbehrnuh* stumbled against the flank of Bili's dancing destrier, frantically clutching at his saddle skirts and stirrup leathers for the support her feet could no longer find on the rippling ground.

With no time to care for the niceties and formalities, Bili leaned to grasp the back of the woman's swordbelt and, lifting her effortlessly, plunked her belly down on his crupper.

Komees Hari came alongside, his big gray stallion tight-reined and seemingly half mad with fear. "It can only be an earthquake, Bili. I thought me there was something odd, something disturbing about this damned plateau. We've got to get off of it . . . *fast!*"

Bili nodded once, turned in the saddle to face his column and shouted, "*THAT WAY*," pointing an arm in the direction taken by the fleeing wildlife. Mahvros was too submerged in his terror to respond to mindspeak, so Bili reined him over to the right. His booted heels beat a tattoo on the black barrel and evoked a more than willing response; exhaustion clean forgotten, the big horse raced flat out toward the track of the game beasts.

The column followed as best they might while trees crashed around them, and huge boulders shifted, slid and tumbled. After their young lord they went, heedlessly putting their panic-stricken mounts at the impossibly narrow, suicidally steep descent down the precipitous face of the plateau.

Had that plateau been higher at this its southern edge, none could have survived; but since it was much lower than in the north, all save the very tail of the column were galloping east and south and west on comparatively level ground when, with an awesome, grinding roar, the entire rocky face dissolved and slid down upon itself.

It was not until they were a birdflight mile from what had so recently been the foot of that small plateau that Bili brought his command first to a walk, then a full halt on the brushy slope of a long, serpentine ridge. Not even there was the earth completely still, but the occasional tremors were quickly forgotten, erased from their minds by the awesome and terrible wonder of the northern horizon.

Looming so huge that it looked close enough to touch, a roiling cloud of dense, opaque, multicolored smoke shot through with flame towered. Then, even as they watched, came a clap of sound of such a magnitude that horses shrieked and repeatedly reared, while men and women slapped hands to abused ears and rolled on the heaving hillside in agony. Some nameless force shredded the cloud, and among the remaining tendrils a vast host of smoking, blackish shapes could be seen rising high into the air. Of irregular conformation were the black objects, and no two of the same size. Some rose faster than others, farther, but all that could be followed with the eye soon plunged back toward earth, trailing smoke like impossibly huge pitchballs from the giant catapult of a god. And wherever they struck among the forested mountains and vales, red flame sprang into being.

One of the shapes narrowly missed Bili's party; falling, it bounced heavily in the narrow vale between their ridge and the one beyond. It finally came to rest within the bed of a tiny rill, and when the last tendrils of steam had dissipated, Bili and the rest could see that it was naught but a boulder.

But what a boulder! It was a boulder big enough for two destriers to have stood upon, uncrowded. And upon its broad face, certain cryptic carvings were plainly to be seen.

At sight of the boulder, the *brahbehrnuh* uttered a single piercing shriek. Then her eyes rolled back in their sockets and she collapsed, bonelessly, at Bili's feet.

CHAPTER II

A westering sun cast its last blaze of light over the gray rock and the dark-green growth of the mountain fastnesses. To the north and south and east of a certain small, steeply walled valley, a pall of smoke filtered that sunlight, and here and there under that smoke blazed fires wrought of the red-hot stones flung far and wide in the explosive death of a distant mountain.

Nor had raging forest fires been the only violence spawned by that mountain's death agonies, for a hellish jumble of tumbled rock and splintered trees was now all that remained of what had very recently been a plateau bearing at least one Ahrmehnee village.

After the reckless gallop down from that doomed plateau, Bili's war party had found that any eastward progress was an impossiblity due to the roaring holocaust. Indeed, they had been compelled to flee northwesterly before the fires which were driven on a strong wind from the southeast. Amid the roiling smoke and confusion, among hills irrevocably altered by the earth tremors, not even the native Ahrmehnee warriors could be certain where they were, and the main party had become somehow separated—roughly two-thirds of them fleeing behind Bili of Morguhn, with the contingent which had included *Komees* Hari Daiviz and Sir Geros Lahvoheetos all gone to Wind for all anyone knew.

It was a motley group which now lay encamped along the banks of the stream that chuckled through the narrow, steep-walled valley. Three distinct languages, plus several regional dialects, were to be heard in that camp. Middle Kingdoms Freefighters rubbed scale-shirted elbows with Ahrmehnee warriors in thigh-length hauberks of beautifully fashioned chain mail, Confederation noblemen supped their meager rations across the fires from man-despising Moon Maidens, and the winter-sere grasses were cropped by a conglomerate herd of lowland destriers and chargers, the finely bred warhorses

18

of the Maidens and the rough-coated mountain ponies of the Ahrmehnee.

Their unsatisfying scratch meal too soon consumed, most of the party settled for the fast-closing night; they huddled about the fires, wrapped in cloaks or saddle blankets, vainly seeking warmth and comfort on the hard, stony ground. Here and there wounded men and women whimpered or groaned in agonized wakefulness or moaned in delirium.

Vahrohneeskos Gneedos Kamruhn of Skaht saw his semi-conscious brother made as comfortable as possible, then left him in the care of a grizzled Freefighter and slowly picked a way between the knots of supine warriors toward where the largest fire blazed, its leaping flames reflected from the burnished breastplate and smooth, shaven scalp of him who was become the uncontested leader of all—*Thoheeks* Bili, Chief Morguhn of Morguhn.

Gneedos mused as he walked, thinking it somewhat odd that these fierce Ahrmehnee headhunters, who had hated and warred upon lowlanders for hundreds of years, not to mention the fabled, man-hating Moon Maidens, had not presumed to question even the least of Bili's orders. But then the *vahrohneeskos* reflected that for all their outré customs and barbaric usages, this particular group of Ahrmehnee and Maidens were all proved and veteran warriors to whom the easy and natural assumption of command by a born war leader such as Bili would seem right and proper. Despite the fact that he had yet to see his twentieth winter, Bili of Morguhn was that rare kind of man—a fighting chieftain of fighters, his invisible mantle of leadership evident to all, be they old or young, male or female, Ehleen or Kindred or Burker or mountaineer.

Tall towered this man the burker mercenaries had dubbed "Bili the Axe," big-boned and heavily muscled, with wide shoulders and hips giving purchase to the sinews which enabled him to swing his huge, heavy axe as easily and effortlessly as a normal man employed his broadsword or saber.

As did many professional fighting men in the Middle Kingdoms of the north, wherein he had fostered some ten years and had his war training, fighting in the army of the Iron King, Gilbuht of Harzburk, Bili kept his scalp shaved smooth for reasons of cleanliness and comfort under a much-worn helmet. But his eyebrows were a blond as light as the tassels of green maize. Where not darkened by sun and weather, his skin was a fair pink-white, and his eyes were of a variable blue. Once, not too long back, those eyes had easily and often warmed with humor and friendliness, but now they were become cold and hard, when not wary and quick-darting, the skin at their outer corners beginning to permanently crinkle and the brow above them to furrow with the weights and worries of command.

Below a narrow nose slightly canted to the right by some old blow, his pale, thin lips frowned above a strong, square chin, and his face was now abristle with a two-day growth of dusty blond beard. Gneedos, though he liked and deeply respected Bili, could not say that he considered the young Chief of Morguhn a handsome man.

"But" he chuckled to himself, "women obviously do. Well, at least one woman does. All the army at Morguhnpolis, on the march up to Vawnpolis and then during that bastardly siege, knew him to be the chosen lover of the High Lady Aldora, and she could've had any man in the host at a mere snap of her fingers."

Unbeknownst to Gneedos, Bili too was just then doing some personal reflecting.

"Sun and Wind, but this is a pretty pickle we're in here." As he often did when worried or troubled, he absently rubbed his thumb along a puckered scar on the right side of his thick neck. "When I was summoned from Harzburk—was it only a year ago? less even than that?—I rode south wondering how I'd keep from dying of sheer boredom as chief of a peaceful duchy for the rest of my life.

"Peaceful, hah! One, maybe two nights of rest I got, ere my mothers were filling my ears with the plots and counterplots and festering rebellion among the Ehleenee. And ere I'd been in my duchy a week, those priest-ridden whorespawn had made to ambush me and my party in Horse County, and a chancy thing that was, too.

"Wind be praised for Geros Lahvoheetos. Had he not fought his way back to Horse Hall—probably," he grinned to himself, "knowing him, leaving a trail of piss all the way—I'd've been cold meat that night.

"Then I and the loyal nobles and poor old Pawl Raikuh's Freefighters had to hack our way out of my own damned capital city, only to find ourselves besieged by an army of peasants and gutter scrapings, led by a gaggle of bloodthirsty priests and a madman and pervert. And when once the High Lord is out of Morguhn and Vawn, I still mean to see that buggering bastard Myros of Deskahti, madman or no, impaled. It's a debt I owe to my brother Djef, and to all the other brave men who've gone to Wind because of him and his ilk.

"But before he died, Djef and the men he led out on that nighttime sally surely blooded the swine." A grim smile flitted across his face as he thought of how the besiegers' transport and stores and siege engines had blazed on that dark night and of how the ill-led and thoroughly confused rabble had spent most of the hours of darkness fighting each other under the impression that their dimly seen opponents were Bili's men.

So badly had the besiegers been demoralized and decimated that, upon receipt of word that Confederation cavalry was on the march from the north, the secular commander and his staff had fled back to the supposed haven of the walled city of Morguhnpolis, taking the senior ecclesiastic with them but leaving the common priests and all their remaining forces, as well as their wounded officers and men, to the tender mercies of the blood-mad garrison of Morguhn Hall.

And, heedless alike of his still-unhealed wounds from the ambush and of the well-meant advice of an older man who was both his cousin and a retired general of the Confederation, Bili had mounted his scratch force of less than a hundred men and ridden out in hot pursuit of the retreating thousands. And it had been a butchery; most of the self-styled "crusaders" had thrown aside their weapons and sketchy armor to facilitate their flight, and precious few of those who still were armed put up any sort of resistance when finally they were ridden down.

But Bili had been fostered, reared and trained in a hard school by a pitiless ruler, and he saw the murderous hunt on to the very walls of Morguhnpolis, he and his men slaying the screaming, running, unarmed would-be rebels until all—both men and horses—were as blood-splashed as autumn hog butchers, until swords and sabers and axes and spears were all dull-edged and clotted all over with sticky gore, until scarcely an arrow or a dart remained unused and both men and beasts trembled with weariness.

Knowing that the city could not be held against the oncoming regulars of the Army of the Confederation and unwilling to tie down their few effectives in an open fight with Bili and his retainers, the surviving rebels within Morguhnpolis had first securely barred all four gates from within, then fled the city by secret ways. Nor did they stop until they were completely out of the Duchy of Morguhn and safely within the neighboring Duchy of Vawn, wherein a similar rebellion had succeeded.

One of the rebellious nobles of Morguhn had been the younger brother of *Komees* Hari Daiviz—a man of above fifty years, owning no known mindspeak ability, no arms training other than the normal basics learned in their youth by gentlemen and no military experience. This Drehkos Daiviz of Morguhn held the minor title of *vahrohneeskos,* which had been part of his patrimony, but he owned no trade or profession to occupy him, and after the death of his wealthy wife he had drifted into the clandestine rebellion mostly out of boredom.

However, before the rebels had fled Morguhnpolis, the senior secular commander, *Vahrohnos* Myros, had suffered some type of seizure and had lapsed into a coma, whereupon all had looked to Drehkos to command. With the direct escape route to the southwest clogged by a vast horde of fleeing peasants and city commoners, Drehkos had perforce led his mounted party north, into the Duchy of Skaht, and then west, into the mountains of the savage, headhunting Ahrmehnee.

Doing only what he sensed was best and with no scintilla of military training or experience to guide him, Drehkos had led his ill-armed and ill-supplied force southwestward in a weeks-long running fight with the cunning Ahrmehnee. He had been racked with sorrow and regret that he had left a good third of his initial numbers dead or missing in those mountains, but those who knew better had all quickly hailed him a military genius to have emerged with such small losses. Moreover, the rebel nobles of Vawn had insisted that a man of such sagacity and prowess was far better fitted to lead and command the rebel forces now concentrated in and about the walled city of Vawnpolis than were any of them.

"If only the Ahrmehnee had managed to take the head of that treacherous dog of a Drehkos," thought the young *thoheeks,* "the campaign would've been concluded last summer and at far less cost, too."

An ancestor of the murdered *thoheeks* and Chief of Vawn had collected during his time some half-dozen tomes having to do with various aspects of warfare. That Drehkos had chanced upon these dusty books had been pure luck—good for him and the rebels, bad for his opponents; indeed, fatal for many. His careful reading and rereading of the small collection had been of immense aid to him in strengthening the existing defenses of the city, in adding new innovations and in harrying the army marching up from Morguhn toward Vawnpolis.

With the two largest cities of the duchy—Morguhnpolis and Kehnooryos Deskahti—back in loyal hands and with the smaller towns and the countryside of Morguhn being purged—bloodily purged—of rebels and rebel sympathizers by Bili and his fast-moving column, augmented by troops of Confederation cavalry, High Lord Milo's summons had brought in armed and mounted nobles from leagues around, thousands of unemployed Freefighters from the Middle Kingdoms north of the Confederation, herds of remounts and draft or pack animals, mountains of supplies and gear and wheeled transport. Then, with all of Morguhn secure and garrisoned, the army—Confederation regulars, Freefighters and heavily armed nobility—had commenced a march upcountry, with Vawnpolis as their goal.

But Drehkos, armed with his new *ars militaris*, had made that march much longer in time and far and away more expensive in supplies stolen or destroyed and in blood spilled and lives lost than his meager forces had had any right to do. His bitter price for the leagues the invading force gained had been mostly exacted in hit-and-run raids, harassment of the supply lines and cutting off of stragglers; but on two singular occasions, he had struck openly, hard and in force.

Bili's mind strayed back to his memory of the first of those attacks, the sole saving grace of which had been to teach a few sorely needed lessons to the generally brave but stubborn and ill-disciplined lowland nobility.

As the van of the column of nobles and Freefighters strung out along the length of a relatively straight stretch of road, the brush-grown slopes to either side erupted a deadly sleet of arrows and darts—a sleet doubly deadly in that many of the Freefighters, who as professionals should have known better, had aped their noble employers in removing helmets and loosing the laces of scaleshirts and gambesons to let air to their profusely sweating bodies.

And so, while men on the road shouted and screamed and died or fought to control wounded and frenzied or terrifiedly shrieking horses, a yelling double rank of armored horsemen, presenting lances and spears, waving swords and axes, careered down the steep road shoulders to strike both flanks in a ringing flurry of steel and sharp death.

From the very onset, it was obvious that the noblemen were the preferred targets of the shrewdly effective ambush, for most of the point troop of Freefighter cavalry had been permitted to pass unmolested between the brushy jaws of the trap and now were milling on the narrow roadway as they tried to wheel about. Nor was the plight of the Red Eagle Troop improved when the rebel archers began to range them; the seemingly sentient shafts sought out every bared head, sank into vitals ill protected by loosened jazerans or pricked horses into a rearing, bucking, screaming chaos.

Then, abruptly, the rain of feathered agonies slackened as the most of the hidden bowmen turned their weapons toward the second troop, which was rounding the hill at the gallop, with the Rampant Blackfoot Banner snapping above the heads of the leading files.

Bili had had no time to uncase his famous axe, so he had drawn his broadsword and snapped down his visor in a single, practiced movement, grasping the handle of the small target hung from his pommel knob at the same time he dropped Mahvros' reins over that knob.

For his part, the blood-hungry black stallion screamed a joyous challenge, and his fine head darted, snakelike, to sink his big yellow teeth into the neck of the first enemy mount to come within range. The bitten gelding was a hunter with no scintilla of war training and no slightest intention of being further savaged by a raging stallion; sidling, he proceeded to buck off his rider just in time for the unhorsed rebel to be ridden down by the second wave of rebel attackers.

Roaring, from force of long habit, "*UP! UP HARZ-BURK!*" and then belatedly, "*MORGUHN! A MORGUHN! UP THE RED EAGLE!*" Bili stood in his stirrups, his brawny arm swinging the heavy sword with such skill and force that its wide blade severed the head from a lance and the head from its wielder in one single figure-eight stroke.

For a brief moment he wondered how so large a mounted force had remained unobserved by both vanguards and flank guards. Then his every thought was of dealing death and avoiding death, and all the world for him became the familiar tumult and chaotic kaleidoscope of battle—the earsplitting clash of steel on steel, the marrow-deep shock of blows struck and blows received, the blinking of cascades of salt sweat from eyes, while gasping for fresh breath within the stifling confines of the helm.

The warhorse, Mahvros, was in his chosen element and

could not have been happier, as he lashed out with steel-shod hooves, tore at horseflesh and manflesh with big, square teeth, used his superior height and weight to deadly effect against the rebels' mounts, few of which shared his training or ferocity.

Bili traded hacks and parries with briefly appearing and quickly disappearing opponents, while the air about him was unceasingly rent by mindless screams of man and horse, by death shrieks and shouted warcries, and rapidly became noisome with the stink of spilled blood, horse sweat and man sweat, and thick with choking dust rising up from the churning, stamping hooves.

Instinctively, Bili would shift his weight in order to help Mahvros retain his footing on the body-littered roadway, often leaning sideways to strike around the stallion's chain-armored neck and withers as the savage black horse reared to make more deadly use of his fearsome forehooves.

Up the road, beyond the trap, Captain Pawl Raikuh and Sergeant Geros Lahvoheetos, closely followed by the man bearing the Red Eagle Banner and Geros' squad—not a man of whom was wounded, thanks in no small part to the strict discipline enforced by the young sergeant, which had seen all helms in place and secured and all jazerans fully laced up—had forced a path to the arrow-raked tail of the chaotic jumble their troop was become. They had collected more unwounded troopers on still-sound horses along the way.

Raikuh, season veteran that he was, took the time to form his force of survivors into road-spanning files behind him, Lieutenant Krahndahl, Sergeant Lahvoheetos and the big Lainzburker standardbearer. Then, waving his sword and shouting, "*MORGUHN! UP MORGUHN!*" he led a crashing charge into the melee broiling ahead.

Twenty yards out from the fierce fight, the standardbearer uttered a single, sharp cry and reeled back against his cantle, the thick shaft of a war dart wobbling out of an eyesocket. Both Geros and Bohreegahd Krahndahl snatched at the dipping banner, but it was the young sergeant's hand which closed about the ashwood shaft and jerked it free of the grasp of the dead man.

And then they were upon the enemy, and Geros could never after recall more than bits and pieces of that gory and terrifying mosaic of blood and slaughter.

But when someone commenced to furiously shake at his left arm and pound a mailed fist on his jazeran, he awoke—

shocked to notice that his clean, oiled and carefully honed sword was now hacked and dulled along both edges and running fresh blood from tip to quillions; moreover, the blood had splashed and fouled his entire right side and even his horse housings.

". . . *and rally!*" That voice, Captain Raikuh's, he suddenly realized it was, and shouting directly in his ear. "Steel damn you, man! Raise the banner! Raise the fucking thing and shout, 'Up Morguhn' and 'Rally to the Red Eagle.' *Do it,* you son of a bitch! Do it *now,* or I'll put steel in you!"

Shaking his ringing head and dropping his gory sword to dangle by the knot, he gripped the shaft in both hands, stuck it at arm's length above his head and sent his high tenor voice out to pierce the hellish din.

"Up Morguhn! Up Morguhn! Duke Bili! All Rally! Rally to the Red Eagle! Up Morguhn!"

A blade smashed against the back of his jazeran, but he faithfully continued to follow his officer's orders, wobbling the heavy, ill-balanced banner and shouting the rallying cry over and over again. From the corner of one eye, he caught the flash of the captain's steel as Raikuh cut down the reckless Vawnee who had attacked the standardman.

At first in slow dribbles, then in an increasing, steel-sheathed flood, the scattered noblemen and Freefighters fought their way out of the press to gather about the eagle banner. No more blades hacked at Geros, for he and Raikuh now were surrounded by a circle of steel, an ever-widening circle the sharp edges of which hacked and stabbed and slashed at the enveloping Vawnee ambushers.

Thoheeks Bili jerked loose the wristknot and threw down a broken sword, then hurriedly uncased and grasped his huge double axe. "Raikuh, Krahndahl!" he shouted hoarsely. "See the standard's guarded. We're going to run those bastards back to their kennels!"

The rebels did not long maintain a stand against the now-organized gentry and mercenaries; they broke and streamed back northward on an obviously predetermined course. They were pursued hotly, Bili of Morguhn in the van, coldly axing any rebel he came near out of the saddle. But when the surviving rebels disappeared among an expanse of gullies and dry creekbeds, Bili wisely halted the pursuit. Then the mixed band picked a weary but wary way back toward the littered, blood-muddy road.

"But we all thought that *Vahrohnos* Myros, the cashiered

Confederation Army officer, was the man responsible for all our reverses," thought Bili, staring into the flames of the fire in that steep-sided little mountain valley. "Even when that young rebel noble we captured that day *told* us, and under hypnosis at that, that the *Vahrohneeskos* Drehkos Daiviz of Morguhn was their overall commander and had both planned and led that ambush, we could hardly believe him, assuming that Myros was craftily using him for a figurehead and acting through him for some obscure reason or other.

"And at that last big raid, when Drehkos was *seen* leading the raiders by noblemen who had met him, and recognized by his strong resemblance to Hari by men to whom he was unknown, hell, even then we tried to find ways to discount the tale.

"Now, that dawn raid is a battle I'm sorry I missed. I've been permitted into the minds and memories of men who were there, but it's not the same thing. That Confederation dragoon officer—what's his name? Linstahk, I think—he's the one who got all the credit for throwing the bastards back, and undoubtedly his charge with his squadron was the deciding blow, but he'd never have had the chance to strike that blow had old *Thoheeks* Kehn of Kahr and his few score Kindred nobility not stopped and held the rebel bastards and kept their host from overrunning the damned campsite.

"Those damned spit-and-polish popinjays of the Confederation Army always take the credit for a victory, even if they arrive so late that they never wet their steel, And as for that pack who call themselves the officers of the Confederation Army, no sane man who hasn't been exposed to them, soldiered in conjunction with the silly, posturing swine, would ever believe the extremes of their arrogance; even the lowliest, pink-cheeked Confederation ensign seems to think that adult noble warriors should jump at his command, his every command, no matter how pointless.

"Such conduct is understandable in Ehleenee, but right many of those officers are Kindred-born and -bred; army life just seems to make them all as stiff-necked and supercilious as the worst *kath-ahrohs* Ehleen."

Then Bili shook his head, chiding himself. "Oh, there I go, generalizing again. Aldora has often warned me about that bad habit. I admit, there are some good men among the Confederation officers. Linstahk, for instance; he's undoubtedly a brave man, and Hari Daiviz is quite fond of him, has much good to say of him. So, too, does the High Lord. And from what little I could sense besides his memories of the battle when he let the High Lord and me into his mind, he seemed an admirable type."

And Bili thought back, recalling most of Linstahk's own recall of that hellish, bloody morning.

With the light of the false dawn, the vanguard contingent moved out—including High Lord Milo, *Thoheeks* Bili with his nobles and Freefighters and near a squadron of Confederation dragoons as well as the High Lord's personal guard; this had been the marching order of the van every day since the first ambush.

The hulk of the noble warriors of the archduchy and their troops of hired Freefighters had taken to the road a bare half hour later. Then had the long, serried ranks of Confederation infantry set hide-shod feet to the measured beat of the drums, thankful that but two more days' marching was said to separate them from Vawnpolis, cursing the muddy morass that last night's rain and the earlier passage of cavalry had made of the road every bit as vociferously as they had cursed yesterday's dust.

At their departure, the exodus of the wagons of supplies and equipment commenced. While the servants of nobles and officers struck tents and loaded baggage and hitched teams, apprentice sanitarians directed squads of sappers in filling in latrines and offal pits.

While fires were smothered and harnesses adjusted, the flanker lancers and the rearguard *kahtahfrahktoee* fiddled needlessly with girths or sat upon stamping horses on the fringes of the bustle. Though all accoutered for the road, they had not yet assembled in marching order but were gathered here and there in small groups, chatting, jesting, spitting and watching the beehive of activity within the perimeter of the soon to be abandoned campsite.

Because his superior officer, Arnos Tchainee, lay ill with fever in one of the medical wagons now lumbering west on the Vawnpolis road, Captain Gaib Linstahk had, this dawn, found himself in nominal command of the entire squadron of heavy cavalry and with authority over the lancers as well, two troops of whom were trickling out in ones and twos on the flanks of the departing baggage train.

Nor were these the least of the young officer's problems, for, as the High Lady Aldora was traveling today in her huge, luxurious, wagonbed-mounted yurt, he found himself forced to deal with the frequently insubordinate commander of her mounted bodyguard, as well as with some three score country nobility, all surly and irascible at being placed this day in the rear rather than the van.

Trailed by his bugler, the squadron colors and a couple of supernumerary junior noncoms, Gaib was leading his charger, who seemed on the verge of throwing a shoe, toward an as yet unpacked traveling forge. As he walked, his lips moved in silent curses at wellbred bumpkins who carried their feelings ill balanced on their shoulders and gave not one damn for his hard-earned military rank, rendering him what little deference they did solely because he was heir to a Kindred *vahrohnos*.

A mindspoken warning from one of the accompanying noncoms caused the captain to glance back the way they had marched yesterday, at the body of mounted men now approaching the all but deserted campsite. Gaib snorted. More volunteer irregulars from duchies south and east of Morguhn, no doubt, though in a larger contingent than usual. And doubtless commanded by yet another noble arsehole who'd marched them through all the rainy night and . . .

And then he heard the first shouts of fear and alarm, saw the first flights of shafted death arcing up from the nearest cover, heard or thought he heard that never to be forgotten, ominous hissing-hum.

Flinging himself astride his mount, loose shoe or no loose shoe, he roared, "Bugler! Sound 'To the colors'!" Then he snapped to the colorbearer and the two noncoms, "Follow me!" Adding, when he realized that they had none of them seen what he had, "Sun and Wind, lower your visors and clear your steel, men, we're under attack!"

Gaib's first reaction was to reach a central point of the campsite and rally his *kahtahfrahktoee*. Better armed and more fully armored than the lancers, they and the even better protected nobles should be able to charge right into the fire of the hidden pack of sniping rebel archers, flush the bastards out of cover and ride them down like the vermin they were.

But that was before it became obvious to his veteran eye that those horsemen approaching from the east were not now thundering up the road to reinforce, but rather to attack.

He mindspoke the commander of the lancers, most of whom were gathered over on the north side, nearer to the road. "Captain Rahdjuhz, assemble your troops and draw them up behind the nobles who will presently form athwart the road. If those pigs aren't slowed down, they'll ride over

the camp before I can form up my squadron for the counter-
attack."

Gaib thought he could actually hear the outraged yelp of
the lancer officer. "Sun and Wind, man," the reply came
beaming into his mind, "have you taken leave of your senses?
A good half of those Vawnee look to be heavily armed, and
they'll go through my two troops like shit through a goose!
I—"

With seconds precious as emeralds, Gaib coldly cut off his
subordinate, furiously beaming, "Wind take you for a coward, Ah! Follow my orders or turn over your command to a
man with a full set of guts. I *said* you and yours would be
the second fucking line, dammit; those heavily armed fire-
eaters of ours will take the full brunt of it."

Then Gaib sought the mind of· *Thoheeks* Kehn Kahr. "If
you please, my lord *thoheeks*, has your group taken many
casualties from the arrows?"

In his mind's eye, he could see the steamy-red face—for
Thoheeks Kahr had gained many years and much superfluous
flesh since last he had actively campaigned or worn armor in
the heat of summer—but there was an ill-concealed and boy-
ish eagerness in the return the middle-aged nobleman
beamed. "*Vahrohneeskos* Berklee's son, Steev, has a broken
leg . . . I think. His poor horse took a dart and fell ere he
could clear leather. And we've lost a few more horses, too,
killed or wounded. But no more gentlemen, all thanks be to
Wind and Pitzburk.

"We await your instructions, Captain *Vahrohnos'* son.
When do you want us to fight? Where? Ahorse or afoot?"

Gaib breathed a sigh of relief. The *thoheeks* and the three
score gentlemen were only technically under cavalry command. They could all see the charging Vawnee from their
position and must certainly be aware that the odds against
them were something over ten to one. Had Kahr sanely opted
for flight rather than fight, Gaib would have been powerless
to do aught save curse him.

"If it please my lord *thoheeks*, form a single rank just inside the camp and block the road. Place your left flank on
the verge of that deep gully and your right at the perimeter
ditch. The lancers will be forming behind you.

"My lord, you and yours *must* hold them until the High
Lady be safely away and my squadron be formed up. My
bugles sounding 'The Charge' will be your signal to disengage.

"Does it please my lord *thoheeks* to understand?"

"Sacred Sun keep you, boy, nothing has pleased me more since my horse sister, Red Sarah, dropped twin foals by my horse brother, Axe-Hoof, and both of them *colts*—one coal black and one snow white! We'll hold the bastards, Captain *Vahrohnos'* son, by Sun and Wind and Steel, we'll hold!"

Next Gaib tried to range the mind of the arrogant Clan Linsee prick who commanded the High Lady's guards. Meeting with no success, he beamed directly to the High Lady herself.

"Yes, captain," came her strongly beamed answer, "I am aware that we are under attack and I have but just farspoken the High Lord of the facts. He comes, but he is far up, with the van, and it will take time.

"I've listened in on your beamings, as well, captain. You are a good officer and a true credit to our arms; your decisions have been sound. Would that I might this day sit a horse at your side, but it is my time of the moon and I earlier imbibed of a decoction of herbs; though they leave my mind clear, so seriously do they affect my balance and my physical coordination that I doubt that I could draw my saber, much less use it."

"But another reason, my lady, that I would have you on the road," Gaib mindspoke emphatically. "As of this dawn, my squadron was understrength, and I doubt not but that we've lost horses and men to the missiles. Yonder looms a strong force, and, am I to have sufficient weight to smash their attack, I'll need every horse and sword I can muster.

"I recall that your team be hitched, my lady; let it please you to take the road forthwith. But you'd best leave some few of your archers somewhere along the road to retard pursuit should we fail here."

Aldora had agreed to adopt his plan, adding, "Sacred Sun guard you this day, young Linstahk; for the Confederation can ill afford the loss of men such as you."

While his lieutenants and sergeants formed up their half-strength units, mating sound, unwounded men with sound horses, where necessary, Gaib and his bugler and colorbearer sat their restive mounts with an outward show of calm. Their training and strict discipline proved, as often before, of inestimable aid in strengthening their force of will to seemingly ignore the incredible tumult and confusion of the feathered death still falling from the sunny morning sky and the milling and bleating of dying noncombatants within the perimeters of the campsite.

Thoheeks Kahr's force of nobles was strung out barely in time; the leading elements of the Vawn cavalry struck their thin line of steel with the sound of a thunderclap, and the line bowed inexorably inward, inward, inward at its center. It bowed until Gaib, watching, was certain that it must snap and let the screaming horde of Vawnee through to pour over the mostly unarmed throng of servants, cooks, smiths and wagoneers.

But then, like a well-tempered blade, the line slowly commenced to straighten, helped by the lancers and, unexpectedly, by half a hundred unmounted sappers, not one of them armored, and "armed" with a miscellany of long-handled spades and iron crowbars, wooden mauls and sawbacked engineer short swords.

Witnessing the costly valor of these support troops, Gaib silently vowed that never again would he either engage in or tolerate the sneers and snickers usual when a "dung-beetle"—which was his peers' unflattering nickname for sapper officers—made to enter the mess.

The ringing, clanging blacksmith symphony raged on, with the superior weight of numbers of the Vawnee bearing the camp's defenders back and back. But *Thoheeks* Kahr was naught if not true to the very essence of his word, for every lost foot was hotly, bloodily contested and the meager gains of the rebels were dearly bought.

Despite the fact that he considered them, one and all, to be stupidly proud, supercilious and completely undisciplined amateur soldiers, still did Gaib find himself flushing with pride that his own veins surged with the same rich blood as *Thoheeks* Kahr and his band, for they fought with the tenacity of the best professionals.

Then Squadron Sergeant-Major Ohahrah was saluting him with a flourish of gleaming saber. "Sir, the squadron be formed on squadron front. Thirty-two of the High Lady's horseguards ride with us; if it meets the captain's approval, eight have been posted to each troop. Will the captain be inspecting the formation?"

Gaib asked, "The High Lady is away, then?"

"Yes, sir; at the gallop, sir."

"No, I'll not be inspecting, sar'major." Gaib smiled at the grizzled noncom. "If the formation pleases your critical eye, it could not but please mine."

Still smiling, Gaib drew his saber and formally returned the salute of his subordinate, remarking in a relaxed and comradely tone, "So, then, Baree, let us see what these rebels know of saber drill. Or had you expected to die in bed, old man?"

Sloping the back of the cursive blade across his armored shoulder, he turned to his bugler. "Horn, 'Walk March,' if you please, then, 'Draw Sabers.' "

Dropping his reins over the pommel knob, Gaib lowered his visor and secured it to his fixed beaver. Halfway through the first, blared command of his bugler, the four troop bugles began to echo it and, with the clop of hooves, creak of leather, jingle and clank of metal equipment and armor, the squadron of Confederation *kahtahfrahktoee* stepped out in the direction of the enemy. A chorus of metallic *zweeeps* from behind him followed the second bugle call.

Gaib did not need to look around to know that the well-schooled, veteran squadron followed in drill-field order, every saber sloped at the proper angle. His mind's eye could picture his force—their closed-faced helmets sprouting short crests of black-and-red-striped horsehair, their gleaming scale shirts of steel reinforced at breast and back and shoulders with light plate such as protected their upper arms, elbows, loins, thighs and knees, reflected sunlight from the high polish of jackboots and long-cuffed gauntlets and leather horsegear.

And the horses. None of them as big and tall and impressive as the destriers ridden by him and some few of the other noble officers, but all mindspeakers and still bigger than the common troop horses of the lancers of the Confederation and of Middle Kingdoms dragoons. *Kahtahfrahktoee* horses were a proud product of generations of selective breeding by the stud farms maintained by the High Lord Milo of Morai, and they stood as a combination of the very best qualities of the many strains that had joined to produce them.

Each horse of the squadron was protected with an armor that included metal plates, chainmail, scale and hardened leather. In action, many of them could be as ferocious as any war-trained destrier, but they were not allowed to be as stubborn as a destrier—any dismounted trooper or officer could safely mount a horse with no rider, as long as the man could satisfy the horse with mindspeak that he was friend rather than foe. The breed was highly intelligent, for horses and mounts rendered riderless for one reason or another could and had been seen to recognize different bugle calls, respond properly and perform intricate drill-field maneuvers unguided by human hands.

Before him, the young officer could see through the slits of his steel visor the open stretch of campsite that lay between him and his objective, the flank of the mob of mounted embattled rebels. To his mind, there were far too many still or thrashing forms of men and beasts littering that stretch of ground; the arrow räin had been costly in unarmored service personnel and draft animals. But he also noted that those before him who could walk, hobble or crawl were stirring their stumps; they could see what was coming, and none of them apparently cared to be ridden down by charging *kahtahfrahktoee.*

When his path seemed relatively clear, Gaib mindspoke the bugler and "Trot March" pealed out, followed by the familiar increase in the noise level from the hoof-thumping, creaking, rattling squadron.

And as never failed to happen at such a point of imminent action, Gaib's chest felt unbearably constricted. His guts were aroil and uncomfortably full, his mouth was dry as dead leaves, and he knew for certain that his distended bladder soon would burst; so, drawing himself up even straighter in his kak, he began to sing, his voice booming in the confines of his helm.

". . . . then let us sing our battle song
Of saber, spear and bow.
Clan Linstahk, Clan Linstahk,
Your courage we'll show . . ."

Noting the now-decreased distance, Gaib mindspoke again, and "Gallop March" blared from his bugler's instrument, as before being taken up halfway through by the troop buglers.

Gaib mindspoke his destrier stallion, Windsender, "I know that you lack that shoe, my brother, and I am sorry to cause you pain, but this must be; we must finish this fight before I can see to you."

"Your brother understands, my brother," the big bay beamed back. "There is not much pain and, besides," he added with a trace of eagerness in his beaming, "a good fight does not come every day."

At the moment he gauged best, Gaib raised his saber high over his head, twirled it twice, then swung it down to the horizontal, pointing straight forward . . . and five brass bugles screamed the "Charge."

Struck on the exposed flank by such a force, many of the rebels were impelled so far to their right that many a horse and rider plunged over the crumbly lip of the deep gully, to flounder in the shallow but cold water until another horse and rider landed atop them.

Almost immediately the charge was delivered, the rebel commander astutely commenced a fighting withdrawal of his force, and, to his credit, Gaib estimated that a bit fewer than half the original force committed actually got away—surviving the bloody, breast-to-breast battle with *Thoheeks* Kahr's men, the smashing charge of Gaib's squadron and the running fight of the pursuit undertaken by the nobles, the lancers and two troops of the *kahtahfrahktoee*.

"And I had to miss it," thought Bili ruefully, "every damned bit of it. By the time the High Lord and I got there, the pursuit was already trickling back into camp."

A Freefighter with a dirty, blood-stained bandage wrapped about his head limped up to the fire and cast upon it most of a small evergreen tree, producing a momentarily brighter, hotter fire and sending a myriad of sparks dancing up into the sky.

And that fiery crackling roar brought young *Thoheeks* Bili back to the present, where some of the leaders of his battered and singed command chatted in low, tired tones about the fire, wounded moaned and whimpered here and there, and horses stamped and whuffled downslope in the narrow strip of yellowed grass.

He suspected that he and they were deep, far too deep, in the territory of the savage, sinister Muhkohee, for the plateau they had been forced to flee had been the westernmost of the Ahrmehnee lands, and they now were far west—he was not sure just how far west—of that area.

They seemed secure for the nonce, however. The narrow vale had been scouted thoroughly while still there was light enough to do a good job of it and had proven to be almost boxed in by the high, rugged hills. Nor could the smoke and glare of their fires betray their location, not with so much smoke, so many fires spawned by the hot rocks still smoldering.

While Bili had been a-musing, his Freefighter orderly had removed the young nobleman's cuirass, brassarts, vambraces and tasses. Now he helped him to struggle out of his smelly, sweat-soaked gambeson. Freed of that much weight and hindrance, Bili stripped off his soggy shirt and, heedless alike of the chill night air and the gathering of men and women around the large fire, he paced down to the chuckling brook and dumped several helmetsful of icy water over his head and his thick, scarred torso, rubbing all the bared skin he could reach with the hard palms of his big hands before again dousing himself with the frigid water. Then he returned to the fireside and wrapped himself in his cloak.

Seating himself on a pile of horse gear, Bili addressed himself to one of the older Ahrmehnee, asking politely, "You're a Panosyuhn, aren't you? The most western of the Ahrmehnee tribes?"

The graying warrior nodded and replied in atrociously accented Trade Mehrikan, with long pauses here and there as he sought to mentally translate his own language into one that this young warleader could understand. "Yes, I'm Vahrtahn Panosyuhn, hereditary headman of a valley northeast of the Great Plateau."

Bili nodded brusquely. "Well then, this is your country. Where is the nearest village? How far, do you think? We need food, and the wounded fighters and horses need rest and care."

The elderly Ahrmehnee shook his head vigorously. "No, Dook Bili, this is not my country. This all about this place Muhkohee country, whence came that horde you saved us from; we have been in their savage land for many miles, now.

"The west edge of that plateau that was has ever been the . . . the border between civilized Ahrmehnee and barbarian Muhkohee. If any villages or hovels lie hereabouts, they are assuredly Muhkohee nests and we'd do well to stay clear of the filthy holes."

Aware that the Ahrmehnee were noted for quick tempers and leery of precipitating even a hint of trouble in this volatile and ill-matched force he now led, Bili was careful to cast no slightest aspersion upon this headman's courage. "Why should *we* be fearful of a few barbarian villagers, Lord Vahrtahn? The wounded aside, we mount some eight score swords, so why should we not simply take what supplies we need from a village . . . if we find one?"

But it was one of the subcommanders of the Moon Maidens who answered him, her Trade Mehrikan no better than that of Vahrtahn Panosyuhn. "Were we so rash as to do so, and no woman would be so stupid . . . though it is easy to see how you childish man-warriors could be . . . dead would we all be before leave this terrible land we could, leader of manwarriors. Wait we must until dead are the fires and cooler the ground, for the way we came we must go; death or worse than a quick death in any other riding lies."

CHAPTER III

Old Vahrtahn Panosyuhn nodded once, his gray beard rippling over the face of his battered cuirass. "The Maiden is right, Dook Bili. In this little valley we are as safe as we can be in this accursed land. What with all the ground-shakings and mountain tumblings and the fires, as well as the heavy slaughter we all wrought upon the savages, perhaps we will not be noticed before we can retrace our steps and be gone. At least, let us all now pray that the Radiant Lady so ordains it."

Bili watched as each of the grim Maidens, each of the hardbitten Ahrmehnee, nodded their agreement and fumbled silver crescents from beneath breastplate or hauberk.

He shook his shaven head forcefully. "No. To stay here will be to see many of our wounded die needlessly; they need unguents, healers, potions to ease their pain and let them sleep. We all need decent food, and the big horses need grain and hay, for the grass here will not last long and they cannot subsist on treebark and moss as do the ponies. I've seen damn-all game hereabouts, and even were this place aswarm with such, our archers used all their shafts to quill the damned Muhkohee, back there.

"No, to remain here will weaken all and kill some. If die I must, I'd rather do it sitting my stallion and swinging my axe. What say the rest of you?"

Nods and smiles and wordless grunts of assent answered him . . . but only from the lowlander nobles and the Freefighter officers. What Bili read on the firelit faces of the others, Maidens and Ahrmehnee alike, was not fear but, rather, a crawling horror.

"Ride out if you wish, you thing of male foolishness!" snapped the Maiden who had earlier spoken. "And take with you all your followers of stupidness. But first allow us, who reason have, the time to win free of Muhkohee lands."

There was a low but concerted growl from the lowlanders

and mercenaries. They all had seen the Moon Maidens fight and unanimously respected the arms skills and clear courage of them; but these armored girls were still mere females, and the nobles and Freefighters intended to tolerate no abuse or contumely from an overweening pack of man-aping women.

Bili knew that growl and recognized its meaning. He knew full well that aching muscles and near-empty bellies had already gone far toward honing a cutting edge on pride and hot tempers, crafting a weapon which could rend apart this shaky alliance of traditional enemies, further decimate their thin ranks and add to the numbers of the wounded. He made to step into the breach, but another forestalled him.

From out of the surrounding darkness, into the shifting, wavering circle of the firelight, came the *brahbehrnuh*, the chieftainess of the Moon Maidens. She moved slowly, a bit unsteadily. She had shed helm and armor, and her loosened hair cascaded in ebon waves about the high collar of her long cloak of soft, green-dyed leather. Her black eyes were deep-sunk, her face pale under her tan, but her voice was firm, and it contained the natural authority of the born leader.

"Kahndoot," she addressed the Maiden standing with arms akimbo, "sit down and shut up! These men are not as are . . ." Her contralto voice nearly broke as she corrected herself. "As *were* the males of our blood. Accuse such as Dook Bili, there, of foolishness or cowardice and you'll shortly have a bared sword to face."

"But, honored one," protested the Moon Maiden hotly, "this stupid lowlander male wants to raid a Muhkohee village, can he find one; and you know what that will likely mean, there being so very few of us."

The *brahbehrnuh* nodded slowly. "Yes, Kahndoot, I know and you know, but he probably does not. Remember, he is not an Ahrmehnee, not even a cursed Ehleen, by the looks of him. You should have explained to him the danger before you so railed at him."

Kahndoot's brows shot up in amazement. "*Me?* Me, honored one? Explain my reasons to a mere man? Why, that's silly!"

Shuffling over to stand before the Moon Maiden, the *brahbehrnuh* placed her palms on the woman's armored shoulders, saying, softly and sadly, "Yes, love, explain. Remember, the Hold is no more, it is gone, utterly. We few here are likely the very last of our race. Are we to survive, we must learn to adapt to the customs of those with whom our lot be cast.

"Mere man though he be, this Dook Bili has proved himself to be as brave and as wise as any woman here, when he knows where lies danger; moreover, he is the unquestioned leader of these lowlanders. Even the Ahrmehnee seem to have accepted his war-leadership, for all that until less than a single Moon agone, he and his men were burning and looting Ahrmehnee villages and steadings, maiming and slaying and raping Ahrmehnee tribesfolk.

"But now you sit you down, love, and hold your tongue, you and our sisters. *I* will explain the awfulness of our common danger to Dook Bili."

Because she had spoken in the secret language of her race, no male present had understood a single word; this was as she had intended, not wishing to shame one of her sisters before menfolk.

While the outspoken Moon Maiden sank back onto her mailed haunches, the *brahbehrnuh* began to make a slow way around the fire. Her unsteadiness was no less obvious than was her stubborn intention to carry on despite it. This very stubbornness touched Bili, touched him as fully and as deeply as had her reckless courage in the battle which had preceeded the earthquake. He felt a strange oneness with this scarcely known, mannish young woman.

Most of the hunkered or sitting officers and nobles made way for the staggering woman, arising, and only reseating themselves when she had passed. But not so one Tsimbos of Ahnpolis, third son of the lord of that Kehnooryos Ehlas city. Deliberately, grinning insolently up at her, he kept his place and even went so far in his discourtesy as to extend his legs when she made to move around him.

But, suddenly, an immensely powerful hand clamped onto Tsimbos' shoulder and, for all his two and eighty *keelohee* and the added weight of his clothing and armor, he found himself savagely jerked erect, raised until only his booted toes still contacted the ground. Held thus, he was subjected to a thorough shaking, while from behind him a cold voice snapped short, brittle phrases.

"On your misbegotten feet, damn you! She is a chief, a full queen, among her own. And, too, she is ill, as any man can see. She has obviously just used her authority to get us all out of what could have quickly become a very sticky situation. So would you deign to render her less honor than you would me, you young cur?"

Swaying a half-step forward, the *brahbehrnuh* laid her calloused palm on Bili's big, scarred knuckles. In stilted Trade Mehrikan, she said, "No, Dook Bili, please to put down your fighter. His actions but bespoke his anger at the thoughtless provocation of my sister's words. Please, so tightly squeezing his shoulder may do injury to his sword arm. Besides, no offense did I take."

Bili was as stubborn as any, but it seemed now entirely natural to gently ease his chosen victim back down onto his feet, slacking off the armor-crushing grip of that hand through which the cool, wondrous fire now suffusing his body and mind had entered. Stepping around the trembling and terrified Tsimbos of Ahnpolis, he took the elbow he could feel through the *brahbehrnuh's* cloak and guided her to the seat his striker had fashioned for him of war saddles and other gear.

When she had partaken icy brook water laced with fiery brandy from Bili's own silver cup, she commenced to speak. To her surprise, she found that for the first time in all her two hundred and forty Moons, she was not only addressing a man as an equal, she actually felt this Dook Bili to *be* her full equal. She felt more, also, but the thoughts were very strange and they tumbled about inchoate in her mind, and she knew that this was neither the time nor the setting to try to sort them out.

Slipping over, she patted the makeshift couch beside her, saying, "Enough room there is here for us both, Dook Bili."

When he was perched beside her, she began, pitching her voice that all about the big fire might hear, as well. "Dook Bili, you well know that we Moon Maidens and the Ahrmehnee are stark and fearsome fighters. Why then do you think it is that, between us, we never have been able to drive those evil beasts we call the Muhkohee from these our mountains? They are many, true, but the most of those many are very poorly armed, as you saw; in a fair fight, no five of their warriors can stand against even one fully armed Ahrmehnee, much less a Moon Maiden.

"When first they came, those foul monsters who eat folk, they set to storm Maiden Valley, our Hold. Of course, they failed, but she who then was the *brahbehrnuh* took council with the Ahrmehnee chiefs—the *nahkhahrah*, Behdrohz, and his *dehrehbeh*—and it was agreed that, lest another attack on a less well-defended place prove successful and give these human beasts a firm foothold in our lands, the newcomers should be driven farther away or at least taught a hard and a bloody lesson.

"Near fifteen score of Moon Maidens rode out from the Hold, Dook Bili, to join three hundred score of Ahrmehnee warriors. They did not then, you see, think that such primitive savages would require more than half the available strength, so that was just how many fighters were committed. For the future of the races—Ahrmehnee and Maidens, alike—that decision was far wiser than any could then have suspected.

"Five hundreds of Ahrmehnee were left to guard the gap through which the force entered these western lands, and they received, after about a week, a few dozens sick and wounded who told glowing tales of a huge battle in which the Moon Maidens and the Ahrmehnee had smashed and utterly routed a vast horde of the shaggy barbarians. Then the wounded and their pony loads of loot and heads rode east with a few of the five hundred as an escort.

"Dook Bili, there were only some fifty men in all that party, *yet they were the largest single body to ever return from that accursed campaign.* Over the next few months, ones and twos and threes of Moon Maidens and Ahrmehnee trickled out of those dread mountains, all sick of mind and of body and mostly afoot. Many had been driven mad by the unspeakable horrors they had seen and been forced to endure, and, one and all, they implored that none others of their races attempt to penetrate into the Muhkohee lands.

"In all, something less than thirty of our Moon Maidens returned to the Hold out of the near three hundred who rode out so proudly, and those who did return were all broken women, Dook Bili. Waking, they shook and shuddered and cast glances of constant and fearful wariness from eyes deepsunk with horror and the terrors of being hunted like game animals; sleeping, they shrieked and moaned and writhed in private and hideous torments. Few of those poor women lived long after their return, and some died by their own hand, unable to longer bear the torture of their memories.

"When the pitiful survivors could be persuaded to speak of what had befallen, they told of strange, unnatural things—of giant, very hairy men, of loathy monsters haunting dark caves and rushing out to slay warriors whose weapons could not defend them, whose fine armor was seen ripped like so much thin cloth by those far enough away to flee safely from the monsters.

"Also, they told of whole villages, filled with people, which appeared and disappeared in the blinking of an eye, of swords which slashed and spears that stabbed out from empty air, of showers of deadly darts which flew from among rocks too sheer and exposed to give cover or concealment or even bare purchase to any living creature.

"Since those terrible days, Dook Bili, we Moon Maidens and the Ahrmehnee have never again willingly entered Muhkohee lands. Muhkohee raids have been infrequent, and most of the raiders have died fighting. Such little as we know of them and their nauseating habits has been torturously wrung from the unwilling lips of the handful who have been taken alive. The few eastern traders who have ignored our warnings and pushed on westward have never returned to tell us if the captives spoke truth. But most of us fully believe the little we know. I do."

Bili spoke with grave courtesy. "My lady, since I myself saw and slew a man more than three Harzburk yards high and so huge that he made his Northorse look like a mere pony under him, I would be foolish to try to deny that giants, at least, truly do dwell among these Muhkohee. But surely they are few in number, for there was but the one back there on that plateau, among thousands of men of normal size.

"As for being invulnerable to weapons, that one surely was not. When his Northorse stumbled and fell with him, he lost his helm and sword and ran on west, afoot. I slew him, and I attest that my axe clove his bare head to the eyes as easily as it would the head of a smaller man. The brains and blood that gushed from that skull looked to be no different from any other brains and blood I've seen.

"As for the rest of the tale—disappearing villages, invisible attackers and cave-dwelling monsters—I suspend judgment until such a time as I have seen such with my own two eyes.

"Now, my lady, tell me, are these Muhkohee all one tribe, or have they several, like the Ahrmehnee?"

Her raven tresses swirled about her robed shoulders as she shook her head. "No, Dook Bili, they have no tribes or clans, and not many real villages. They live mostly in family groups of no more than a bare score of folk, farming only enough land to support themselves. Muhkohee is not the name of a tribe, it is rather the name of the family—or families, I don't know which—of the giants."

"They are the chiefs, then, my lady? The leaders of these barbarians?" prodded Bili.

"No," she replied, her voice perceptibly weaker than at the beginning. "They have no real leader, I think. The individual families are ruled, like packs of wild dogs, by the strongest male. He kills any challengers until age or infirmity presages his own defeat and death. The ruler of these families has unquestioned access to any female of the family he may fancy at any time—be she his sister, his daughter or even his mother.

"You see, they are very primitive and uncouth, rabidly hating anything which smacks of the decent or the civilized. Even so, their own legends try to name them a very ancient race, saying that their forebears fled the Places of Light long before the Old Gods fought and destroyed those fabled places and themselves. And so . . .

"But I am very tired now, Dook Bili. Besides, the Panosyuhn and Soormehlyuhn tribes have, over the years, taken and questioned more of the cannibals than have the Moon Maidens. I see men of both tribes here. Let them answer such further questions as you have; belike they can do it better than could I."

After the *brahbehrnuh*, assisted by two of her officers, having courteously declined Bili's offer of personal help, had returned to the Moon Maidens, the young duke asked if one of the Ahrmehnee warriors would finish informing him about their mutual enemies.

Vahk Soormehlyuhn's vitality flashed through his dark eyes above the great, sharp beak of his nose. He seated himself, crosslegged, on the ground before Bili, the older man, Vahrtahn Panosyuhn, squatting beside him.

"A filthy and brutish people they are, *Dehrehbeh* Bili. From birth to death, they never bathe, and since, summer and winter, they wear mostly pelts and ill-cured hides, the foul reek of them is unbelievable. More than a few of their raiders have been slain or taken by Ahrmehnee simply because the rotting-flesh stench of them betrayed their presence to our warriors; and that be pure truth."

Bili found this fact easy to believe, recalling the awesome stink of the shaggy savages against whose thousands he had thrown his squadron of lowlanders. Compared to that gagging odor, the commonplace battle smells of sweat and blood, splattered brains and burst entrails, had seemed almost sweet.

Old Vahrtahn Panosyuhn took up the story. "As for the

Muhkohee, huge as they are, they are not chiefs, rather shamans, sorcerers. There were never very many of them, and we assume that they must not breed true, for each succeeding generation sees fewer of them, and those with weakened powers, or so the barbarians we have taken from time to time said before they finally were allowed to die. The Silver Lady grant that all the giants soon be dead, for then and only then can we normal folk stamp out the last of these foul, unnatural eaters of manflesh and make these mountains once more safe for decent, civilized folk to dwell in."

Bili heard several scornful snorts from the group of lowlander nobles and turned his head to loose a venomous glance in their direction. Although, like his nobles, he personally considered the head-hunting and -collecting practiced by the Ahrmehnee tribes about on a par with the cannibalism that they and the *brahbehrnuh* said was among the brutish practices of these Muhkohee—or whatever their true name was —now was no time to stir up discord with the only allies available in this sinister land.

Turning back to the two Ahrmehnee, he asked, "If Muhkohee is not the name of the shaggy men, then what is?"

Vahk spread his big hands and grinned. "It's a hard word for an Ahrmehnee-speaker to shape his mouth about, *Dehrehbeh* Bili, which is the main reason we've kept calling them Muhkohee all these years." He grinned even wider and added, "Among other and far less complimentary things, that is.

"As closely as I can come to what they call themselves, it is Ohrgahnikahnsehrvaishuhnee."

Bili, himself, grinned wryly. "I can now see just why you and your folk stuck to Muhkohee, Sir Vahk. I think me that I'll follow your precept on the matter."

Old Panosyuhn spoke up again. "Such as we know of their customs and usages, Dook Bili, are exceeding strange. For, although they all partake of manflesh with great gusto, they will not eat of the flesh of their kine or fowl, taking of them only milk and eggs and hides; and, too, although they hunt bears and wolves and the like for the furs and pelts, not even a starveling Muhkohee would eat of those creatures' flesh."

Bili shook his head in consternation at such wastefulness. "What do they do, then, just leave good meat out to rot?"

"No, Dook Bili," replied Panosyuhn, "they *bury* the carcasses of the game and of any of their dead kine or fowl, too. With great ceremony and solemn sorrow do they bury them, all the while praying to their gods. Rather to one of their chief gods, him called Kahlohdjee, in their tongue."

"They have many gods, then?" inquired Bili.

"I think so, Dook Bili. I think they have very many gods, though I know the names of only a few of their gods or of their many devils," Panosyuhn answered, furrowing his wrinkled forehead and ticking off the difficult names on his fingers. "Let's see . . . *Kahlohdjee* is one, *N'Vyrmuhndt* is another, then there be the god Plooshuhn . . ."

"Your pardon, please, *Der* Vahrtahn," interjected Soormehlyuhn with the customary respect shown to older Ahrmehnee by younger. "But I think I recall that Plooshuhn be not a god but one of the greatest of their devils."

Panosyuhn tilted his head, closed his eyes and scratched at the scalp explosed under his thinning hair, then he opened his dark-brown eyes and nodded briskly. "My thanks, young Vahk. The valiant Vahk be right, Dook Bili. I am an old man and I had misremembered. Plooshuhn is a god, but a very evil god, to the Muhkohee . . . or so say these evilest of living men.

"Plooshuhn is, say these terrible Muhkohee, the patron devil of any who smelt ores, cast bronze or suchlike. This, Dook Bili, be why Muhkohee-fashioned tools and even weapons be always of cold-hammered iron, unless they have been able to steal better, properly made ones.

"These manlike monsters have no respect for age and its wisdom, either. Whenever a man or woman of their groups is found too old or infirm to do a full day of useful tasks, they kill and eat him or her, and in especially hard times they think nothing of eating their youngest children."

Bili's shock and amazement was borne in his voice. "Yet they cast away the flesh of any beast? They must be a race of madmen, these Muhkohee."

"There are some beasts they will eat," put in Soormehlyuhn. "Any fish, frogs or snakes they can catch, lizards, too. They remove the scales or skins and fins, but they eat everything else, even the guts and all they contain. They also eat insects, worms, grubs and caterpillars. I doubt me not that a Muhkohee stew would turn the stomach of a hog."

When he had heard all that the two Ahrmehnee knew of the singular customs of their traditional enemies, Bili dismissed the gathering, announcing that he would sleep on the matter and apprise all of his decision on just what course they had best take on the morrow.

But when at last the young duke lay rolled in his cloak on the springy bough bed made for him by his striker, sleep seemed to elude him for some time, despite the physical exhaustion of the events of the long, strenuous day just past. For one thing, he was very worried about what might have befallen old *Komees* Hari, brave Sir Geros and all those others who had become separated from the main party during the confusion following the earthquake. Unless Hari had kept his wing together and had lucked onto such a relatively secure campsite as Bili's, the old man and his troops were in direst danger.

Straining his vast telepathic abilities to the utmost, Bili vainly endeavored to range *Komees* Hari's mind . . . nor could he contact any of the few other minds he knew well in that band, which might mean all or nothing. They could all be already dead, or his failure could be simply caused by some something in his own makeup and present condition.

For, as the High Lord Milo and the High Lady Aldora had often attested in his hearing, despite all the years of study and practice, not even they could admit to knowing very much about their own telepathy, much less that of anyone else.

"If I had one of the prairiecats here, now," mused Bili, "to merge our two minds and so increase my range and power . . ."

But all of the great felines who had accompanied his force on the march west and in the battle on the plateau were missing, like Hari and Geros and the rest.

Helpless to contact any of his friends, Bili's restless mind roved back again to last year's events, to the eventual investment and siege of Vawnpolis, where once more the genius of *Vahrohneeskos* Drehkos Daiviz of Morguhn had manifested itself.

"And even then, disregarding mountains of evidence to the contrary," thought Bili ruefully, "there were those of us who were still able to convince ourselves that that bastard *Vahrohnos* Myros of Dehskati was really the shrewd mind we faced."

"It wasn't until . . . until the near disaster that followed our taking of those two outer salients of Vawnpolis that most of us really began to believe that another mind than Myros' might be guiding the opposition. Sun and Wind, what a close call that was."

And once more young Bili's mind flew back over time and

distance to the day of the assault on the outer works of the invested city of Vawnpolis, held by the Ehleen rebels.

An hour before the dawn, Aldora's maidservant wakened her mistress. The High Lady and Bili arose, washed, broke fast on a bit of hard bread dipped in strong wine, then helped each other to arm and wended their way to the sprawling pavilion of the High Lord. There they separated, with Aldora riding off to the cavalry camp and Bili remaining with Milo to accompany his sovereign at the head of the assaulting infantry.

No words were either spoken or beamed at the parting of the lovers; none were needed, for their two straining, striving, pleasure-racked bodies had communicated all that was needful in the night now dying. As for Milo, he allowed himself a silent chuckle or two, for Aldora trotted off astride none other than Mahvros, Bili's own huge black warhorse—a one-man, mindspeaking killer stallion that had never before allowed any other than his "brother," Bili, to fork him.

Preceded by a pinkish vanguard, the copper-hued sun peeked over the eastern horizon, and, with a crash and roll of drums, a shrilling of fifes, a pealing of trumpets, the gruesome day commenced.

When his two younger brothers—Djaik and Gilbuht, down from the Middle Kingdoms to have a share in this marvelous war now raging so unexpectedly almost in their own home duchy—requested permission to ride this day with the mounted Freefighters, Bili was more than happy to grant such permission, for it summarily relieved him of two worries.

He had already seen one brother slain by these rebels, and he had no wish to have two or even one more go to Wind. There was a good chance that the mounted Freefighters and Confederation lancers would not fight at all this day; and even if they were called upon to smash back any sortie which might be made to relieve or reinforce the two salients, Djaik and Gil would be much better off heavily armed and in the saddles of their fully trained destriers and fighting the kind of combat with which they were most familiar than they would be afoot, in half-armor, clawing through abattises and clambering up shaky ladders.

Bili did not much like undertaking that prospect himself, but since the High Lord had elected to personally lead this attack, the Morguhn of Morguhn had felt honor-bound to serve at his overlord's side.

Aldora had shaved his head early last evening, and the rising sun glinted on the shiny scalp as he carefully checked and rechecked the fit and fastenings of harness on the two horses that would bear him and the High Lord until the attack actually commenced.

The High Lord's big chestnut nuzzled at Bili's thigh and mindspoke. "Am I to have no armor at all? Or did you forget mine as you forgot the most of your own, twolegs?"

Bili slapped the muscular neck affectionately, scratching away at the base of the neatly roached mane until the horse was almost purring. He silently answered, "It be a hot morn, already, and the day will be even hotter and very long. You two will be doing no fighting, so why burden you down with armor and padding, eh?

"Your brother, the High Lord Milo, and I will not have your thews to help us bear the weight of plate in the coming battle, so we wear only helms and cuirasses, plus gorgets, shoulder pieces, brassarts and kneecops, with our swords slung across our backs."

The chestnut stamped and snorted derision, rolling his eyes. "Stupid! That, twolegs, be a stupid way to fight. Yes, it be hot, but not so hot as the lands where I was foaled. Put on our armor and your own; we can fight as well as you."

Bili chuckled to himself; this chestnut could be every bit as stubborn and set in his ways as could his own stallion brother, Mahvros. "I know well that you can fight, brother, but can you climb twelve-foot stone walls? Do you think that your armor will stop sixty-pound boulders or eight-foot spears . . . or did you intend to catch them all in your teeth, perhaps?"

"My lord duke . . . ?"

Bili turned from the horse to face Captain Pawl Raikuh. This Freefighter officer who commanded Bili's company of hired fighters was also half-armored, with the hilt of his broadsword jutting up behind his left shoulder and his left hand gripping a five-foot spearshaft with two feet of double-edged pike blade riveted to it. Behind the captain stood Color Sergeant Geros Lahvoheetos, similarly armed and holding the ten-foot shaft about which was furled the Red Eagle Banner of the House and Clan of Morguhn.

"What are you doing here, Pawl?" Bili demanded in a voice tinged with surprise. "I would have thought you'd send Hohguhn or Krahndahl to lead this contingent under me.

Surely you're not depending upon either of them to captain our cavalry today?"

Raikuh grinned. "No, my lord. My lord's brother, Lord Djaik, vice-captains his horse for this engagement."

Bili first started, then relaxed, smiling. "Oh, nominally, you mean. I thank you for that courtesy to him, Pawl."

"Scant courtesy, that." Raikuh shook his head, his lobster-tail napeguard rattling. My lord Djaikuhb will *lead*. And should it come to action, I'm sure he'll do your lordship proud."

"Oh, come now, Pawl," snapped Bili deprecatingly. "Our troop is composed entirely of veterans, and, as such, they'll not be putting their lives on the line at the behest of an over-grown fourteen-year-old. Men have to respect a warleader."

Raikuh sobered. "And respect my lord's brother they do, one and all. Any who chanced to not see Lord Djaik fence Old Pyk, the senior weaponsmaster, to a standstill last night have heard of it. And besides, they'll be flattered to have a blood brother of my lord to lead them."

Bili frowned. "Well, what then of my other brother, Gil? He be anything but feckless. Think you he then will mildly obey the dictates of a younger brother? I doubt it."

Raikuh's grin returned with a vengeance. "Hardly, my lord. My lord's brothers had . . . ahhh, some few words on the matter. My lord Gil has decided to ride with Duke Hwahltuh's force."

Bili could just bet they had "some few words on the matter." Since first the two Morguhn cadets had been reunited, it often had been all that their elder brother and chief could do to keep them from each other's throats—and in cold, deadly earnest, at that.

Both Djaikuhb and Gilbuht were experienced warriors and natural leaders . . . and that last was a part of the problem. But the biggest bone of contention between the two lay to the north of the Confederation, in the lands where they had fostered, had their upbringing and arms training.

The Duchy of Zunburk, which had sheltered Gilbuht for almost eight years, was a traditional ally of the Kingdom of Harzburk. Harzburk's ancient foe was the Kingdom of Pitzburk, wherein Djaikuhb had been fostered and trained for six years.

CHAPTER IV

When *Strahteegos Vahrohnos* Ahrtos of Theesispolis reported his troops to be ready, the High Lord—wearing no more armor than did Bili or Captain Raikuh—emerged from his pavilion and mounted his chestnut, hanging a hooked and spiked warhammer on his pommel. In obedience to his mindspoken command, his mount began a slow trot toward the waiting ranks of the Confederation infantry.

As there had been no desire to keep secret their day's objectives, engines had been pounding the fortifications crowning and ringing the two hillocks since there had been enough light to lay and sight them; and they were still hard at the job. Bili could see dust spurts, hear the distance-muffled thuds of the boulders against timber, masonry and earthworks, while the smoke from the blazes caused by the pitchballs and firespears rose high into the windless morning sky.

To his experienced eye, it did not appear that the engines' missiles had effected much real damage to either of the salients. A few dressed stones had been knocked askew here and there and more had surely been loosened, the timber facings of some of the earthworks were smashed and splintered in places, but the bulk of the thick, wide, cunningly laid abattises—designed to hold attacking men in one place long enough for the defenders' darts and slingstones and arrows to thin their ranks—seemed to be virtually untouched.

The High Lord's mindspeak answered the young man's unasked question. "Oh, yes, Bili, my engineers know well their work. But much of that is green wood, still in the bark and, consequently, hard to fire. Also, the bastards apparently have plenty of water, and they've managed to quench nearly every fire we've managed to start. I can but hope that you're as good at axing wood as you are at axing men."

Accompanied by Bili, Captain Raikuh, *Strahteegos* Ahrtos and his entourage, a squad of his personal mounted guards and their commander, *Mehgah* Aib Fahrlee, the High Lord slowly inspected the formations of infantrymen—twelve thousand, in all, drawn up in battalion front.

The assault companies were foremost, bearing woodsman's axes, pry bars and hooked poles for pulling apart the outer entanglements. They were shieldless, but armed with wide and heavy shortswords and half-armored in good plate.

Next were the infantry archers, their compound bows larger and more powerful than the cavalry weapon. Their mission was to keep the defenders too busy ducking arrows to loose any of their own at the laboring assault companies until enough of the abattises were cleared away for the actual attack to begin.

Then came rank upon serried rank of heavy infantry, the backbone of the Army of the Confederation, spearbutts and ironshod shields grounded. Their helms were fitted with napeguards, cheekpieces and nasals, the collars of their knee-length scaleshirts were chin-high, and the plate greaves strapped to their lower legs included a kneecop which was spiked to facilitate climbing. The long pikes which Bili had seen them sloping on the march had been replaced by six-foot spears.

Bili studied the faces under those field-browned helms, to find that all—old or young, Ehleen-dark or Kindred-fair— were weather-tanned and seamed with scars. Here and there a copper cat crouched atop a helm, denoting the valor and the singular battle prowess of its wearer. A very few helms boasted silver cats, but Bili saw only two golden cats in the course of the progress.

One golden cat adorned the helm of a slender, hard-eyed young *lohkahgos*, standing stiff and motionless as a stone statue before the assault company he led. The other crested the helm of a grizzled, short-legged and thick-bodied soldier, whose equipage sported no single other mark of rank or achievement.

"Well, I'll be damned!" The High Lord reined up before the man and leaned over the chestnut's withers to peer into the green eyes under the white-flecked, brick-red brows. "If it isn't Djim Bohluh. I thought you'd been pensioned off long ago. What's wrong, Djim, has that scaleshirt taken root in your scaly old hide?"

Letting his shield rest against his leg, the old soldier clasped both big hands about his spearshaft and put his weight upon it, lifting one foot from the ground. Ignoring the venomous glare of a squadleader who looked young enough to be his grandson, he showed worn, yellow teeth in a broad grin.

"Speak true, Lord Milo, can you see these here hands a-pushin' a plow or a-milkin' a cow?"

Milo chuckled. "You've got a point there, right enough, Djim. But look at the rest of it, man: your own piece of land, a snug cabin and a young wife to tend you and to get you sons to fill the ranks."

The soldier cackled. "No need to leave the army to do that last. I bin doin' that for . . . well, for more years than I cares to think on. Fac' is, Lord Milo, chances are at leas' a good comp'ny's worth of these here boys *is* my get, did they but know it. For that matter, young *Lohkeeas* Froheeros there"—he pointed with his chin at the livid, almost apoplectic squad leader—"do put me much in min' of a lil gal I useta pleasure, down Sahvahnahs way."

Bili saw almost all of the surrounding faces jerk or twitch to a muffled chorus of groans and gasps which told of suppressed laughter, while the young sergeant's lividity deepened until he looked as if he were being garroted. Not even the stern-faced *Strahteegos* Ahrtos could repress a grin.

The High Lord clasped his hands on his pommel. "You insubordinate old reprobate. How old are you, anyway?"

Bohluh shifted uncomfortably, lost his grin and looked down at the ground. "Oh . . . ahhh, I be unsure, Lord Milo, bein' such a iggernant man and all. I . . . I thinks I be about forty-four . . . give 'r take a year 'r so."

Milo snorted derisively. "Take none and give a dozen or more, you white-haired scoundrel! Djim, you were a man grown when I gave you that cat, after the big battle at Wild Rose River; and that was more than thirty years ago.

"*Strahteegos* Ahrtos." Turning in his saddle, he bespoke the infantry commander. "Why hasn't this man, Bohluh, been retired?"

That officer squirmed in his saddle. "Well . . . ahh, well, my lord, it . . ."

But Bohluh interrupted. "Lord Milo, don't go a-blamin' young Ahrtos, there, 'cause it ain't none of it his fault. He be a damned good of'cer, allus has been. But alla my records they got burned up in that big fire at Goohm, fourteen year agone. An' when we set out a-doin' them over, it might be some names and dates got put down wrong, is all."

Milo sighed. "Djim, you must be pushing sixty . . . hard; and that's half again the average lifespan, even for a civilian.

Old friend, war is an activity for young men. I think I should retire you here and now.

"Report back to the duty officer in your camp and start packing your personal effects. When I'm done in this field, I'll have orders drafted to get you back to Kehnooryos Ehlas; or you can retire in Morguhn, if you wish. There're right many new-made widows there, and *Thoheeks* Bili is going to need some loyal husbands for them."

Bohluh's spear fell, clattering, and the boss of his shield clanged on the hard, pebbly ground. His lined, seamed face working, he stumbled forward from his place in the ranks, one big, callused hand raised beseechingly, the other grasping the chestnut's reins.

"Please, Lord Milo, please don' send me away, please let me stay. This be my *home*, my lord, the onlies' home I've knowed for near forty-seven year. If . . . if I didn' hear the drum of a mornin', I'd . . . I couldn', wouldn' want to . . . I means . . ." Then the old man's voice broke and he could only sob chokedly, over and over, "Please, Lord Milo, please don't send me away . . ."

And something in those swimming green eyes touched a deep nerve in Bili of Morguhn. He urged his horse up beside the High Lord's and touched his arm.

"My lord, if you please . . ."

Milo mindspoke impatiently, "This is none of your affair, Bili. It's army business, a matter of broken regulations. We can't afford the precedent of a sixty-odd-year-old soldier swinging a sword in the ranks. Damned few officers, even, are allowed to serve past the age of fifty."

"I . . . I understand your position, my lord. So, too . . . I think . . . does he. He knows that this is the end of his long, long road. But . . . but I do not think my lord understands him."

"And you," beamed the High Lord with a tinge of sarcasm, "from the preeminent wisdom of your less than twenty summers, do?"

"Your pardon, my lord, I had no wish to offend."

"No, *your* pardon, Bili." The biting edge was departed from Milo's mindspeak. "I don't suppose I'll ever get over being jumpy before a battle; and I sometimes forget your constantly expanding mental abilities. So, what do old Djim's words say to you?"

"He craves one last boon, my lord. A soldier's death, and this one, last battle in which to find that death."

"And you *know* this, Bili?" demanded Milo. "How?"

The answer came quickly and unhesitatingly. "My lord, I can just sense that this Bohluh and I are much alike, and were I in his position, this is what I would beg of a man I had served so long and so well."

"Bili," Milo beamed, "discipline in my army is much stricter than what passes for such in your Middle Kingdoms hosts. Every ear within the hearing has noted my ordering him back to camp, and it would damage morale if his pleas seemed to bring about a reversal of that order. Besides, it's highly probable that his company won't even fight today. These regiments are drawn up for effect; we'll not use a third of them, if that many."

"Djim Bohluh has served you well, my lord?" asked Bili.

"He'd not have that cat otherwise," Milo retorted. "He's been up and down the noncommissioned ladder so many times that he's worn a path in the rungs of it. But that's because, when in garrison, he's a boozing, brawling, womanizing, insubordinate rakehell. But on campaign, in many a battle, he's been worth his weight in emeralds. Had I had as few as one regiment just like him, the western border of the Confederation would be somewhere on the Sea of Grass today."

"Yes, Bili, Djim Bohluh has, indeed, served me well."

"Then, my lord," suggested Bili, "second him to me, to my guard, and let him find that which he now seeks with us. I know damned well we'll wet our blades this day."

As Bili remembered, he and Captain Raikuh had been atop the ridge above the little hollow where their Freefighters were clumped, wetting brick-dry mouths out of their water bottles and listening to some long and endlessly obscene tale spun by old Djim Bohluh. He and the captain had been observing and commenting upon the actions of the assault companies and the archers who were not very successfully attempting to cover their efforts.

Then young Geros Lahvoheetos had climbed up, and they three had been discussing various aspects of the Freefighter's trade and what did and did not constitute bravery when the High Lord mindspoke him.

"Bili, move your company down to *Strahteego*s Ahrtos' position. I'll be leading the attack on the left salient and Ahrtos will be in command of the attack on the right one; but I want you with him, because you own a quality that he all-but lacks—imagination.

"Take care of yourself, son. If anything happens to you this day, Aldora will no doubt make my life miserable for the next century or two."

The attack had been absolutely hellish. Only narrow gaps had been cleared through the interlaced abattis, and the Confederation infantry sustained heavy losses while threading through the openings. Slingstones and arrows and darts hailed down thickly from the summit of the fortified hillock, despite the shafts rained on the defenders by the Confederation archers.

Then, when the survivors were at last through the deadly hedge and were forming up for the uphill charge against the bristling breastworks and the masonry walls beyond, no less than *three* catapult stones—from Confederation engines, too!—fell short and bounced a sanguineous path through the forming ranks; the hundredweight missiles sent steel scales flying and mashed leather and flesh and bone into one indistinguishable sickening jelly.

The ranks closed up again and the charge was launched, but less than halfway up the slope, *Strahteegos* Ahrtos—his visor open for better vision—had his jaw torn almost off by a slingstone and fell, clashing and gurgling bloodily, at Bili's feet.

The sub-*strahteegos* who immediately assumed the lead got but a few yards farther up when a pitchball took him full on the breastplate, and Bili's last view of the unfortunate officer was of a writhing, shrieking, flame-shrouded figure rolling on the ground.

The *keeleeohstos* who then took over made it almost to the outer works—a chest-high, earth-and-timber rampart—when a thick-shafted, four-foot engine dart spitted him through the belly, going through his high-grade steel plate as cleanly as a warm knife through soft cheese.

Then Bili had no more time to watch or count the succession of commanders. He leaped aside barely in time to avoid a trayful of red-hot sand, though a hideous scream from just behind him attested that the sand had landed on some poor bastard. But Bili surged forward, and the powerful sweep of his heavy axe cleanly severed a leg of the man holding the tray.

And somehow Bili found himself atop the breastwork, wreaking bloody carnage on the swift succession of foes who appeared for but bare eyeblinks before him, dimly recording the shock of countless blows on his own plate and helm.

Oblivious to the familiar cacophony of battle, he concentrated only on remaining alive . . . and seeing to it that his opponents did not.

Then only the backs of rebels running up toward the stone-walled summit met his eyes, and someone's—was that Raikuh's voice?—shout was ringing through his closed helm.

" . . . Bili, Duke Bili, if we tail those bastards now, we'll take fewer casualties. The frigging archers and darters won't be able to range us without ranging their own, as well."

Bili attempted to speak, but he had to work his tongue about in the aridity of his mouth before he could wet his throat enough to get the words out. "Whoever the new army commander is, he'll take time to dress his troops, however many of them are left. You've seen how these hidebound regular arseholes operate, man!"

Raikuh shook his head briskly, his lobstertail napeguard rattling. "There're damn-all officers left, Duke Bili. The highest-ranking bugger I can see is a lieutenant, and he's missing a hand."

"Then who the hell led the regulars up here?" demanded Bili. "Somebody must've led them onto this rampart."

"If anybody did, it was you, my lord," snapped Raikuh bluntly. "They followed you once, they'll do it again. If we wait around for those spit-and-polish types to forward another senior officer, damned few of them or us will make it up to those bloody walls!"

Bili whirled to face the regular infantry men and lifted his gory axe on high, roaring, "After them! After the bastards!"

For a breathless moment, the Confederation troops wavered, partially reassured at the voice and tone of command, but on edge, uneasy at the lack of formation. And that was when old Djim Bohluh repaid Bili's kindness.

"Sacred Sun fry your shitty arses!" bellowed the loud and far-reaching voice of the sometime senior noncom, its flavor unquestionably that of parade grounds and make-work details, "What're you pig-fuckers a-waitin' on? You heerd the friggin' order! Or has them there money-fighters got them more guts than you? Move, damn you, *move!*"

And it was just as Raikuh had said it would be. The defenders of the walls had the bitter choice of loosing full at their own comrades now retreating from the captured ramparts or having the bulk of the attackers run up the slope unscathed. So they tried what they took to be a middle course, loosing at a high angle and hoping that their shafts fell upon the proper heads; most of the rebel archers lived just long enough to rue their error in judgment.

Not, thought the still-wakeful Bili—lying rolled in his woolen cloak in a lean-to shelter somewhere far to the west of any civilized land or people—that there still weren't some close moments yet to come that day. Not to mention what Geros did . . . and Bili still had trouble believing he did it, though he saw it with his own eyes and knighted him for it.

The shouting, screaming, cheering, howling broil of men had swept over those gateless walls, their jabbing spears and dripping swords leaving red ruin in their wake, while shrieking panic fled before them.

Bili's pitiless axe scythed ruthlessly through the press of rebels atop the wall. At its inner edge, he kicked over a ladder down which the less nimble defenders were fleeing, then jumped lightly to the stone paving of the inner court, briefly wondering where the defenders had lived in the absence of huts or tents within the fortification.

But the thought was necessarily short, for he was almost immediately confronted by a determined opponent armed with a broadsword and a huge body shield—a rebel officer, if the garish richness of the elaborately chased and inlaid full suit of plate was any indication.

An experienced warrior, this one, for he handled his long sword and weighty shield with a practiced ease, deflecting Bili's hard-swung axe on a sloped shieldface and quickly rushing inside, too close for the axe to be effective. His flickering blade feinted briefly at Bili's visor slits before its point sank through leather and cloth and into the flesh and muscle high on the young *thoheeks'* thigh.

Roaring his pain and rage, Bili closed the distance even more, and his left hand let go the iron axe shaft to pinion the wrist of the rebel's sword arm in an armor-crushing grip. Heedless of the searing agony of the steel buried in his leg, he pivoted half around, slid his right hand halfway up the axeshaft and ferociously rammed the central spike betwixt the gilded bars of his adversary's visor.

With a gurgling, gasping scream, the swordsman stumbled back, his big shield dragging, his sword hanging by its knot. Bili disengaged his axe, whirled it up in both hands and swung a crashing blow against the side of that black-plumed helm. The swordsman was hurled to the pavement and lay motionless and soundless while immense quantities of blood gushed from between the visor bars of his sundered helm.

And Bili strode on to his next encounter.

Lying with his cheek pressed against the scratchy saddle blanket, Bili thought, "And that was when I very nearly died. Would have, if not for Geros; he deserved his knighting for that alone. That big rebel could've crushed me like a bug with that monstrous club of his. He was the biggest man I'd ever seen, before I saw a Muhkohee, that is."

Instinctively, he winced and flinched at the memory. "One minute I was hacking my way through that mob of rebels, the next minute it felt as if lightning had struck me in the small of the back. Then that pavement came up and slammed against my visor and it was all I could do to turn my head enough to see that gigantic rebel raising his club to finish me. Thank Sun and Wind that Geros had been hard on my heels through the whole, bloody broil. How did the tale I squeezed out of him go, now?"

Freefighter Color Sergeant Geros Lahvoheetos, well protected by his two Freefighter color guards and the old infantryman, Djim Bohluh—a fearsome and formidable fighter for all his age—had trailed the *thoheeks* and Captain Raikuh as closely as possible amid the chaos of shove, thrust, slash and hack. Leaden slingshot and various other missiles had holed and rent the Red Eagle Banner during that protracted and ghastly ascent of the hill, but Djim's big infantry shield had sheltered Geros himself from any harm.

One of his assigned guards—Hahfah, he thought it was— had fallen off the stone wall with a stove-in helmet, so close that his plunging body almost took Geros with it. The other one rolled off the walltop into the paved court, locked in a deadly grapple with a rebel.

Then, down in the swirling battle raging all over that court, both Pawl Raikuh and old Djim were swept out of the narrow view afforded Geros by his closed visor. Nonetheless, he kept doggedly on his lord's heels, using his fine sword where necessary and taking blows on his armor and helm until his entire being was a single, throbbing ache.

Just ahead of the colors, Bili's gore-slimy axe downed rebel after rebel—shattering shields, crumpling plate and helms, severing limbs, smashing heads and chests. Behind Geros, wielding sabers and broadswords and a miscellany of pole arms, came two score Freefighters of the Morguhn Company and, after them, the battered remnants of the Confederation infantry, mostly spearless now but proving no less deadly with shortsword and shield.

The rebels fought hard, as vicious as so many cornered rats, holding every bare inch of ground with a suicidal tenacity; but slowly they were driven back and back, their thinning line constricting around a central brick-and-stone platform mounting two large engines. Twice they tried to form a ring of overlapped shields, but each time Bili's terrible axe lopped off spearheads and beat down shields and the Freefighters poured ravening through the gaps, their blood-dimmed blades sending more and more dozens of rebels down to gasp out their lives on the red-running ground.

Then the main battle was boiling about the platform, under the very arms of the big catapults, and old Djim—bleeding in a dozen places, but grinning broadly—was once more at Geros' side, only to be swept away and disappear again a moment later. A sustained roar of deep-voiced cheering arose from the rear, loud enough that the color sergeant could hear it even over the incredible din engulfing him. He took a brief glance over his shoulder to see fresh companies of Confederation infantry, wave after wave of them, appear atop the wall and jump down into the court.

He turned back just in time to see *Thoheeks* Bili beaten to earth by a giant of a man swinging a massive timber like a whole treetrunk and still in the bark. Oblivious of the blades beating upon his cuirass, Geros hurled himself forward, ducked under the swing of the giant's log and jammed the mostly ornamental brass point of the standard staff deep into the monstrous man's belly, just below the horn-buckled belt.

With a high, falsetto scream, the stricken rebel dropped his log, grabbed the shaft and pulled it free of his body with an ugly sucking sound. Then, whining, his pasty, beardless face contorted, he lumbered toward the man who had hurt him, his ham-sized hands extended before him.

Instinctively, Geros realized that it would be his very life to chance within reach of those hands. Wedging the ferrule of the standard in a wide crack between the paves, he brought up his sword and danced back out of reach as lightly as his tired, trembling legs would move. Assuming a point fighter's crouch, he awaited his huge foe's slow advance, then aimed a powerful thrust at the impossibly broad expanse of unarmored chest . . . and almost fell into those deadly clutches!

Too late, he noticed that the giant's arms not only were packed with rolling muscles but were almost as long as the combined lengths of his sword *and* sword arm. Even though he hurriedly pulled the thrust, the right hand locked about the swordblade and sought to jerk Geros closer, to his death.

Frantically, the sergeant pulled back with all his might. After a heart-stopping moment of resistance, the honed edges sliced through callus and skin and flesh and sinew to grate on massy bone and slide free, the sword's passage lubricated with hot red blood.

Raising his ruined, useless, spurting hand to eye level, the hulking creature rent the air with another of those shrill, womanish screams, then placed the gory palm and fingers tight against his punctured belly, from which a purplish-pink loop of gut was working. But he did not halt his shuffling advance.

To fall or even stumble would presage a messy death, so Geros backed cautiously, his knees flexed and his booted feet feeling a way across the uneven footing of blood-slick paving, dropped weapons and still or twitching bodies. The young sergeant was suffused with a cold, crawling terror, for he well knew that no sane man would so stalk an armed and armored opponent while lacking any sort of weapons but bare hands . . . and but the one of those.

His every instinct told him *run*, turn and *run!* And he knew that he should, but he could not, for the giant was now between him and *Thoheeks* Bili, still lying stunned where he had fallen. So, despite it all, despite the fear that was almost unmanning him, Geros could not willingly desert his young lord.

It was the monster, though, who stumbled over a dead body and would have fallen on his face, had he not slammed the wide palm of his only good hand on the slimy ground. And Geros spied his opportunity and danced in, his point quick as a striking viper, sinking deep, deep into the left eye of that upraised face.

The shudder that racked the gargantuan body all but wrenched the broadsword from Geros' grasp. Then the tree-thick left arm flexed and the dead giant's huge head thumped the paving stones.

"I've known, lived with, warriors for the best part of my life," thought Bili, still wakeful in the chill mountain night, "and Sir Geros Lahvoheetos is unquestionably one of the bravest men it has ever been my honor to meet or soldier with. But just try convincing him of the fact! He's absorbed too many sagas of matchless, unblemished heros and is firmly convinced that because his bladder fails him in action, he must be a coward.

"Yet his second and greatest feat, that day, was the very stuff of sagas. It was an impossibility; only a madman would have believed it could happen. Yet I *saw* it, and so did at least three dozen other men."

Old Pyk, the Freefighter weaponmaster, clucked concernedly while he wrapped bandage about Bili's thigh. "It's stopped bleeding, my lord. Still, I think it should be properly burnt, else you run the risk of losing the leg to the black stink." He finished lapping the bandage and neatly tied the ends, adding, "And a wound-burning be much easier, my lord, if you've no long time to think on it."

Bili lowered the big canteen of brandy-water from his lips and smiled. "Thank you, Master Pyk, but no. When we be back in camp, I'll have the Zahrtohgahn physician, Master Ahlee, see to the wound. I've had wounds burnt ere this, and I much prefer the soft words of his mode of healing to your old-fashioned red-hot spearhead."

The young *thoheeks* leaned back against the merlon, refusing to allow his face to mirror his pain, while his orderly folded the slit leg of the blood-caked breeches over the bulk of the bandage, then pulled the boottop back up and secured its straps.

A nearby Freefighter remarked, "My lord, Captain Raikuh is coming back."

Bili opened his eyes and levered himself into a sitting posture on the parapet of the inner works and took one more pull at the canteen, then resolutely corked it; it would not do to have fuzzy wits if push came to shove and he was forced to have another shouting match with Sub-*strahteegos* Kahzos Kahlinz, now senior Confederation officer in the conquered salient.

Pawl Raikuh strode across the carnage he had helped to make, stepping around the bodies, where possible. All at once he stopped, bent to peer closely, then drew out his dirk and sank to squat beside a dead rebel; after he had wiped his blade on the dead man's clothing, he sheathed it, dropped something shiny into his belt purse, arose and continued on his way.

When he had climbed the ladder, he paced deliberately over to Bili's place, removed his helmet and saluted. The padded hood which still covered most of his head was sweat-soaked, and there was a crust of old blood on his upper lip and around his nostrils; his scarred face was drawn with fatigue.

Bili waved to the stretch of parapet on his right, saying, "Pawl, sit down before you fall down. And here, try some of this brandy-water; most refreshing, it is."

After the briefest of hesitations, the captain sank with a sigh onto the proffered seat and gratefully accepted the canteen. He took one mouthful, swished it about in his mouth and spit the pink-tinged fluid downhill, then threw back his head and upended the bottle, his throat working.

"What," asked Bili, "did our esteemed colleague have to say when you transmitted my message that his troops could now begin clearing the field, Pawl?"

Raikuh grinned. "Very little of a respectable nature, Duke Bili. His remarks tend to leave the distinct impression that he has little use for Freefighters and even less for Middle Kingdoms-trained country noblemen who fail to give him and his pack of brainless pikepushers the full degree of respect he feels they and he deserve."

Bili snorted. "The bastard is mad, must be. Brought in his companies on the tag end of the battle—most of them never even blooded their steel, except to dispatch some rebel wounded—and then expected us to bow low and give him and his the first pick, the top cream of the loot! If he's a fair example of the kind of officers the High Lord is raising up these days, then Sun and Wind help our Confederation, is all I can say."

Extending his hand, he poked at a bejeweled hilt peeking out from under Raikuh's boottop. "Found some goodies yourself, did you, Pawl?"

His grin broadening, Raikuh rubbed his hand along the bulge. "It be a genuine Yvuhz, my lord, with a real gold hilt, but it's not mine. It's equal shares in my company; whatever the lads and I find goes into a common pot, and the proceeds will be evenly split."

Bili nodded gravely. "There's a good decision, Pawl. Too many companies end up hacking each other over scraps of loot." He smiled teasingly. "But we've the intaking of a city ahead of us. How are you going to apply your rule to female loot?"

"Share and share, I suppose, my lord . . . within reason, of course. But we'll just have to ford that particular river when we come to it."

Raikuh took another deep pull at the dwindling contents of

the canteen, then said, "My lord, we took the time to measure that man who knocked you down; that bugger was over eight foot tall, and I'd not be surprised if he weighed more than six hundred Harzburk pounds! He must have had the thews of a destrier, too, for it took three men to even lift that log that he was swinging like a staff. I wonder he didn't break your back with it, my lord, cuirass or no cuirass."

Gingerly, Bili shifted his position. "I'm still not sure he didn't, Pawl. But you mean that our Geros slew such an ogre single-handed, with only his sword?"

"No, my lord." Raikuh shook his head. "First he tickled the big bastard's guts with the point of the standard staff—to the full length of that brass blade, and just below the navel. My own belly aches just to think of such a wounding."

"And where is Geros now, Pawl?"

"I sent him and a detail back to our camp to fetch horse litters for our wounded. And pack mules for our dead."

"BILI!" Milo's powerful mindspeak burst within the skull of the young *thoheeks* suddenly and with terrifying intensity. "You and every other living man must get off that hill at once—you're all in the deadliest danger!"

CHAPTER V

The assault on the other salient, headed by the High Lord, had proved almost a textbook exercise in how such a maneuver should be done, and, where Bili's experience on the left had been an exposition of the weaknesses of the Confederation Army, that on the right had been a strong testament to that army's positive qualities.

Honored to have their supreme sovereign in their van, men and officers alike had gone about their prescribed actions in a strict, regulation manner—archers and engineers taking excruciating care in providing maximum cover for the advance up to and through and past the widely gapped abattis, the attacking units quickly and precisely forming their hill-encircling front behind their cat banners, with the High Lord and his plate-armored guards in the interval between two units.

At the roll of the massed drums, the engines had switched over to high-angle fire directly into the stone-walled fort atop the salient and the archers had confined their efforts to well-aimed loosings at clearly defined targets well ahead of the serried ranks of infantry.

On the second drumroll, every heavy shield came up to battle-carry, every spear sloped across right shoulder at an identical angle, all performed under the critical eyes of halberd-armed sergeants and officers with their bared broadswords at the shoulder-carry.

With the third roll of the drums, a deep-throated cheer was raised and the lines started forward, up the slope and into the hail of death hurled down by the rebel defenders, dressing their lines at the jogtrot as missiles took their inevitable toll.

Leery of appearing cowardly in the eyes of the High Lord, the commander of the second wave kept his men close upon the heels of the first—as Sub-*strahteegos* Kahzos Kahlinz had not—so that relatively fresh units were always on hand to replace those rendered ineffective through losses. Thus stiffened, the ranks simply swept over the outer ramparts, leaving precious few of those rebels alive to retreat to the main fort atop the hill.

Ten yards from the bristling stone walls, under the fiercest of the rain of stones and darts and arrows, Milo's mindspeak to the surviving senior officers gave the order which proved to make the final assault far easier and less costly to the Confederation troops.

Halting, still in aligned and ordered formations, the fore ranks knelt behind the secure protection of their big shields. As one man, the rank behind them grounded their spears and employed the small tool carried for just such a purpose to extract the removable pins securing the heads of their dual-purpose spears. Then, to the timing of the drumroll, their brawny arms drew back and hurled the heavy missiles with a much-practiced accuracy which was not really necessary, for so very thick was the press up on the walls that even a tyro could scarcely have helped fleshing his spear.

While the men of the first volley drew their wide-bladed shortswords and knelt, in turn, the line in front of them rose as one man and hurled their own spears. Then the drums once more rolled their bass thunder, and, cheering, the companies swept forward, their living wavecrest breaking over and then engulfing the little fortification before the defenders could recover from the bloody shock of the two spear volleys.

So sudden, complete and—to the rebels—unexpected was the victory of the High Lord's force that the suicide garrison had no time either to seal or even to conceal the huge oval chamber thoroughly undermining the fortifications, the tunnel through which they had been garrisoned and supplied, and the oil- and pitch-soaked timbers supporting all.

"It's a stratagem which can be hellishly effective, Bili," the High Lord urgently mindspoke. "Something similar once cost me most of two regiments when we were conquering the Kingdom of Karaleenos, more than a century ago. Since this hill is mined, it stands to reason that that one you're all on is, too. For some reason, I've been unable to lock onto the minds of Ahrtos or any of his senior officers, so you *must* get word to him that all troops are to quit that hilltop, immediately!"

Bili was blunt. "*Strahteegos* Ahrtos is dead, along with most of the other officers of the first wave. A sub-*strahteegos* called Kahzos Kahlinz presently commands the few infantrymen who survived the actual fighting, as well as his own slow-footed companies. He thought that he commanded me and my Freefighters, as well, until we had some . . . ahhh, words on the matter."

"All right, Bili. Everything will be set aright once this danger is past. For now, I'll mindspeak Kahlinz. You see to getting your own company off that hilltop. Down as far as the abattis, you should be safe. Get your wounded off, but don't bother with your dead; there may not be time."

Sub-*strahteegos* Kahzos—the thirty-five-year-old third son of *Thoheeks* Hwilkz Kahlinz of Kahlinz—whose twenty years under the cat banners had earned him the command of a line regiment and a second-class silver cat, was coldly furious.

First, that old arsehole Ahrtos had relegated him to the inferior and honorless command of the second wave, while taking his two best battalions away from him for the initial assault and "replacing" them with two understrength units of irregular light infantry from some godforsaken backwater in the northwestern mountains.

Then a noble bumpkin—and it was difficult, despite his title and his powerful mindspeak, to credit that the young swine was even Kindred, what with his damned harsh, nasal Middle Kingdoms accent and his scalp shaven like some barbarian mercenary—had *defied* him, had denied the authority of a Confederation sub-*strahteegos,* obscenely and loud enough for every regular on the hill to hear.

Blatantly lacking respect for either Kahzos' rank or his age, the young savage had not only profanely and flatly refused to place himself and his mercenary scum under Kahzos' rightful authority, but he had insisted that his outlaw company of northern barbarians be given leave to loot the salient *before* the Confederation gatherers were allowed to set about their accustomed task of scavenging valuable or usable items.

And Kahzos had seen scant choice but to accede to the most unreasonable demands, despite the flagrant breach of the sacrosanct regulations of the Army of the Confederation. For the arrogant young cur had made it abundantly clear that, should the sub-*strahteegos* demur, he and his mercenaries would assuredly fight—turn their swords on Confederation troops—to achieve their larcenous ends.

At that juncture, Kahzos could only think of that wholly disgraceful business some years back, of the ruined career and public cashiering of an officer who had set his battalion on mercenary "allies" when they had refused to fight. Of course, the man in question had been a damned *kath-ahrohs* Ehleen—which automatically, in Kahzos' opinion, meant a stubborn fool and a born thief and liar—and had hoped that by butchering the mercenaries, he could conceal the fact that he had embezzled their wages.

But, still, with such an unsettling precedent and with his honorable retirement not too far distant, Kahzos had stuck at issuing the order that might ensure an armed and all-round disastrous confrontation between him and his regulars and that puling pup of a *thoheeks* and the mercenaries.

However, his innate prejudice, towering ego and hidebound insistence on rules and regulations aside, Kahzos Kahlinz was basically a good officer and an intelligent man. When the High Lord mindspoke him, he immediately grasped the dire possibilities, the deadly danger to every living man within the new-conquered salient.

After snapping a spoken order to his staff drummer, he beamed his reply to his sovereign. "My lord, because of some unforeseen difficulties with the barbari . . . ahh, with *Thoheeks* Bili and his company, the gather squads have but just dispersed about the area. The musicians and the company drummers are all handling litters, of course, but I have ordered my own drummer to roll the 'Recall' and I will immediately dispatch a runner to warn the *thoheeks* and the mercena . . . ahh, the Freefighters."

"Never mind *Thoheeks* Bili, Kahlinz," beamed Milo. "He was warned before you were. Just get your units from off that damned hill as rapidly as may be. We've taken much loss for damned little gain this day as it is."

Bili supervised the lowering of the wounded Freefighters down the outer face of the stone wall before he allowed himself to be eased down to the ground below, leaving Pawl Raikuh and a few men still on the wall to see to the dead and the bundles of loot and equipment.

Unless they were noble-born, deceased Freefighters were usually just stripped of any armor, weapons or other usable effects and left wherever they fell on the field; so, after getting the hard-won loot down, Raikuh simply had the near-nude, stiffening corpses shoved off the inner edge of the wallwalk to join the hacked husks of their recent opponents on the pavement of the inner court.

As the captain set his feet to the first rung of the rope ladder his men had jury-rigged, mostly from battlefield debris, he could but grunt his disgust at the foolhardy idiocy of that supercilious turd of a sub-*strahteegos* who should have been shooing his troops out of the elaborate deathtrap, but was instead ordering them into painfully dressed formations as fast as they reported to the roll of the drum.

Sergeant Geros and his detail returned just as Bili hobbled down to the place where the wounded had been gently laid. The young *thoheeks* took the opportunity to appropriate the sergeant's mare but found, to his chagrin, that he had to be helped into her saddle.

Increasingly thick and dense tendrils of smoke were arising from between the paving stones of the inner court before the rearguard of the infantry column gained to the top of the stone wall and dropped down its outer face, and that company still were trotting toward the perimeter defenses of the doomed salient when a flame-shot pillar of smoke and dust mounted high into the air from behind the walls of the fort. To those on the slope below, it was as if some gigantic monster out of legend had roared with hellish din and fiery breath; the doomed infantrymen on the quaking ramparts were half obscured, and their terrified screams, curses and prayers were heard only by themselves.

First, a wedge of rampart collapsed into itself, but few saw it, for just then and with an even more awesome noise, the entire stone fort and much of the hillside between it and the ramparts simply dropped straight down, its place taken by high-leaping flames so hot that even those down near the abattis felt uncomfortable heat.

Then another and wider slice of rampart gave way, and suddenly the entire remaining stretches of rampart slid, roaring and crashing, into the huge, blazing pit, sending an unbelievable shower of scintillating sparks up and through and even high above the solid-looking entity compounded alike of dust and roiling smoke.

Bili urged the mare, Ahnah, as close as he dared to the still-crumbling verges of the deep crater; other men crowded up in his wake, despite the waves of enervating heat, the clouds of choking smoke and the nauseating stench of burning flesh which assailed them all.

At first, the young *thoheeks* could spy no trace of the hundred-odd officers and men who had been trapped atop the rampart—thanks in no small part to the asinine dawdling of Sub-*strahteegos* Kahzos Kahlinz, who, Bili had noted, had been the very first man in the column to quit the fort—when it had gone down. It was with shock that he saw, as a gust of wind briefly blew away the covering smoke, that one of those lay almost at his feet.

By his armor, the man appeared to be an officer . . . and condemned to an agonized and singularly unpleasant death. A massive timber, likely one of those which had pillared the huge trap, lay across both of the unfortunate's legs. The far end of the timber was already blazing, and several feet more had commenced to smoke and smolder.

Pawl Raikuh touched his lord's arm. "Duke Bili, I could take two or three men and try to get him out . . . ?"

Bili squinted down into the smoky slice of hell for a moment, then shook his head sadly. "No, Pawl, that would do no good. Look at the size of that timber, man! There must be a full Harzburk ton of hardwood there. It would take a score of men to even shift it and a couple more to pull the officer free."

"But we've got that many, Duke Bili," said Raikuh. "For all he's one of those damned spit-and-polish popinjays, he's still a man."

Bili cupped his hands to his mouth and shouted down, "Can you hear me, soldier? There's no way we can safely get to you. Enough men to lift that timber would likely start that mess to sliding again, kill you and them, too."

The bloody, dirt-caked head of the figure below could be seen to nod slowly, wearily, so Bili added, "The timber is already on fire, man. You'll slowly roast alive if you don't cut your throat!"

The trapped man's hands fumbled uncertainly at his waist but came away empty; apparently his belt had been torn off, and with it had gone his dirk. Moreover, his position made it impossible to draw the long broadsword strapped across his back. Now frantic, he pushed at the dead weight of rough-hewn wood which would so soon be the agent of his torturous death. But he could as easily have shifted a mountain, and presently he slumped back, defeat mirrored on his gory, battered countenance.

Bili groaned. "Pawl . . . somebody . . . Sun and Wind, get an archer or a dartman up here! We can't just watch the poor bastard die like that!"

A number of Freefighters drew, hefted and threw dirks or knives, but the blades all fell short. Then, only three feet from the suffering officer, a section of the timber puffed a great blob of smoke . . . just before bluish flames began to lick over the visible surfaces with hungry intensity.

Bili shivered all over and unconsciously bunched up his

cloak-wrapped body on the bough bed in his mountain lean-to, his skin surfaces all goosefleshed. "And that was when it happened," he thought. "That was when Geros *did it*, did something that I'm certain no one who failed to see it really believes . . . and I can't blame them. It was clearly impossible . . . yet it happened."

The young *thoheeks* had mindspoken the responsive mare about, determined to, despite his wounds and injuries, ride if necessary to the main camp of the Confederation troops and fetch back an archer to forestall the sure agonies of the officer trapped below. Then he heard Raikuh's sudden bellow.

"Damn your wormy guts, Geros! Come back here! That's a fucking *order*, sergeant! Come back here!"

The big mare started, recognizing her twolegs brother's name, and willingly turned back to her former position. And then she and Bili astride her and Raikuh and all the rest were impotent to do more than stare.

Sergeant Geros' battered armor and helmet, his prized sword and even his canteen lay in a heap where he had shed and dropped them near the steadily crumbling verge of that yawning pit of fire and death. The man himself could be seen in a wavery, distorted fashion through the waves of heat beating up from the almost-fluid earth into which his jackboots sank nearly to the knees with each step he took. He moved slowly, obviously unsure of the insecure, constantly shifting footing; but move he did, ever closer to that pinioned and doomed officer.

"He'll most likely die with him, too," thought Bili, a bit sadly, for like Pawl Raikuh, he had come to like and respect the efficient but humble young sergeant. Thinking aloud, he said to no one in particular, "That's true, selfless bravery, yonder. And yet that man was worrying but a few hours back because he'd pissed his breeks a few times in combat!"

Those watching saw the courageous young man win to the officer's side, saw the flash of white teeth as the forcibly recumbent man smiled up at this man who had risked so much to assure him a relatively painless death. They saw the officer's lips move, saw him pull something off his right thumb and drop it into Geros' palm, then open his hand, awaiting Geros' dirk or bootknife. They saw Geros' own lips move, although, like the officer's, his words were not audible to them above the roaring of the huge holocaust and the constant crash and rumble of shifting stones and timbers deeper in the crater.

And then it *happened!* Geros turned and took a few steps until he could squat and work his two hands into the steaming, smoking earth under one end of the massive timber. Slowly, ever so slowly, he arose, the muscles swelling, bunching in shoulders, backs and thighs under his smoldering gambeson.

And as the young sergeant arose, *so did the timber!* It did not rise far, true—perhaps a foot or even less—but it was enough for the officer to pull and claw with his two sound arms and hands and thus work his smashed legs from the impression beneath that crushing weight of solid oak.

The moment that the officer's feet slid from under the timber, Geros let go his grip and the ton or more of hardwood settled back in its place . . . but for only a moment, then it began a slow but increasingly faster slide downslope, toward the fires raging below.

Somehow, working against the current of the now-flowing river of oven-hot earth and its flotsam of splintered wood and boulders, Geros half-dragged, half-carried the man he had so miraculously rescued from certain death back to the verge. There scores of willing hands drew them both back to safety.

By that time, of course—badly injured to begin with and after the rough handling Geros had perforce had to employ to get them both out—the officer had fainted, but old Djim Bohluh had identified him.

"That's young Captain Lehzlee, a good lad and a good, just of'ser, he be, by Sacred Sun's redhot arse, *Thoheeks* Bili, sir."

"A son of *Ahrkeethoheeks* Ahndroo, Chief of Lehzlee?" asked Bili, thinking that if it was a Lehzlee of that clan, Geros certainly had lucked out this time, for they were certainly the richest clan in Southern Karaleenos, if not in all the principality.

"The *Ahrkeethoheeks'* onliest son, now," attested Bohluh. "The captain's elder brother 'uz kilt mebbe six months agone a-fightin' the Ahfuht tribe, out west. This here's young Hailz's las' campaign, his paw wants him back."

"Well, the *ahrkeethoheeks* and Clan Lehzlee will get their heir back now, thanks to the bravest man this or any other army will ever have. I already had intended to knight him, make him a *vahrohneeskos* in Morguhn—he saved my life, too, today. But in view of these last few scarce-believable minutes, I doubt me not that the High Lord and the Lehzlees will improve substantially upon a mere ennobling."

And that they assuredly did, thought Bili, who at long last began to feel the needed sleep nibbling at the corners of his consciousness. A first-class silver cat, and the only reason it wasn't gold was that Geros was a Freefighter and not a regular. And that meant thirty ounces of silver a year for as long as he lived.

Thoughtful, as always, of his subjects, the High Lord deliberately delayed that ceremony, Bili sleepily recalled, so that the chief of Clan Lehzlee, old *Ahrkeethoheeks* Ahndroo, might himself be there in the camp under the walls of besieged Vawnpolis to place the cat on its massy silver chain about the neck of the man whose matchless valor had saved his son and heir.

"That wasn't all, of course," Bili thought. "That old archduke is as proud as a solid-gold hilt and he couldn't let it go at just that gesture. So Sir Geros—Sun grant that he and *Komees* Hari still live and are sleeping safe, this night—now rides in a suit of duke-grade Pitzburk worth a small fortune and carries a Yvuhz sword better than any blade I've ever owned.

"The old man offered him, as well, any full-trained destrier he fancied in all the Lehzlee herds, but Geros insisted that his mare, Ahnah, was all he needed or wanted, so now he holds title to rich lands in Lehzlee to add to the baronetcy I still mean to give him in Morguhn.

"And the weird part about it all is that months back, poor old Pawl Raikuh—Wind guard his gallant soul—told Geros and me and several others that this man, who a bit over a year ago was a gentleman's valet with as much knowledge of arms as a draft ox, would ere he died become a widely respected knight, a moderately wealthy minor nobleman and the castellan of a great lord's burk.

"Sun and Wind, there's so much about this that makes no sense at all."

And then, Bili finally slept.

CHAPTER VI

Lying warm in Meeree's tender, familiar embrace, the *brahbehrnuh* slept until past Moonset. She awoke suddenly, fully and for no reason she could fathom. Above her, the evergreen boughs roofing their lean-to shelter crackled with frost, from afar came the cry of a hunting owl, and a single star winked palely above the summit of one of the hills that flanked the valley.

The fire which had burned before the open side of the rude shelter was now but a few glowing coals, and the cold, despite the thick, woolen lining of her cloak and Meeree's, was nibbling all along her left side; although her right cheek was warm with the soft, regular breaths of her lover, her left was all aprickle with the icy kiss of the frigid air.

The winged predator of the night skies cried again, closer this time. The *brahbehrnuh* gently disengaged her hand from the limp clasp of the sleeping Meeree and used its warm palm to drive the chill from her numbing cheek; then she drew up a corner of a cloak to cover that side of her face, but did it ever so carefully, so as not to disturb Meeree.

Somewhere on the blackness of the nearby hillside, there was the short, shrill deathcry of some small creature; then, with a loud flapping of powerful wings, a large, dark form flew low over the sleeping camp, momentarily blotting out the light of that single dim star. The *brahbehrnuh* knew then that the hunting owl had triumphed and soon would feast, and she breathed a silent prayer to the Lady, whose sacred messenger the huge-eyed birds were held to be.

"Oh, my dear Lady," she added plaintively but still silently, "what must I do? What will be best for your few, brave Maidens who now are left, the less than three score who depend upon me, trust my judgment and decisions?

"Must we who have served You so faithfully, as did our mothers and grandmothers back to time past reckoning, must we finally submit to the bitter rule of men, or will our Lady guide us to a haven of safety, wherein we can rebuild our hold, regenerate our sacred race and serve You faithfully as ever?"

Then, abruptly, Meeree was no longer at her side and she stood erect on silver-bladed grass, growing out of silvery soil; the air about her was cool, but no longer cold, and everything glowed with a soft, silvery brightness. Only once before in all her young life had she found herself transported to this holy place, stood on this blessed turf; yet she remembered, knew at once where she now was, knew that her pleading prayer had been heard.

From within the building of white, silver-veined stone came the Lady, moving across the intervening distance as lightly as a running doe, a smile of greeting on Her pale lips, but a deep sympathy welling up from Her silver-gray eyes. As She came closer, one of Her hands closed tinglingly on the *brahbehrnuh's* and the other went to gently stroke the girl's cheek.

"Oh, my poor, dear, ever-faithful Rahksahnah, you have suffered so very much, my child, and it truly tears my heart that you must suffer still more. Yet, so must it be, dear one, so must it be; the pattern is tightly woven, now, and grim death snuffs close upon your trail."

The *brahbehrnuh* sighed deeply and bowed her head in meek surrender to the inevitable. "Then I soon will die, my Lady? Will . . . can it be honorably, a death in battle?"

"Be not so abject, Rahksahnah." Silvery fingers took her chin and raised her head. *"Where is the proud, brave young Moon Maiden, that warrior and leader of warriors with whom I shared sweet love on my couch a bare twenty-five moons agone?"*

All at once, the tears she had so long withheld, not dared to shed before even her Meeree, before the *brahbehrnuh's* dark eyes, cascading down her weather-darkened cheeks, over the calluses left by the cheekpieces of her helmet.

She sobbed, "Dear my Lady, the Hold of the Moon Maidens is no more. Some monstrous force rent the living rocks of the mountain asunder and flung the very altar stone from Your holy shrine untold leagues through the air and sent it crashing into a brook before my very eyes—and it so hot that it turned all the waters of that brook to a cloud of hissing steam.

"When I saw that unspeakable horror, all strength left my

body and all awareness fled my mind. If such as that could happen, then all that Kokh Taishyuhn spoke is surely truth and I and my few Maidens are the very last of our race.

"Oh, Lady, Lady, what are we few to do with no Hold to shelter us in this pitiless world of savagery and death?"

But the Silver Lady did not immediately answer. Instead, she led the weeping girl to a soft couch set amid a grove of silver-leafed trees, their scintillating blossoms filling the air with a subtle fragrance which spoke of the peace and tranquillity of a still and restful night. There, seated, they two shared sips from a silver cup of a pale wine. Then the *brahbehrnuh* pressed once again to the cool, pale, ever-remembered lips of the Lady.

Then, somehow, in the blinking of an eye, they lay nude together upon the couch, it now having become long and wide as a fine bed. And hilt-hardened palms and fingers pressed, caressed sacred Goddess flesh, while the silvery, cool-soft hands of the Lady traced tingling pleasure over the tenderest areas of the hard-muscled, olive-hued body.

And, for the *brahbehrnuh*, time ceased to be for a timeless eternity of shared rapture. Seeking lips and darting, maddening tongues, the brush of nipple against hardening nipple, black hair mingled with silver hair, gasping to draw air into bodies convulsing with spasms of unbearable pleasure.

When they could once again breathe normally and time once more held sway, they again shared the wine cup and then another long kiss. The Lady arose and draped Her silver loveliness in Her single, flowing garment, then helped the *brahbehrnuh* to don her own clothing, doing up the points of shirt and breeks with swift, nimble fingers.

Carrying that wine cup which never seemed to become empty, the Lady led Her guest, Her lover, across the springy sward to where a fountain splashed misty water into a basin of whitest marble, seated Herself upon an alabaster bench and drew the Moon Maiden down beside Her.

Clasping the *brahbehrnuh's* hand in both of Her own, She said, *"Sweet my love, you must no longer grieve the death of the Maidens' Hold and your dear folk who died with it, for you must understand that death is the natural end of mortals and all their works, be that death soon or late; only god-flesh is eternal, god-flesh and mortal spirit. Mortal bodies are born, my child, they live a brief while and then they die and their substance goes to the nourishment of other life forms, just as the substance of other life forms went to their nourishment*

*during their own short spans of life. But the spirits of mortals
go on to seek and find another fleshly husk to house them for
still another brief time.*

"*If My way seems harsh and pitiless and wasteful to mortals, it is because they do not or will not understand My way,
not truly. You see, dear one, nothing is ever wasted, not really, for the past fed the present and the present feeds the future. Yes, the Valley of the Moon Maidens is gone, along
with the fleshly husks of all those who were within it; but
even in death, the remains of those husks are or will soon become new life, and the immortal spirits, freed now of their
fleshy envelopes, are soaring far and wide over lands and seas
and soon each will become the deathless core of new life. So
you see, Rahksahnah, dearest, your grief should be rejoicing.*

"*As for your own death, no matter how tight the weavings,
the deeds or misdeeds of mortals always can change, or
rather realign, certain threads, slightly altering the final pattern. You, yourself, if you heed My advice and My portents,
can do much to prolong your life, child. So, too, can the man
Bili of Morguhn. Also, there are two other men, whom you
have yet to meet . . . and another who is not really a man,
at least, not wholly such.*

"*But you and your Moon Maidens must give over the ways
of the Hold, to a large degree. I know that it will be very
hard for you all—especially so for sworn lovers like you and
your dear Meeree—but you all must adopt many of the ways
of the outer world, the world of men, if any of you are to
survive in your present husks.*

"*Times of great danger lie ahead for all those who camp
about the place where your body now lies, Rahksahnah, and
not all of them will live through those times. The Moon
Maidens who do survive will be those who have courage to
surrender the ways of the dead past for present life and a
chance for future happiness.*

"*Although you all must remain warriors for some while
yet, you must all give over the other ways of the Hold, are
you to live on to serve Me. I can feel that you know My
meaning, my child. In the beginning, the change will be very
difficult for most of you, for the men who now share the
camp and will soon share the deadly danger with you are
none of them at all akin to the meek and biddable men who
were your sires and brothers. You and your sisters must learn
to treat these men as equals. Each of you must pair with a
man who appeals to her, take him as war companion and*

*lover, share all things with him, both the good and the ill.
Yes, it will seem strange and unnatural, at first, but those
who persevere will soon find each succeeding day brighter
and more fulfilling. On this, you have My word and My
promise, dear Rahksahnah.*

*"But now, My sweet and ever-faithful one, it is time that
your return to your flesh, that you may repeat My words to
the Moon Maidens and prepare them for the new, changed
life they must all so soon begin to live are they to survive
the near-future dangers."*

And with no sense of transition, the cool comfort was
gone, the silver radiance was become the utter darkness
which precedes the dawn, the jewel-flowered trees above her
head were metamorphosed into the frost-crusted evergreen
boughs thatching the roof-wall of her lean-to.

As she slowly turned her head to stare at the gray ashes
and few, dim coals which were all that remained of last
night's fire, the warm, sweetly moist breath of Meeree wafted
over the fine hairs on her nape . . . and then she could have
wept yet again when she thought of what she and her sisters
must so soon give up.

But then she thought of Dook Bili, thought of the height
and breadth and immense strength of him, thought of the
savage ferocity with which he had shaken the man who
would have offered the insult. She thought of that invisible
but unmistakable aura of leadership which was so naturally
his and which had brought almost everyone—Moon Maidens
and diverse races of men alike—to accept him instantly as
war chief of their heterogeneous band.

She thought, too, of the consideration he had shown her
and her poor, homeless sisters in so very many ways, of his
courtly courtesy to her, personally, on the night just past. All
the Ahrmehnee warriors she had ever seen or dealt with had
been obviously resentful and contemptuous of her and every
other Moon Maiden, and brutally callous toward their own
poor women; but this Dook Bili, for all his strength and vigor
and fierce starkness in battle, had dealt with her and all her
sisters as respected equals and had proved solicitous, gentle
and caring toward her in her illness of shock and grief—she
thought that not even another Moon Maiden could have
treated her more tenderly than had this massive man.

Lastly, she allowed herself to recall that tingling warmth
which had coursed through every fiber of her body when he
had taken her arm to guide her stumbling steps around the

council fire, last night; she recalled too that the touch of no other mortal—not even dear Meeree—had ever so thrilled her; only the Holy Hands of the Lady could do the like.

Was this then the answer? The Lady had said that She could see that the *brahbehrnuh* knew the answer, and She had also said that this singular young man-warrior, this Dook Bili, somehow had the power to alter the pattern so as to make the weaving one of life rather than of death. Yes, this must be the answer, she thought. So she began to mentally frame the words she soon must speak to her Moon Maidens.

As the boles of the stunted hardwoods on the lower reaches of the surrounding hills became black-on-black, Meeree stirred beside her and the *brahbehrnuh* turned onto her right side to receive the wet, sleepy kiss which was her lover's customary morning greeting. She responded briefly, meeting Meeree's questing tonguetip with her own, but then gently disengaged and drew herself back. Smiling languidly, Meeree pressed her hard palm upon the *brahbehrnuh's* left breast and commenced to caress it through the fabric of the shirt with slow, circular strokes.

Feeling her body beginning to respond to the familiar and long-loved touch, the *brahbehrnuh* quickly gripped the young woman's wrist and stilled the hand.

"No, my darling, I'm sorry, but I must talk to you, *now*. There are many things I must tell you, and some will be very hard to bear . . . for us both. But you must listen and you must obey, as you love me and as you love Her, the Lady. For this night I was again with Her, our Silver Goddess, and all the words that I will speak to you and to our sisters come from Her."

In each succeeding generation of Moon Maidens had their *brahbehrnuhs* been the acknowledged mortal voice of Her, the Silver Lady of the skies of night, so Meeree listened dutifully to her lover's words. So, too, did the rest of the Moon Maidens, in a private place, far up the narrow, twisting vale, where a spring-fed pool gave birth to the brooklet. But it was only after their scanty breakfast was eaten, the wounded women comforted as best was possible and the horses looked to.

"Last night, my sisters," she began gravely, "I wakened to hear an owl. Twice did the holy bird call, then did I hear the beat of her wings, loud as distant thunder. She flew low over the clearing before my shelter, and I prayed that she would bear my message to the Lady.

"And, my sisters, *my prayer was heard!* The Lady did take up my spirit to bide for a while with Her, in Her place. There She did comfort me and console me and impart to me that which I now must tell you."

The *brahbehrnuh's* audience of warrior-women stood or sat or squatted attentively, no slightest shadow of disbelief on their faces, for ever had it been thus that their leaders were taken up and counseled by the Goddess in times of crisis, that they might partake of Her wisdom and by it guide their race, Her hereditary servants.

But a single, ill-omened time in all the long history of the folk of the Maidens of the Moon had a *brahbehrnuh* been ordered by the Council of Grandmothers to act against the counsel of the Goddess. And fewer than five out of each hundred of that doomed sortie had won back to the Hold; even fewer had been sound of body, none had been sound of mind, and most had died within bare moons of their return. Only that wretched *brahbehrnuh* had lived long enough after her return to conceive and bear a daughter, of which soon-orphaned child the present holder of that title was the direct descendant.

Therefore, as she lowered the pitch of her voice—for these, the Silver Lady's words, were not for the ears of men—they crowded in closer, so as not to miss a syllable of the Sacred Words, Her Holy Counsel, as transmitted by the lips of the most recent descendant of uncounted generations of priestesses.

"Know, sisters mine, that the Hold of the Moon Maidens and all our dear folk are truly gone from this land; erased are they as if they had never been. When I swooned while the burning rocks fell, yesterday, it was because I saw and recognized Her altar—the sacred and secret altar from deep within the council cavern—flung into that little stream, before me."

A low, doleful moan welled up from the women grouped about her. Only their warrior heritage and training, their rigid code of self-discipline, inhibited louder lamentations and a shedding of the hot tears burning their eyes, those and their fierce pride.

The *brahbehrnuh* went on in her pain-racked voice. "So there is no hold, no valley of home, no place of safety and love to which we can ever return, sisters. From this day hence, we few remaining Moon Maidens must make our way in the world of men. Although we shall honor Her all our lives, will continue to serve Her as best we may, we must change or alter certain of our customs and practices, must unlearn or forget many of our ancient traditions . . . so She did tell me."

"But *brahbehrnuh*," spoke up the lieutenant, Kahndoot, "these mountains stretch, it is said by the traders, for hundreds of leagues to north and south and at least for scores to east and west. Why can we not seek out another valley, establish another hold and steal boys and men from the surrounding folk to labor in our fields and pastures and give their seed to the perpetuation of our holy race? Such as this was done by the many-times-great-grandmothers when they came riding down from the north."

The *brahbehrnuh* shook her head sadly. "Simply because, dear sister Kahndoot, such is not Her will. The Goddess has said that, henceforth, our futures must be bound up with those of men—with the lowlander warriors and their chief, Dook Bili—are any of us to live to bear daughters and sons.

"Advised was I by Her that this new life, in which these men will be our equals, our war companions, our lovers, will be hard of bearing . . . but in the beginning only. Attested did She that, do we but set our minds and our hands and our hearts to this new and strange life, each new day will be the more enjoyable, the more rewarding.

"Thus spake our ancient Goddess, our Silver Lady. So who am I, who is any one of us, to doubt or to stand against the Sacred Counsel of the All-Knowing?"

The lieutenant's strong, hilt-callused fingers moved to trace the Sacred Moonsign, and she bowed her helmeted head in silent, humble submission to Her dictates.

"Now, my dear sisters," the *brahbehrnuh* continued, "be you selective in your choices of your new, male war-lovers, no less selective than you were in your choices of your present lovers. Choose a man you can admire and respect. Choose not for his rank but for his warrior skills, his cleanly ways, his courage.

"The Lady would have us all choose lowlanders, not these Ahrmehnee, so it matters not if your chosen man have a woman awaiting him in his home place, for these strangers oft have two or more wives at once, unlike the Ahrmehnee.

"Now, heed me, be you not too forward. Remember that this is no Moon Festival mate selection, such as was practiced in the hold, of yore; these fighters are your equals in all ways, not mere fieldworker-swivers whose only function is to quicken you for the good of the holy race.

"But be you not too reticent, either. Let the man of your

choice be assured that you would be his true and ever-constant battle companion and his lover. Let him know with certainty that your sword will ever guard his back, that you will care for him in wounds or sickness, that you will see to the decent disposition of his body should he be slain.

"But, sisters mine, be you in no way meek; demand equal vows from him, for all here are seasoned warriors. Are we to have the continued respect of these new, male lovers, it must be by dint of *mutual* admiration, *mutual* loyalty, *mutual* love, and a shared pride.

"When we return to the camp, I go to confer with Dook Bili. I will impart to him the words of the Lady and some of that which I have said here, to you. I do this so that the men may be receptive to our overtures."

She cupped her left hand about her pudenda and raised her right hand, making the Holy Moonsign. "Now, dear sisters, let us all pray the Lady that we all will serve Her to the very best of our abilities in these new and most strange ways."

With the Maidens and the Ahrmehnee guarding the hilly perimeter, the horse herd and the camp, Bili was able to assemble every unwounded or ambulatory man of his original force of Freefighters and nobles still with him. He then led them up to that same secluded spot in which the Moon Maidens had so lately gathered.

Smiling slightly, but still looking—and feeling—a little bemused, he motioned to them to sit or squat, as suited them, and then began to speak.

"Noble gentlemen, Freefighter officers and troopers, I have just spoken with the *brahbehrnuh* of the Moon Maidens, and I have most remarkable tidings for you all. . . ."

It was as the young *thoheeks* was wending his way back down the twisting vale at the head of his men that he received a faint but familiar mindspeak beaming.

"Chief Bili of Morguhn, have you a twolegs female for me, as well?"

"Whitetip!" Bili silently responded. "Where is my cat brother? Is Sub-chief Hari with you, or any others of my fighters?"

Still weak but growing infinitesimally stronger as the cat apparently neared, the answer came. "No, Chief Bili, yours is the only familiar mind I have ranged. Until I did, I had feared that I and this short-ranged, near-useless female of a Confederation Army cat and these two miserable, half-broken ponies were all that had survived the ground-shakings and the fires. But how bides my chief? I long for the sight of my twolegs brother."

"I am well and safe, for the nonce," beamed Bili. "But I, too, long to clap eyes upon my brother cat. I will show you where we are." With that, he beamed his memory's images of the areas they had traversed in escaping from the fires, then of the landmarks of the single entrance to the tortuously twisting little valley.

"Ah, yes," announced the prairiecat. "Whitetip and the female are west of you by nearly half a sun's ride. But we will come, Chief Bili."

"Take great care, cat brother," Bili admonished, "for this be an evil land and it harbors savage men and monsters of many sorts and, are the Ahrmehnee to be believed, maleficent witches."

As the men dispersed about the camp, Bili made his way back toward his own shelter; but just before he reached it, a Moon Maiden stepped from within a tiny copse to confront him, blocking his path. Full-armed she stood, with bronze helmet and cuirass of antique design, the knuckle-bowed hilt of her long saber jutting up behind her left shoulder and her heavy short sword and broad dirk belted above her slim hips; a small, round targe was strapped to her left forearm, and her gauntleted right hand grasped the worn haft of a light, crescent-bladed axe. Bili could clearly see great pain in the dark eyes of the young woman.

Speaking fast and low, she said, "Dook Bili, my name is Meeree. I am . . . *was* war companion to the *brahbehrnuh*. Seldom have ever she and I parted since mere children were we, but now our Sacred Lady deems that different things of life be. Be it so then, as She commands, no matter how strange and not natural it seems to us Moon Maidens; for we all are but clay and She is the potter.

"But, man, warned by Meeree be you, here! My love for her dies not; until my death am I hers to bid and her honor is as mine own. Hurt or shame or forsake her ever at your peril, man-who-replaces-me-in-her-arms! Oft have my fine weapons drunk deep of man-blood . . . and easily can they do so again."

Without allowing Bili to answer or respond, the full-armed young woman spun on her booted heel and stalked back into the copse and out of sight.

A rough-barked arrangement of poles had been lashed between the boles of two trees to support Bili's heavy warkak and other horse gear; now those sturdy poles bowed under the weight of two kaks, the new set richly embossed and adorned with silver and semiprecious stones.

Within his shelter—slightly larger and higher than most, for Bili was a taller man than most of his followers, standing more than two yards from bare sole to pate—his own armor and weapons had been rearranged to make room for another panoply; this one was similar to that worn by the woman who had just confronted him, but was far richer. He also noted that his bough bed had been enlarged and that his own scarlet saddle blanket was now partially covered by a black one, its edges all stitched with fine silver wire.

"She brings," thought Bili, "a considerable dowry, in any case. Not counting the stones, there's five pounds or more of silver on her gear. And, as I recall, her big mare seems a fine, well-bred mount, fit to throw us good foals by my Mahvros."

The sound of footsteps on the path brought him spinning about to see the *brahbehrnuh* approaching, droplets of water beading her high-arched eyebrows and dangling braids of blue-black hair. From her throat to almost the ankles of her tooled boots, her body was enveloped in the rich, soft leather of her wool-lined cloak.

When she spied him standing just inside the shelter, she seemed to waver and, recalling her recurrent bouts of weakness since she had swooned on the day of the earthquake and the rain of hot rocks, Bili stepped hurriedly from the rough hut, crossed the fire clearing in two, long strides and placed an arm about her shoulders.

"Is my lady ill again?" he inquired solicitously, concern obvious in his voice, his powerful right arm gently supportive. "Come, let me help you to my shelter. I think there's a little brandy left in my bottle; perhaps a sup of it will restore you."

And yet again the *brahbehrnuh* felt that unbearably pleasurable tingling surge through all of her being, that odd sensation which she never had experienced from the touch of any save the Goddess. And this man. This strange, huge, strong man. This stark warrior-man, born leader, born killer, but never less than courteous and gentle toward her and the other Moon Maidens.

Once more the tingling suffused her. So strong was it this time that all strength departed her legs and, but for the support of his thick, hard-muscled arm, she would have collapsed onto the rocky ground. Without another word, Bili thrust his left arm behind her buckling knees, bore her into the shelter and carefully lowered her onto the bough bed. Then he turned and rummaged through his gear until he found his silver flask and cup.

After filling the cup with cold water from his canteen, he trickled into it the last small measure of the strong spirit, then placed it to her lips and squatted by the bed, holding her body raised until she had downed it all. Before arising, he doffed his cloak, deftly rolled it up and placed the improvised cushion under her booted feet.

When once more he stood, his shaven poll brushing the evergreen thatch of the roof, he said, "Stay you still there, my lady. I'll go and fetch back one of your Moon Maidens to care for you."

But she stretched out a hand toward him, imploring, "No, Dook Bili, I am not ill. Please, stay and sit with me awhile."

Slowly, he sank back to perch on the edge of the bough bed, knowing with his fine-tuned presentiment that something momentous was looming. And when she sought out his broad, big-knuckled hand and took it into both of her own, he knew without thinking that some singular occurrence soon must be.

Hesitantly, he thrust probingly . . . and his mind slid easily into hers. She started and gasped as if touched with a hot iron.

"So," he beamed silently, "you Moon Maidens *are* mind-speakers. Are we two to be mates, as you desire, this will make our relationship far easier and deeper, my lady. I can speak hardly any Ahrmehnee and you speak Mehrikan but ill. Do many of your race mindspeak?"

Wonderingly, she spoke aloud. "I . . . I do not know, Dook Bili. I had, of course, heard that silent communication was among your folk practiced. But . . . but among my race it is . . . is a thing unheard of."

"No," he mindspoke, "don't speak with your lips, my lady. Think what you would say . . . then do *this* . . . so."

Her dark eyes widened. "It . . . it is so simple. Oh, thank you, Dook Bili!" This time, her lips did not move.

Grinning, he gently squeezed one of her hands. "The pleasure was mine own, my lady. I can but hope that my lady is as quick to learn and to master other arts, as well."

The images projected along with his mindspeak abundantly clarified his meaning, and the *brahbehrnuh* found herself blushing furiously. Then he leaned forward, and his smooth-shaven face blotted out the sunlight filtering through the thatch as his mouth pressed down upon hers. The tingling now was almost unendurable. Her sinewy arms crept up and closed around his thick neck, while her lips and tongue once more moved . . . but not in speech.

CHAPTER VII

"Furface" Gy Ynstyn had found a place where the light was good, and there he squatted. With round brass rod, hardwood dowels, a bit of soft leather, a small copper hammer and a homemade wooden mallet, he was engaged in carefully restoring his battle-battered bugle to its original shape.

A veteran Freefighter from the County of Gainzburk in the Middle Kingdoms, he had been Duke Bili's personal bugler since first the army had marched into Vawn last summer. Although the mindspeaking nobles of the Confederation had less need of a hornman than did the nobles of the Middle Kingdoms, still Gy took his position seriously and prided himself upon the good appearance of himself and his equipment at all times.

He heard the familiar clanking of armor well before its wearer reached him, but kept his keen hazel eyes upon his work. Not even when a shadow fell across that work did he look up.

"Move to right or left, dammit!" he muttered. "You're in my light."

"What are you doing, man?" demanded a husky voice. "And why have you a beard when other men do not?"

"I'm trying to get the dents out of my bugle so that it will sound right when next Duke Bili wills that I wind it," he growled ill-humoredly. "Not that it's any business of yours."

Then, angry at the interruption, he glanced up at this overly nosy inquisitor . . . and hammer, bugle and all dropped from his hands as he awkwardly rose to his feet, flustered. At the same time he hoped against hope, he still knew for certain that this fine-looking young filly could want nothing more of Gy Ynstyn than a bit of idle conversation.

Meeree leaned axe and target against a rock, bent and picked up the brass instrument. Placing the mouthpiece to her lips, she blew experimentally into it, and when this availed her no toot, she blew harder and harder until veins stood out in her forehead, but all her efforts proved fruitless.

Frowning, she thrust the bugle back to Gy, stating, "More work it needs, man. No sound at all it does."

Gy smiled then. He had had long experience of seeing non-initiates fail to elicit notes from a bugle. "Not so, and it please my lady. Though it will not sound pure and true until I can get out these damned dents, this horn will wind well enough; and my lord Bili order me to blow it."

"Show me, man!" demanded Meeree imperiously.

But Gy shook his head. "The bugle never is sounded without good reason, my lady, even in a safe garrison. Duke Bili has expressly ordered me to not sound it here, lest we draw some unwelcome notice of our presence from the shaggies hereabouts. I am sorry that I cannot accommodate my lady's wishes."

A bastard son of a cadet of the house of Gainzburk, Gy had had a soupçon of courtly training before he had hired himself and his sword to a Freefighter captain; now he showed that training with a full and courtly bow to the Moon Maiden.

Meeree seated herself on the rock against which her weapons rested, clasped her hands on one knee and leaned back. "Oh, very well, man. But if your war companion I am to be, sooner or later teach me to blow that thing you must, that your place I may take on the battleline should you wounded or sick be."

With shaking hands, Gy gathered up his tools and tried to replace them properly in their roll of oiled leather. His now madly whirling mind had never really considered the possibility that, with such a profusion of southron noblemen and not a few Freefighter officers and noncoms from whom to choose, one of the Moon Maidens—now all man-hunting, said Duke Bili—would set her sights on a lowly, thin-pursed trumpeter.

"My . . . my . . . lady," he stuttered, "surely my lady is but having a . . . a jest? I am not an officer, nor yet a sergeant . . . not even a corporal, but only a hornman, and . . ."

"And," she added, "you serve Dook Bili as servant, as well. You are by him day and night, when"—she grinned—"you fixing your horn are not."

"I am become Duke Bili's striker, yes," Gy said sadly. "But only because my old friend who was his former striker was slain the first time we charged the shaggies, back on that plateau. Poor Gilbuht, his horse fell on the slope, and the whole damned squadron rode over him. A good friend he was, we had soldiered together for some years, and . . . and I miss him sorely, my lady."

Taking one hand from her knee and leaning forward, Meeree grasped his arm in a gesture of sympathy. "Yes, it is always painful to lose a true friend, Gy Ynstyn. But you soon will find, sure I am, that I can as good a friend to you be. With a war dart, can I at twenty double paces pierce an eyedot on a targe, with my good axe at the same distance can I that same targe split. Few among the Moon Maidens can ride better than Meeree, and only the *brahbehrnuh* and one or two others of our sisters can best me with saber or short-sword.

"At many and sundry oddments am I skilled. I can healing infusions of herbs and bracing teas prepare. And a hunter most accomplished I am, Gy Ynstyn. Full many a mountain boar have I lanced to death and, once, a red bear. Hoppers and squirrels in many scores have fallen to my slingstones, lynxes and wild goats to my darts, and once did a lucky cast of dart drop a full-winged turkey.

"So, man, you see, Meeree is no common warrior."

He nodded. "My lady, this I know. But also I know myself to be not worthy of such a woman as you. I am but a horn-man and . . ."

"*And* a warrior uncommon, like me, man," she interrupted, adding gravely, "These two eyes saw that you did cleave a Muhkohee from crown to chin, for all that a helm of thick leather he wore and you with no axe but only a saber."

Gy's face reddened above his ruddy beard. "A lucky stroke," he muttered.

"Why lie you, man of many talents?" Meeree asked bluntly. "Fight you and ride you as good . . . well, almost as good as fight and ride I." Then she grinned wickedly. "Too, good to look at you are. If take a man I must, the Goddess said not that an old or ugly one must I take."

"Lady," Gy remonstrated a little desperately, "when this campaign be done and the duke have no more need of a bugler, I know not how I will feed even myself. My captain and most of his condotta with which I marched south were slain under the walls of Vawnpolis, so I suppose that I at least own right to my armor and weapons and my horn; but, my lady, I do not even own a horse, the one I now ride being the property of a southron nobleman. Nor have I lands to return to, nor aught to sustain me or a wife in Gainzburk."

Both his voice and the formerly level gaze of his hazel eyes dropped. "You see, my lady, I . . . I am a bastard."

"Bastard?" She carefully shaped the two syllables of the alien word with her tongue and lips, wrinkling her brow. "Of late, often I have that word to hear from the men of your race. Bas-tard. It means what, Gy Ynstyn?"

He sighed, but once more met her gaze resignedly. "It means, my lady, that I know not, in truth, who was my sire. I have but my mother's word that he was who she says, for he never bothered to wed her."

Throwing back her helmeted head, she roared and shook with laughter. "Oooohohohohoho!"

Gy's eyes hardened, and the lips half hidden in his thick, bushy beard straightened to a thin line. "The dishonor of my birth amuses my lady, then?"

Meeree instantly sobered somewhat, sensing that she had deeply offended him, but still she could not keep a tinge of humor from her voice as she said, "Oh, silly man, offense take you not. No ill to you did I mean in my laughing. But, man, take the sole words of our mothers we all must. Beside, since know you your mother, what matters it who was the man who sired you? Few of us Moon Maidens know—or care—who was the man who quickened our dear mothers with us; it is not important."

While a stunned Gy digested this bombshell, she went on, "Two good swords we own, man, and all needful gear. This Dook Bili seems a man who would reward service, and think I he will not send you away on foot. As for lands and food, earn them our swords can; or to join an Ahrmehnee tribe we might. Kin to mine is their race and respect my Moon Knowledge they would, for they too reverence the Silver Lady. And ever pleased are they to gain another strong sword arm or two.

"So, do you want a war companion, man? Or is Meeree then unpleasing to your eyes and ears, perhaps?"

"Lady mine," Gy said fervently, "you are most pleasing to both eye and ear and, I doubt not, to hand and lips as well. Yes, I would be more than pleased to have such a one as you, and I pledge that I would be a faithful friend, but it were only fair to you to tell you the unpleasant truths I did."

Meeree smiled. "Then settled it is, man-Gy." She rose lithely to her feet. "Fetch back my gear to your shelter now I will."

Picking up her axe and targe, she strode briskly off toward

that area which had been the camp of the Moon Maidens, her long, muscular legs flashing as they ate up the distance. Meeree was well pleased with herself, having killed two birds with a single stone this morning.

The secret was no longer secret, the *brahbehrnuh's* self-chosen name, formerly known only to the Lady and, mysteriously, to the ancient *nahkhahrah*—or senior chief of all the Ahrmehnee tribes—Kokh Taishyuhn, now was known by Bili, as well, taken from amid the roil of her mind during the last few hours.

Side by side, Bili and Rahksahnah lay on the enlarged bough bed. His thick arm was about her shoulders, and their two warm, damp, utterly fulfilled bodies pressed one to the other in the beautiful, rosy aftermath of their first coupling.

Idly, her finger wandered over his scarred torso. "How very fair you are, my Bili. Never have I seen skin so pale. Are all your race so skinned?" she mindspoke curiously.

"My coloring is my mother's, Rahksahnah," he beamed, smiling in happy exhaustion. "My late father, Duke Hwahruhn, was near-pure Ehleen and almost as dark of skin and hair as are you; some of my brothers are almost that dark, too."

"How many are your brothers, my Bili?"

"Seven . . . I think. There were eight, but one—the second-eldest, Djef—was slain in battle last year by the accursed Ehleen rebels when they besieged my hall. I promised my most solemn oaths to my mothers that I would allow naught to befall Gilbuht and young Djaik, who were campaigning with me; now I can but hope and pray Sacred Sun that they and old *Komees* Hari and the others somehow escaped both the fires and the Muhkohee."

Her brows wrinkled in obvious puzzlement. "*Mothers,* love? How can any being have but the one mother?"

He chuckled and lightly squeezed her. "Horseclans customs, Rahksahnah, ancient usages of the Kindred. All of a man's wives are accounted mothers to all of his children."

"Yes," she beamed, "I had heard that men of the lowlands had more than one wife. How many do they usually have?"

He shrugged. "Common clansmen and most lower nobles have only one, but higher nobles often have more. My father had two, and they blood sisters of the Middle Kingdoms House of Zuhnburk, daughters of a duke and wives of a duke, which is what the Ehleen title *thoheeks* means in Mehrikan.

"Other Confederation nobles have as many as three or four, sometimes; and I have even heard, of one *ahrkeethoheeks* who has six. But I think I'd not care to share my hall with so many."

She shook her full head of lustrous hair, now much mussed and disordered. "Most remarkable are these ways of your clans, Bili, but it is the will of Her, so I suppose that I and the others of my sisters must become accustomed to them."

He grinned. "Only those who, like yourself, have been so unfortunate as to have succumbed to the manly charms of Kindred noblemen, like me, need even worry about their men taking other women, save as concubines, Rahksahnah. Middle Kingdoms men, even high nobles, take but one wife at the time. And all of the Freefighters out there are burkers. Nor do all of the Kindred necessarily adhere to the old customs brought from the Sea of Grass by our ancestors; it's a matter of very personal choice, you see, and only practical among high-ranking, wealthy men."

"And you are high-ranked and wealthy, my Bili?" she asked.

"High-ranked, yes," he answered. "As regards wealth . . . well, I truly know not. Oh, my Duchy of Morguhn was once moderately wealthy, but first came that damned hellish rebellion, then the putting down of it, both attended by much loss of life so that the duchy is now near depopulated, especially of the commoner sorts who worked the land, tradesmen and artisans and suchlike. Those matters alone would have been about sufficient to dissipate my late father's personal wealth and ravage the lands he bequeathed me.

"But to add to the damages and horrendous expense, the Duchy of Morguhn has been used as a junction of troopmarshaling and supply for the forces besieging Vawnpolis and then, after a surrender was negotiated, for the campaign against the Ahrmehnee. And with so many tramping back and forth across Morguhn, I may well be a poor man when, and if, I return.

"But the lands are good and fair, Rahksahnah. They will produce more wealth in time, and meanwhile I am accustomed to hard living, not so addicted to luxury as are most Kindred nobles. I can wait for better times."

She raised her head and brought her face close to his, and

just before their lips met she murmured low but aloud, "And I shall wait with you, my Bili."

The kiss deepened, lengthened, while questing hands sought out and found the secret places of bodies still almost strange. Rahksahna slowly drew herself up onto his body and—

"Chief Bili!" The thought-message burst into his mind with such force that he started up involuntarily, hurling the girl from off his body. "Chief Bili, beware! Many twolegs, some on horses and all armed, come to the place where you are. Your watchers on the western and the northern hills should have spied them long since, but they seem to just look through the column. The twolegs will be among you ere long."

The prairiecat paused, then added, "The other cat and Whitetip can attack, possibly delay them a short time . . . ?"

"No!" Bili impulsively ordered. "If you've not been spotted by these twolegs, stay low and await my summons; but trail the strangers, stay as close as it is safe to them."

Bili knew better than to question the numbers of the column, for few prairiecats had ever learned to count well.

Breaking off the farspeak with the feline, he mindcalled Mahvros, his war stallion. "Brother, bring the herd into camp, *quickly!* Soon there will be fighting." He did not await an answer, did not feel it necessary, for he knew the bloodthirsty temperament of his destrier only too well.

As with all telepathic communications, the exchanges had consumed but bare split-seconds of time, so he was able to check the startled girl's fall, mindspeaking, "Rahksahnah, one of the prairiecats, Whitetip, just farcalled me. There are armed strangers approaching this vale from the west. Arm as quickly as you can and assemble your Moon Maidens. My stallion is bringing the horses and ponies into camp."

Then he was off the bough bed and its stained and rumpled blankets. Hurriedly, he pulled on shirt, trousers, boots and then gambeson. *"Furface!"* he roared. "Sound 'To Arms' and then 'Officers' Call.' Sound both of them twice, then come here and help me to arm."

But even as the brazen notes rang through the cold air and the camp about became a hubbub of shouts and scurryings and metallic clanking-clashings, a full-armed figure darkened the entry of the shelter.

Meeree dropped her axe and targe and hurried over to the *brahbehrnuh*, who had buckled the last strap of her cuirass and was reaching for one of her cuishes, but was waved away. "No, Meeree, help Bili first. Remember, he now is leader of us all."

So, when Gy came hurrying in, red-faced, as the swelling thunder foretold the imminent arrival of the horse herd, Bili's cuirass, tasses, tassets and cuishes were already secured in place. Meeree seemed to be having trouble, however, with the Pitzburk helm, being unaccustomed to the newer innovations in armor; for the panoplies of the Moon Maidens, though of good quality and richly embellished, were of Ahrmehnee manufacture and of antique design.

Wordlessly, Gy took over, securing the equipment in barely an eyeblink, whereupon the frustrated Meeree unleashed a hot torrent of foul Ahrmehnee curses and profanities and turned her attentions to the *brahbehrnuh*.

Bili emerged from the shelter to see Mahvros—more than seventeen hands of black, glossy hide stretched over a full Harzburk ton of bone and rolling muscle—trot into the fire clearing, shepherding Gy's dapple gelding. Leaving Gy to saddle and equip the two mounts, Bili strode clanking down the pathway to the brookside, the scene of last night's council. He was not surprised to find all the Freefighter officers not only present but fully-armed, but it was a distinct and very pleasant surprise to find almost all of the southron nobles in as battle-fit a condition. Perhaps, he thought fleetingly, they're learning something . . . finally; they might, some of them, make decent soldiers yet.

Hastily, he outlined what information the prairiecat, Whitetip, had forspoken him, adding, "Also—and this puzzles me, gentlemen—Whitetip avers that so close is this force that our guards should surely have spied them ere now.

"Lieutenant Roopuht, take a squad down to the hill above the mouth of the vale and see what's to be seen, then send a galloper back to me."

Slapping gauntlet to breastplate, the Freefighter spun and trotted off, while Bili issued crisp orders marshaling his force. Almost all of the small command were armed and standing to horse before the galloper came boiling back up the vale.

Springing from his kak, the wide-eyed trooper gasped, "My lord duke, Lieutenant Roopuht bids me report to your grace that he sees no men or horses, but that some beast, a huge, scaley monster, is even now advancing up the brook track into the vale."

Without a word, Bill vaulted into the saddle and, trailed closely by Rahksahnah, the nobles and the officers, headed

Mahvros back the way the galloper had come. Troubled deeply by the vastly conflicting reports, he mindcalled White-tip.

"I am here, Chief Bili," was the feline's prompt response. "As you ordered, about halfway up the column and out of sight. Most of the twolegs have halted here. Perhaps only as many in numbers as I have claws on my four feet have kept on along the running water."

"Are all of them fighters?" Bili demanded. "And see you anything of a large animal coming this way before them?"

"All are fighters, right enough, Chief Bili. And I see no beasts, large or small, only huge men on Northorses, as many of them as my back claws . . . I think. The smallest is as big as the giant man whom you slew before the great shaking."

Every step Mahvros took increased the agony of Bili's presentiment of great danger just ahead. After hand-signaling those behind him to fully arm, he uncased his gigantic axe, but did not yet lower his visor, wishing to maintain maximum visibility of what must soon come to pass in this decidedly unusual situation. Behind him he heard the ripple of sound as visors were lowered and locked, and as sabers and broad-swords came out of sheaths. Whatever might now occur, he and the van were as ready as they could be.

Approaching the place where the stream debouched between a pair of precipitous knobs onto relatively level ground, Bili's presentiment became almost overpowering. Then, amid a shower of hastily gathered boulders and a chorus of horrified shouts from Lieutenant Roopuht and his men on the knob above, the ultimate terror poked its preter-naturally huge snout into the vale, flicking a forked tongue as long as a lance shaft before it!

Rahksahnah's scream of terror was not the only one, and they were all combined with the whufflings and snortings of horses suddenly reined up short. But Bili forced his trained and disciplined mind to calm appraisal of the monster now waddling around the rocky flank of the knob and into the mouth of the vale.

The scales which covered every visible inch of its thick body shone the color of blued steel. The one eye Bili could see was as big as a lancer's targe—near two feet across—and was the hue of fresh-spilled blood, with a vertical black slit of a pupil. Thick as treetrunks were the legs thrusting out from that immense body, then bending down at right angles to bear the weighty burden of wide-spreading, black-clawed travesties of human hands.

Sighting the knot of horsemen, the beast again sent that ten feet of questing black tongue flickering out, opened its gaping jaws—armed with double rows of back-curving, sharp-pointed teeth, glistening whitely and the smallest of them longer than the fangs of an adult prairiecat—then snapped them shut and increased its waddling-rush, seemingly oblivious of the missiles being showered upon its back from the knob above.

Somewhat reassured, despite the horror apparently confronting him and his force, by the fact that his destrier was standing calmly, awaiting a command, and seemed in no slightest fear of a creature looking to be a meat-eater and at least twice the big horse's height at the withers, Bili again mindcalled his furry scout. "Whitetip, where are you now?"

"At the tail of their van, Chief Bili. They are now halted in the cut, all save about as many as I have claws on one forepaw. But can *you* not see them, Chief Bili? Even in the low place where I lie hidden, still can I see your helm and the axe on your shoulder."

"And you spy no beast like a great huge lizard going before them, cat brother?" Bili asked once more.

The cat's mindspeak rang mildly exasperated. "Chief Bili, have you guzzled too much of the stinking water? Only men and horses are before you!"

"Be ready to attack on my command, cat brother." Bili broke off the mental bond with the hidden feline, then he mindspoke Mahvros. "Brother mine, what see you before us?"

Mahvros stamped a big, steel-shod hoof, clearly impatient for the bloodletting to commence. "Great, huge men on big horses, brother, but the horses are those slow, sexless ones; they will not stand against Mahvros or any other warhorse. Behind those is a man the size of my brother, and he bestrides a stallion; that should be a good fight for us both, brother." He stamped again. "We charge now, brother?"

"Soon," answered Bili. He reined about and beckoned the van to come to him. To the credit of their collective and individual courage, they all did. When all were within hearing, he spoke in a low-pitched but carrying voice, ignoring the jaw-snapping thing that seemed to be bearing down upon them all.

"Furface, sound you the 'General Advance'; the moment

that the rest of the squadron comes into view, this van will charge."

But one of the horsemen threw up his visor with a clang to expose a dark, Ehleen countenance. "*Thoheeks* Bili, I've followed you through what has seemed like half the damned mountains in all the world, nor did I stick at riding behind your banner against five or six times our numbers of bloodthirsty barbarians. But if you mean to charge that devil's spawn yonder, you'll damned well charge without Mikos of Eeahnospolis . . . or any other man with brains in his head. *Look* at that monster, damn you; it could champ a destrier in twain with one bite!"

Clenching his jaws, Bili stifled a sharp and insulting retort. He really couldn't blame the young nobleman. Despite his own dead certainty that the waddling monstrosity was mere illusion aimed solely at human minds, an atavistic terror and loathing still tickled at his vitals.

As calmly as he could he said, "Look you, Lord Mikos. The Ahrmehnee headmen spoke last night of works of wizardry. That apparition yonder seems to me to be an example of such, for though it seems clear and menacing to us, neither the cats out there nor my Mahvros can see it. Instead, they see armed and mounted men . . . and not very many of those."

But Mikos of Eeahnospolis looked anything but convinced, and others seemed to be of a like turn of mind.

"Very well," snapped Bili. He faced Mahvros about and dropped the reins loosely over the pommel knob so as not to hinder the big horse's fighting abilities. With his left hand thus freed, he lowered his visor and rose to his customary fighting position in the stirrups. "*Now,* brother!" he beamed.

Eagerly the big black trotted forward. The trot became a faster trot, then a gallop. Waving his heavy axe as lightly as if it were a child's toy, Bili raised his warcry.

"*UP! UP HARZBURK! A MORGUHN! A MORGUHN!*"

"*NO, BILI, NO!*" Rahksahnah screamed once, then she snapped down the visor of her archaic helm and spurred her tall mare in Mahvros' wake, her own lighter axe balanced to throw or hack or parry. And hard on her heels came Meeree, with Gy Ynstyn just behind.

When it seemed to the knot of breathless watchers that their leader would surely ride directly into those cruel, tooth-studded jaws, the black stallion came to a sudden halt. Whirling his thirteen-pound weapon around his head yet again,

Bili let go the steel shaft and sent the axe tumbling, end over end . . . but not at the now-rearing monster's head, rather much lower, some six or seven feet above the ground.

The thick axeblade took the beast at the confluence of body and loose-skinned throat, and passed cleanly through, disappearing like a pebble tossed into thin mud. But all heard the meaty thud of some solid something on flesh and bone, followed almost at once by the unmistakable shriek of a wounded *man*.

In less than the blinking of an eye, the horrid, looming monster was gone! It had not fled: rather, it had vanished as if it never had been. To the eyes of the dumbfounded vanguard of Bili's force, what had appeared to replace the monstrosity was strange enough, if not as fearsome.

Just inside the vale's narrow entrance were five of the gigantic Muhkohee. Two of them were standing, still holding over their heads the oversized bullhide shields which had protected them from the rain of rocks, for none of the five wore armor of any sort, unless thick leather jerkins and high-peaked hats of similar material could be construed as body armor. Behind the first two, two others had dropped their own shields to kneel beside the fifth, who lay writhing and moaning on the rocky ground, his hairy hands covering his face, bright blood gushing between the fingers.

Beyond this group of giant men, just outside the notch between the two rocky knobs, a sixth Muhkohee, garbed in the same fashion as the others, sat a piebald Northorse and held the reins of five more of the oversized equines.

A score of yards to this Muhkohee's rear were a column of normal-sized men, at least a dozen. All were armed, armored mostly in well-worn scaleshirts and mounted on largish mountain ponies. But it was their leader who caught and held every eye.

Although certainly no Muhkohee, he was quite a big specimen of a man—half a foot over six feet, anyway, and of proportionate breadth—and he was mounted upon a destrier that might have been Mahvros' twin for size and conformation, but of a uniform, creamy-white color.

The big man's armor had obviously been forged in the Middle Kingdoms and was lavishly decorated, every inch being covered with red-gold inlays and enamelwork, while the helm held in the crook of the man's bridle arm was encircled around the brows of the bowl by a broad, thick band of gold. The man's wavy, brick-red hair was streaked liberally with

strands and patches of yellowish-white. His eyes were half
hidden under bushy brows so thick that they seemed not to
break their march over his nose; his lips, too, were almost
hidden by a big, drooping red mustache. He and his stallion
made a striking picture, and, as they all watched, he lifted his
helm and replaced it on his head, though he left the visor
raised.

Bili drew his broadsword and once more rose in his stirrups. Raising his visor, he cupped hand to mouth and
shouted, "Ho! You on the white stallion, as you can see, we
outnumber you by better than ten to one. I have no wish to
kill you and your men. If we are camped upon your lands,
I'm sorry, but we had no choice or option. What with the
fires, it was trespass or perish, and we mean to depart eastward as soon as conditions permit. On that, you have the
word of Bili, *Thoheeḳs* Morguhn.

"However," he went on and grinned, "if only blood will
satisfy you, why not spare the blood of your followers and
make it between us two, eh?" His voice was tinged with a
happy anticipation.

Nor was that anticipation lost on his hoped-for adversary.
The big man in the gaudy armor tilted back his head, and his
basso laughter rumbled from his open-faced helmet. Then he
bellowed back at Bili, "There crows a young cockerel who
can hardly wait to blood his spurs! Naetheless, it was well
spoken, young sir, well spoken, indeed."

He kneed his stallion slowly forward, his right fist resting
on his armored thigh, making no attempt either to draw his
ornate sword or to grasp the iron-hafted morningstar which
dangled from the off side of his saddlebow.

The white stallion's unusually long pasterns flexed sharply
at every step, imparting grace and style to his movements.
His high-arched tail was full and rippled in a sudden gust of
air, while his well-formed head nodded proudly. Skirting the
unarmed and still bewildered-looking Muhkohee, the big man
did not halt his creamy mount until he was less than three
lance lengths from Bili and Mahvros.

Bili made a move to lower his visor, but the big man cried,
"Hold, young sir, wait. Whilst I've no doubt that we two are
about evenly matched and would make a fine, memorable
single combat, it were best that we talk, first. Best not only
for us, but for those who follow our respective banners."

"Are you a Sword Brother?" inquired Bili. At the big
man's nod, Bili reversed his weapon, grasping it by the blade

and bringing Mahvros to a slow walk while the stranger drew forth his own fine sword.

"Brother," Bili mindspoke Mahvros, "this will be a Sword Truce, so keep your teeth out of that stallion."

"But, brother," the big black remonstrated sulkily, "what if that overproud, pink-eared mule insults me? Or what if he bites me first?"

"Just mind your training and my orders!" admonished Bili sharply. Instantly, he regretted taking out his nervousness— sudden truces with unknown opponents after first blood always unsettled him—on the loving and ever-faithful horse, so he added, "Besides, we may fight yet, dear brother. There is but one negotiable way out of this vale, and this man's little force is blocking it. But restrain yourself a bit longer and let me see what he wants to discuss.

"Will Mahvros do that . . . for his brother?"

Beaming love and assurance of his obedience to Bili, the black stallion advanced until the two riders were almost knee to knee, then halted to stand like an onyx statue.

CHAPTER VIII

His every sense on full alert to guard against trickery, Bili wordlessly extended his sword, hilt first, his blue eyes meeting the stranger's blue-green eyes as he did so. In return, he accepted the big man's proffered weapon, and after each had solemnly kissed the bared steel just below the hilt, they again exchanged and then sheathed their blades.

After they had shucked gauntlets and shared a complicated, ritual handclasp, both men visibly relaxed, tension draining out of their bodies. Each now was secure in the knowledge that the ancient Sword Oath was as sacred to the one as to the other and that consequently neither would commit or countenance any treachery as long as the Sword Truce remained in effect.

The stranger spoke first. "Well, young sir, you and yours are in a pretty pickle, and no mistake! That those Ahrmehnee and Moon Maidens shoud be this deep into Muhkohee country is remarkable enough, considering the severity of the drubbing they took the last time they invaded. But by the Blue Lady, what are burkers and Confederation nobles doing here with them? I had thought the Ahrmehnee *Stahn* to be a bitter enemy of the Confederation, and of the Karaleenos Ehleenee, before, since time out of mind.

"Or are you really a *thoheeks*, sirrah? You look and bear yourself more like a burker than a damned foppish Ehleen. And your accent is of the Middle Kingdoms, too, not of the damned decadent southlands."

Bili smiled. "But nonetheless I am, sir, truly *Thoheeks* and chief of the Clan Morguhn, and the Prince of Karaleenos is nominally my overlord though recently I and mine have been in direct service to the High Lord of the Confederation, Milo Morai. But I also have the great honor to be the grandson of a Duke of Zuhnburk, on my mother's side, so I was fostered at the court of King Gilbuht of Harzburk. I soldiered with the army of King Gilbuht for five years and was

100

honored with the Order of the Blue Bear of Harzburk, ere I was summoned back to Morguhn to succeed to my patrimony and titles."

"Yes," chuckled the big man, "I heard the 'Up Harzburk.' Old habits are sometimes hard to break, eh? And a knight of the Blue Bear, are you? But that still leaves much unanswered, sir duke. What do you here, so far west and in such company?"

But Bili shook his head. "I'd not seem discourteous, sir, but I've answered enough questions, for the nonce. Now I'll ask one: Just who are you and what are your intentions toward me and my force? What follows this parley—war or peace?"

"Hmmph!" The red-haired man snorted, but showed no sign of displeasure. "Well, you're blunt enough, anyway; there's no misunderstanding you. Who I am is a long story, and I will be more comfortable before I go into that story, sir duke. Suffice it here to say that I am a nobleman driven from his rightful lands by a vile usurper. You, being who and what you are, may call me Byruhn; but your followers must preface the name with my title, prince."

Somewhere, deep in the depths of Bili's memory, the combination of name and title—Prince Byruhn of . . . ?—seemed vaguely familiar. Somewhere, sometime, he had heard of it and knew he should recall the tale, but with all else that was now on his mind, the old memory eluded his grasp. "And your intentions, Lord Byruhn?"

Byruhn raised his bushy single brow. "Why, sir duke, to save you and those assorted folk, back there in the vale, from protracted and singularly horrible deaths, if you'll all accept my aid . . . and my terms."

"Terms, my lord?" Instantly, Bili's every faculty returned to full alertness, and he beamed a mindprobe at the stranger . . . but slammed headlong into a very strong and impervious mindshield.

Byruhn at once seemed to know what Bili had tried, but he smiled good-naturedly. "No, I'm not gifted with telepathy, as you must be, sir duke, but certain of my wizards have schooled me in how to guard my thoughts against those who are.

"But be not so distrustful of me, young man. I now mean you all no slightest ill, not since I've learned who and what you are. I only commenced an attack because I had thought the force in this vale to be a raiding party of Ahrmehnee and Moon Maidens.

"I live finely balanced on the edge of a sword here, with precious few friends and a vast host of enemies, deadly enemies. The Blue Lady knows, the earthquake and those blasted fires have roiled things up enough and more than enough hereabouts. And an Arhmehnee raid at this fell juncture, could well topple me and mine from the skillet full into the fire."

"But," said Bili dubiously, "there are indeed Moon Maidens and Ahrmehnee warriors here. How does the mere presence of me and my noblemen and Freefighters make a difference? And, Lord Byruhn, who are you to talk of terms? My force could ride over yours with ease."

Byruhn smiled thinly. "And just how do you know that I've not a larger force in concealment out there?"

Bili answered the smile with a wolfish grin. "If you have, they're not within easy reach, my lord. I am better served than you seem to think. Your route of march was scouted for at least a mile, and by ones immune to the delusions of your tame Muhkohee, too."

"Impossible!" snorted Prince Byruhn. "Aside from a couple of large and some score of smaller wild animals, the only life my wizards sensed since we marched around Crooked Peak was a brace of played-out mountain ponies . . . probably strays from the outlaw raiders who were caught by the earthquake and the fires, Sword be praised."

Bili asked, "A group led by one of the Muhkohee? Between two and three thousand of them?"

Byruhn showed his big, strong and amazingly white teeth again, but this time in more a grimace than a smile. "Aye, the same pack, and I just wish I knew where their renegade leader was skulking now. There'll be scant slumber for me until I find him and put paid to his damned account."

"Well, then, Lord Byruhn," said Bili, "if we both speak of the same man, of the same war party that my force ran off the plateau back there just before the earthquake, you may commence to sleep in peace this night. My good axe split the bugger's oversize head like a ripe melon."

Byruhn's thick eyebrow developed a steep arch over each eye. "Big you assuredly are, sir duke, as men of our sort go, almost as big as me, you are; but still I find it difficult of belief that you could have single-handedly slain an armed Muhkohee. It was single-handedly, I presume?"

"Yes, I did it alone, Lord Byruhn, but it was no great feat of arms!" Bili snapped coldly. He had not actually been called a liar by this Prince Byruhn, but close enough. "When his Northorse fell, he lost his helm, and apparently his guts as well; at any rate, he cast away his sword and shield and tried to outrun warhorses, afoot, and him in full armor, too. But my Mahvros here"—he absently kneaded the muscles under the big black's roached mane and the stallion all but purred—"overhauled him and, for all the thickness of his skull and that odd ridge of bone running down its center from front to back, I clove him to at least the eyes."

The prince eyed Bili shrewdly for a long moment, then he smiled, really smiled, this time, and broadly, then raised an arm and beckoned over one of the huge Muhkohee. The giant was beside them in only three unhurried strides, and for all of Mahvros' height and his own, Bili found that still he had to look up in order to observe the Muhkohee's face at close range. And this was not the biggest of the leather-clad ones, though certainly the eldest and most venerable. Still, this old one was nearly two feet taller than the one Bili had axed down.

"Elmuh," said Byruhn solemnly, "this be Bili, Duke of Morguhn, from down in the lowlands. He led the warriors who drove the outlaws off the plateau and, with his great axe, he slew your son, Buhbuh."

Without a word, the old Muhkohee stiffly knelt at Bili's left, then extended a monstrous hand, palm up.

"Remove your gauntlet, please, sir duke," Byruhn answered Bili's questioning look, "that he may contact you flesh to flesh. He'll not harm you, never you fear; not even I could command him to do such now."

Not comprehending any of it, Bili drew off his scaled glove and placed his big, scarred hand in the wide-spreading, hairy palm, whereon it appeared as a babe's, before the long, thick fingers closed gently around it.

The Muhkohee looked deeply into Bili's eyes, and the young man met their gaze unflinchingly. While they remained thus, Bili became aware of the Muhkohee's odor—strong, musky, but not truly unpleasant. It was unlike the body odor of any man or woman he ever before had smelled. Then, with a distinct shock, he realized what was so startlingly different about the Muhkohee's eyes; the pupils were not round but almost oval, and the surrounding color was not white, but rather a tawny-golden hue.

"Quite correct, honored sir." The mindspeak was as strong as any Bili had ever received. "I, we, are not human, not en-

tirely. But I am human enough to feel deep gratitude to you
for freeing my poor little son, at long last, from the flesh
which imprisoned his tortured spirit. May your gods bless you
for that praiseworthy and generous act.

"But when I consider what and who you are, honored
one, I realize that selfless deeds are but natural to your
nature."

Breaking off contact, the old Muhkohee spoke aloud to the
prince. "This be the champion whose coming was prophesied,
lord prince. He is the one who will stand beside us in the
Last Battle."

Bili could only assume that the old Muhkohee had mindspoken his fellows, for they all approached, to range themselves behind old Elmuh and sink, like him, to their knees,
but all in attitudes of submission or veneration; even he who
had held the Northorses was there, and not even the one
whose face the haft of Bili's thrown axe had smashed was
missing, and he now seemingly oblivious of either pain or
swelling or bleeding.

As for Prince Byruhn, he had once more removed his gold-
encircled helm and was regarding Bili with a mixture of
helpless gratitude and awe.

Bili did not understand any of it then or for some time yet
to come.

Upon his learning that the force under Bili's command
was all but starving, Prince Byruhn spoke a few words to Elmuh, and shortly four of the younger Muhkohee set out,
moving faster afoot than could their lumbering Northorses.
One of them bore a huge handful of darts—each almost the
size of a conventional wolf spear—another, a long self-bow
and a quiver of arrows, the third, a leather sling, and the
fourth, a couple of big sacks.

Although Bili, Rahksahnah, the two Ahrmehnee headmen
and Prince Byruhn had early on dismounted to gather about
a fire before Bili's shelter and share cups of cold brook water
laced with mountain applejack contributed by the prince, the
rank and file had not been so hospitable or trusting of the
newcomers, either the human or the Muhkohee. The southron
nobles and the burkers and the Ahrmehnee warriors had returned to their respective fires and camps in the fringes of the
wooded sections and simply eyed the knot of the men-at-arms
of the hulking prince. But all kept their armor on, their

weapons belted or near-to-hand and their mounts on quickly reached picket lines.

But when the four Muhkohee came loping up the valley less than two hours later, heavily laden with eatables—several large deer, a yearling black bear, a monstrous boar and some dozens of such smaller game as hares, squirrels and birds, plus two bulging sacks of various herbs and tubers, some of which were strange to even the woods- and mountain-wise Ahrmehnee—a sudden thaw took place among the ravenous squadron and all joined willingly to help the Muhkohee carry, then clean, dress and begin to cook the various meats and wild plants.

By the end of the shared meal, it being the first full feeding that most of Bili's folk had had in days, the truce was on the way to becoming the alliance which Prince Byruhn was so obviously seeking, with even the Ahrmehnee and Moon Maidens seeming now at ease in proximity to the huge, ugly, very strange but surprisingly gentle Muhkohee.

When the small party of leaders grouped around Bili's fire had eaten their fill and were sharing more of the generous prince's apple spirits, one of the Muhkohee glided from out of the surrounding brush. For all their size, Bili had quickly noted that these semihuman creatures could move as silently as shadows.

This one halted a few feet away and waited for his lord to bid him speak. At Byruhn's nod, he stepped over to Bili, and it looked to the young man as if the single stride spanned at least two Harzburk yards. Respectfully, the huge one knelt and proffered Bili's axe—the big, heavy weapon looking like some small child's toy axe in those monstrous hands.

Noticing that his weapon had apparently been not only cleaned but polished to a high sheen as well, Bili profusely thanked the Muhkohee, adding, "I now regret that I had to hurt one of your folk, master wizard. I hope that he is not too severely injured."

The thin lips drew back off the massive yellow teeth. "No, lord champion, the haft of your axe but broke my nose. But it only caused me pain until Pah-Elmuh had the time to heal me. I now bleed no more and hurt no more and the bone will soon knit and the colored swellings subside. But for a pure-blooded man, you are most strong to so easily wield so fine an axe, lord champion."

Goggle-eyed, Bili just stared up into the giant's face for a moment. With exacting scrutiny at the close range, he could with some difficulty discern a certain spongy appearance of the wide-spreading nose and slight swellings of the face along with what seemed to be old bruises.

At length, he demanded of Byruhn, "As steel bites, my lord, are these Muhkohee of yours like unto the Undying, then? He looks to have been smitten far more than a week agone, not less than two hours, only."

Byruhn smiled. "No, sir duke, it is but an example of the singular healing powers of my Elmuh, who is most remarkable even for his remarkable breed. He has right often done the same for me and for many another, both Muhkohee—as you and the Ahrmehnee call the Kleesahk—and full men. He can halt bleeding, both inner and outer, remove pain and often repair smaller hurts without even touching the injury. This is why I insist that he go to war with me, for all that he truly hates warfare and will fight only when all else has failed and then only to protect himself or those he loves."

Bili arose suddenly. "My lord Byruhn, if all that you say be full truth, then I have some folk who lie much in need of your healing wizard."

What Bili and most of his followers saw in the next hour was nothing less than miraculous. Men and women who had for days and nights been writhing in tooth-grinding agony suddenly were bereft of their pain and sank into deep, restful sleep or watched, in fascination, as nimble, eight-inch-long fingers expertly cleansed and poulticed and bandaged wounds and burns and the stumps of lost digits, or splinted limbs afresh or took out the remainders of smashed teeth.

The last patient was Tyluh, a captain of Freefighters, a native Yorkburker whose loss Bili had sorely felt; for not only was he an excellent commander, but he was one of the few Freefighters who could mindspeak well, and he could even farspeak to a limited range. His helm had buckled under the oak-and-granite mace of a shaggy, and he had lain like a log ever since, breathing but shallowly. The most of one whole side of his close-cropped poll was a single soft swelling. Bili had seen similar bloodless head wounds before, and he had never seen a man live for long after receiving one.

After tenderly examining the unconscious officer, the Muhkohee wizard, Elmuh, looked up at Bili and Byruhn and said, gravely, "This poor man is near to his death, lords. A piece of his skull is now pressing hard upon the thin sack which holds his brain.

"It is possible that I can remove that bit of bone from its

dangerous lodgement, but he may die, even then. So what would my lords have me to do?"

"He will certainly die, and that, soon, as he is," Bili stated flatly. "So your efforts can do him no possible harm, whatever passes. You have wrought wonder already for my poor folk, here, and I am forever in your debt, master wizard. So, should you attempt to save brave Tyluh, too, and fail, how could I hold his loss against you? Do what you think should be done."

The Muhkohee with the broken nose set off at a lope, moving faster than a trotting horse, for all his pigeon toed gait, his thick arms swinging widely to balance his body on his even thicker, short legs. Quickly, he was back with a leathern roll. From this roll, Elmuh took several knives and odd-looking instruments of bronze or brass and set about his surgery, the younger Muhkohee assisting him as they were needed. When Captain Tyluh's head was swathed in bandages and the huge wizard had washed his hands and his gory instruments in the nearby brook, he returned to kneel before Bili and Byruhn.

Smiling tiredly, he said, "There still is an even chance that he will die, my lords. It was a sore injury; but at least I now can reach his mind with my own and I have wrought such as I can within his mind to stimulate the healing of his bones and flesh. Also, I have bidden him remain in his protective stupor until I waken him; for were we to move him, as we soon must, and him conscious, he most surely would die."

Bili paced forward and reached up to lay his hand upon one of those impossibly massive shoulders. "What can I do for you to repay such bountiful kindnesses, Master Elmuh?"

The dark pupils of the amber eyes had become mere slits against the brightness of the sun, so Bili could discern nothing in their glance, but the Mohkohee's lips slipped back off the massive dentition in a smile. Again came that very powerful mindspeak. "My lord champion, it is my true pleasure to relieve any who suffer, be they men or Kleesahk or animals. What you and my prince and this mate you have so lately taken for your own will do for me and mine was decided and ordained long before first your newborn eyes opened to the light of your Sacred Sun."

Bili felt then an odd, disconcerting prickling somewhere deep within his mind. Silently, he asked, "Then you would wish that my repayment to you be rendered in the form of service under Prince Byruhn, your lord? Is that your true meaning, Master Elmuh?"

The old Muhkohee beamed, "As I have said, lord champion, putting aright the ravages of disease or accident or the shameful effects of the basic savagery of man has ever been my pleasure and my joy; these past hours' work have been most satisfying to me for that reason, and it is rather I who should thank you for allowing me to do what I could for your suffering men and women.

"As for the service to the prince and to my race of you, your folk and your beasts, that is a fact foreordained by both ancient prophecy and my own scrying, and though I have seen much that you will lose in that service, also I have seen much that you will gain. Believe me, lord champion, for I possess the power to see what is to be . . . sometimes; the Eyeless Wise One taught well my father, and my father did pass all of those teachings on to me."

Bili and Prince Byruhn faced each other across the coals of the firepit before Bili's dwelling, Rahksahnah hunkered at Bili's side and the huge bulk of Master Elmuh leaned on the trunk of a tree a few feet behind the prince. A little to Bili's right, busily engaged in washing his face with a licked paw, sat the massive, fierce-looking prairiecat, Whitetip.

Despite the relative frigidity of the tail end of the mountain winter, the cat's long winter coat was beginning to pull out in patches, giving him a somewhat disheveled look, but he was still impressive, with his long, white canines, his seven feet of overall length and the full nine hands he stood at his thick-thewed withers. His base color was a rich, golden chestnut, with ghostly traces of darker rosettes scattered on the body and on the two-foot tail, which also sported a snow-white tip, from which came his name.

Prairiecats of the pure breed, like Whitetip, were highly intelligent mindspeakers and had been willing allies of the Kindred for hundreds of years on the high plains, mountains and prairies whereon the Kindred Horseclans had led a no-madic, wandering existence for centuries. And when Milo Morai, now the High Lord of the Confederation, but then the Undying God of the Kindred, had led the long migration of above forty of the Horseclans from the prairie to this eastern-seaboard land, scores of the great felines had accom-panied their human brothers and sisters.

However, it was soon discovered that a settled life upon thickly populated lands where much of the wildlife had been killed off or driven away was simply not the proper place for prairiecats, and when a very famous old man of the Horse-clans elected after some years to return west, a large proportion of the adult prairiecats accompanied him.

Those few who were left in the east were mostly scattered and, over the years since, had mated more than once with the native treecats—smaller, lightly built and lacking both the long cuspids and much of the intelligence of prairiecats, although even most of the wild ones had at least a minimal mindspeak ability.

A specimen of such disastrous interbreeding was the female cat that was curled asleep to the other side of Whitetip. She was less than half his weight and only a bare half his height, and her upper cuspids were only a little larger than those of her treecat cousins; for all of Whitetip's disparagement of her—he made it plain that he felt her to be runty, deformed and retarded—Bili thought that the young queen was intelligent enough and had decent mindspeak. But she seemed awed by the huge purebred male and constantly deferred to him.

Bili and Byruhn were talking, while Rahksahnah strove hard to follow the men's conversation; but, couched as was that conversation in the nasal, northern dialect of Mehrikan and well sprinkled—in Byruhn's speech, at least—with archaic terms and obsolete phraseology, more than a few of the bilingual Ehleen noblemen would have shared her difficulty, to a greater or a lesser extent.

"So then, Byruhn," said Bili, "your noble sire is the rightful King of Kuhmbuhluhn, you say? But Kuhmbuhluhn is not a kingdom, Byruhn, it's been a grand duchy for three quarters of the last two centuries. Only recently has the High Lord Milo designated it a principality and its ruler a prince, which he could legally do, since the *Ahrkeethoheeksee* of Kuhmbuhluhn had been his vassals for scores of years."

Prince Byruhn frowned, then shrugged the thick shoulders beneath his quilted, padded and much-embellished gambeson of fine black leather. "All of which is, of course, the direct result of my great-grandfather's brief moment of folly. That and my great-granduncle's foresworn and shameful duplicity.

"Know you, young cousin Bili, that when the middle lands were but a single huge kingdom, Kuhmbuhluhn was but a small, south-central mark of that kingdom, always menaced and sometimes ravaged by the Ehleenee and right often the springboard for raids in force against them.

"But this order changed, five hundred years agone. The sea

waters—both the salt sea and the freshwater sea to the north-west—swept far and far inland, permanently claiming for their own many a mile of less elevated lands, while hideous earthquakes rocked and racked and ruined all the lands of men, changing the ages-old courses of rivers, toppling some mountains and raising up new ones where none had been before. Strong burk walls crumbled like so much dried mud, as, too, did whole cities and towns, and an ordered society was thus plunged into an utter and howling chaos.

"But Kuhmbuhluhn was only minimally affected by the vast calamities, and while the great nobles—the Grand Dukes of Redn and Bethlum and Pitzburk and Eeree and their satellites—butchered the King in Harzburk, then commenced to fight each other like some pack of savage mongrels, my distinguished ancestor, Leeahn—the first of that name and also known as 'the Great'—utilized his small but effective army well. With it, he carved out a modest kingdom of both Ehleen and Mehruhkuhn lands, nor did he have to fight for all of them, by any means, for when complete disorder besets a land, men clutch at any straw which gives promise of stability.

"As years became decades and many bloody defeats made it clear to the new states—Harzburk, Pitzburk, Tchaimzburk, Yorkburk and Getzburk, among others—that they could neither strip lands from Kuhmbuhluhn nor dissolve it, they at last grudgingly recognized the rank and status of my house. Then, as the Ehleenee, too, slowly recovered and became ever more aggressive and warlike, seeking to reconquer lost lands and gain new ones, our value to the other Middle Kingdoms became apparent and they not only desisted in making war upon us, but commenced to aid us against the Ehleenee to the south and the fierce mountain tribes to the west."

The prince opened a belt purse and withdrew from it a greenstone pipe and a bladder of tobacco, then began to carefully fill and tamp while he went on with his history. He was an accomplished storyteller, and Bili listened in silent fascination.

"With the help of both Harzburk and Pitzburk, Leeahn's great-grandnephew, King Byruhn the First, established and fortified the marks of Ransuhnburk and Rahmneeburk and Frahstburk, then went on to build the great fortress at Buhnkuhburk, to guard the Western Trade Road into the mountains.

"So, with the greater powers of the Middle Kingdoms

resolved to peace with Kuhmbuhluhn, if with no other states, least of all each other, and with strong salients guarding our border marches against attack from south or west or southeast, settled pursuits such as farming and stockbreeding became profitable enterprises; and that is the period when the reknowned Kuhmbuhluhn Chargers, of which strain both your stallion and mine own are such matchless specimens, were developed and refined.

"As more and more Kuhmbuhluhners were required to return to work the lands, it became necessary to replace these yeoman-soldiers with more Freefighters, that the various fortresses and smaller strongpoints be adequately manned and that the marches be regularly patrolled; this was done. Then, as the kingdom waxed richer from the fruits of peace, my ancestors were able to increase the size of their armed bands and slowly add more bits and pieces of land to their kingdom. Not wishing to risk a violation of the Sword Council Edicts which protected them from the vastly more powerful kingdoms of Harzburk and Pitzburk, they took almost all of the added lands from the Ehleenee and the mountain tribes."

The pipe now packed to his satisfaction, Prince Byruhn extracted a small coal from the edge of the glowing nest between his horny thumb and forefinger, blew white ash from around the red-orange core and then placed it atop the tobacco. With the stem between his teeth, he began puffing, talking around the stem, in between puffs, as he continued his recital.

"And so the kingdom prospered and grew, fighting only when pressed or openly attacked, carefully keeping clear of the rivalries of the larger and smaller states to the north . . . until the coming of the plains barbarians, the Horseclans.

"At the time that the Horseclans fought their way into Kehnooryos Ehlas, that wretched kingdom had been for some five years under the misrule of a weak and a cowardly High Lord. This wretch placed more value upon gold than upon honor, unlike his sire, who, Ehleen or no, had still been a stark warrior and had pressed Kuhmbuhluhn hard throughout his life, campaigning with his troops in good weather or foul, fighting at their van and winning the respect of every foe he faced.

"Early on in his reign, the craven and pleasure-worshiping son of that unusual Ehleen, having emptied his treasury and lacking the means to buy the luxuries to which he was addicted, had sold back to Kuhmbuhluhn lands which his sire's

sword had won. Seeing the way the wind blew, my great-
grandsire seized both the opportunity and still more Ehleen
lands, routing every force that this faint-hearted High Lord
sent against him.

"When my great-grandsire chanced to hear that not only
was Kehnooryos Ehlas beset in the west by a migrating host
of nomads, but that King Zenos of Karaleenos was ravaging
the southern borders and that a renegade Ehleen nobleman
was raising a force hostile to the High Lord within the very
heart of the unhappy kingdom as well, my ancestor scraped
together every uncommitted man in the Kingdom of
Kuhmbuhluhn who could fork a horse or swing a sword or
push a pike, reinforced this motley with a few stray units of
Freefighters and marched due south, in search of lands and
loot and glory.

"Alas." The big prince blew a stream of bluish smoke into
the fire pit. "Poor old Great-Grandfather found none of
them, but rather ended by losing everything he owned, save
only his honor.

"Foolishly, beyond doubt, he split his force, riding well
ahead with his nobles and most of the Freefighter dragoons
and leaving the foot and trains to follow down the Eastern
Trade Road. Just beyond the Suthahnah River, a mixed
horde of nomads and the heavy cavalry of the renegade
Ehleen noble ambushed the foot and extirpated the light infantry and the rear guard of lancers, then looted and burned
the trains.

"By some miracle—or, as I've always believed, the raiders
saw no need in losing men by attacking a force that couldn't
pursue them anyway—most of a largish condotta of Freefighter heavy infantry survived the disaster. They salvaged
what they could by way of supplies from the burning wagons,
withdrew to a defensible position near the river they'd just
crossed and then sent gallopers to the van.

"The first messenger who reached my great-grandsire
related that not only had the renegade Ehleen nobleman—
who had been a general in the armies of the then High Lord's
brave sire, and a damned good one, or so I have been told—
joined with the nomads, but he had sent word to the more
hostile of our neighbors that the bulk of our earstwhile defenders were deep within Kehnooryos Ehlas, perilously far
from their own lands.

"Therefore, my great-grandsire sent his brother—his own,
dear, loved and trusted younger brother—Duke Hehrbuht to

first succor the remains of the infantry, then return posthaste to Kuhmbuhluhn and secure it against attack. Trustingly, my ancestor gave his brother the pick of the Kuhmbuhluhn nobility along with three full squadrons of first-rate dragoons."

CHAPTER IX

"This foul and detestable traitor arrived in the kingdom to discover that there was no danger looming, that no one of the kingdom's spies and agents had heard aught of any word of any nature having been passed to Kuhmbuhluhn's enemies. It all had been, it developed, but a clever ruse designed to force my ancestor to do just what he had done, what he had felt compelled by his hereditary responsibility to do; split his forces further."

The prince selected another small coal from the firepit, blew it free of gray ash and pressed it into the bowl of the greenstone pipe.

"At that juncture, young cousin, a decent and honorable man would have speedily returned to his brother and lawful sovran with his nobles and condottas. But not the treacherous, backbiting Hehrbuht; oh, no, not he.

"Hehrbuht and certain other self-serving traitors who had ridden north with him lied and deceived and cajoled through the length and the breadth of the kingdom. They magnified the ambush of the foot and the trains, vastly overemphasized the few, unimportant skirmishes of the van, and combined both sets of prevarications into the proportions of utter and unrelieved disaster for the bulk of the Kuhmbuhluhn field army. Then they proceeded to their real purpose: placing total culpability for all of this supposed havoc squarely upon the head of my great-grandsire, King Mahrtuhn, deliberately leaving the impression that he was, at his very best, utterly incompetent as a leader of men!

"By the time that a few loyal men had gotten down to my great-grandsire and he had headed back from Kuhmbuhluhn with his remaining forces, it was already too late. The foresworn and evil Hehrbuht had twisted words and arms until the Council of Kuhmbuhluhn had declared him true king, thus deposing my ancestor, whom Hehrbuht immediately declared to be an outlawed exile. With the usurper squatting in the new capital, Haigehzburk, King Mahrtuhn led his loyal followers to Kuhmbuhluhnburk, the old capital, in the west of the kingdom. There he prepared for war and issued a summons to all loyal Kuhmbuhluhners to rally to the just cause of their rightful king.

"Before the year's end, all of the members of the council were aware that they had been hoodwinked and chivvied into the perpetration of a calamitous crime. To a man, and to their everlasting credit, they deserted the usurper and reassembled in Kuhmbuhluhnburk, where they did reconvene and attempt to right the great wrong they had earlier done my ancestor.

"But the traitor, Hehrbuht, refused to recognize or to heed this new mandate, not only continuing to illegally style himself King of Kuhmbuhluhn, but robbing the kingdom's treasury to hire on more condottas loyal only to him. And he continuously called upon his brother, my ancestor, the rightful king, to surrender the western lands and cities and fortresses which he and his held, unconditionally!"

The prince drained off the last of the contents of his cup, refilled it with water and brandy, then offered both bottles to Bili and Rahksahnah before going on with his tale.

"Quite naturally, since the right was his own, not that of his scheming brother, good King Mahrtuhn did no such thing, rather did he rally his available loyalists and redouble his efforts to marshal them and gird for the attack, which now was a sure and looming certainty.

"Because he had not enough men to both adequately defend the old capital and field a decent army—not without stripping the frontier fortresses, which he would not do, since such would seriously endanger Kahmbuhluhn from alien enemies—he declared Kuhmbuhluhnburk an open city, that it might thus evade the ruination and attendant horrors of a sack, and he moved his headquarters and his court—such as it was become—to the impregnable fortress at Buhnkuhburk. Then he and his army marched northeastward against the hosts of the usurper.

"To shorten a longish tale a mite, young cousin Bili, poor, brave King Mahrtuhn met with defeat in a great, crashing, day-long battle, near a ford on the Blue River Plain. But for the devilspawn usurper, it was a truly pyrrhic victory; he lost over half of his army, so there was no meaningful pursuit or harassment of my great-grandsire's withdrawal with his own survivors to Buhnkuhburk.

"Now, understand, the usurper's army had vastly outnumbered that of King Mahrtuhn's loyalists and the ruinous costliness of his 'victory' had been in large part due to his bumbling, ill-conceived strategy and his hotheaded tactics on the actual field. Moreover, his Freefighter officers easily recognized the incipient folly of his deadly mistakes well before the fact and had remonstrated with him, only to be one and all reviled and insulted by the headstrong 'monarch.' And so, immediately they had buried their dead and reorganized their condottas to some extent, they all demanded and received the payment balance on their contracts, then they all marched out of Kuhmbuhluhn in search of an employer who might offer something other than certain death.

"Now, since the usurper had already stripped the treasury bare to the very walls and floor, he could hire no more Freefighters to continue armed support of his unnatural pretensions. Frantically casting about for any device or stratagem which would serve to keep his ill-gotten crown upon his head and that evil head upon his shoulders, he fairly leaped at an offer of military and financial aid proferred by the ambassador of the King of Harzburk.

Nor, in his terror of losing that which was never rightfully his to own, did my craven great-granduncle even pause to consider the steep price Harzburk was sure to demand and assuredly receive: nothing less than the vassalage of the whole of Kuhmbuhluhn, reduction in the ranking and status of both kingdom and king and the probable appropriation of northern borderlands, not to mention the dire possibility that poor Kuhmbuhluhn would become a battleground for Harzburk against its many enemies.

"For no sooner did this preternatural misalliance of Harzburk and Kuhmbuhluhn's usurper become common knowledge than was my valiant ancestor's court at Buhnkuhburk visited by a high-ranking and powerful plenipotentiary of the King of Pitzburk, who then was a sworn and a deadly rival of the House of Harzburk."

Bili nodded and said, "And still is, for all that both kingdoms now are ruled by new dynasties."

"Yes, I know," the prince answered, then just sat for a few long moments, puffing at his pipe and staring into the firepit. It was obvious that his thoughts were far away . . . or of very long ago. Then at last he looked up with a new and strange look in his blue-green eyes, a look at once sad and regretful, but, albeit, savagely proud.

"My gallant ancestor, the noble King Mahrtuhn, was not simply hereditary ruler of the Kingdom of Kuhmbuhluhn, my young cousin; no, he was one with his kingdom and all who dwelt therein—from the mightiest to the humblest. He was an integral part of the plowlands and grassy leas, of the forests and waters and mountains. Unlike the selfish and greedy usurper, King Mahrtuhn had suffered real pain to see Kuhmbuhluhner hack, maim and kill Kuhmbuhluhner, to see the trade roads clogged with marching, warring hosts, the rich fields and lush pasturelands ridden over and trampled down by warhorses and watered all too well with gallons of the best and richest blood in the realm.

"Too, this wise, generous and sensitive man could clearly see those harsh facts to which his traitorous brother was so obviously blind, that to allow the ages-old and endless conflict between Harzburk and Pitzburk to spill over into that which had been his loved kingdom and his birthplace Kuhmbuhluhn, would be to serve the death sentence on the kingdom and, most likely, on most of the folk, as well. And so, honorable King Mahrtuhn of Kuhmbuhluhn, last legitimate king to sit upon that throne, did the only thing which a man of honor and compassion for his lands and people could do under such bitter circumstances.

"With all his household, with all other loyalists who wished to stay by him and share his self-imposed exile—noble and common, soldier and farmer and stockman, men and women and little children—some three thousands, in all, King Mahrtuhn set out to the southwest, on the Mountain Trade Road. His destination was unknown to him or to any other, and the only surety was that there would be much hard fighting against the mountain tribes and months or years of suffering and privation before they reached some strange place they might claim as their own . . . if ever they did so.

"But they were a people no less brave and honorable and self-sacrificing than my revered great-grandsire, their leader, and set out into the outer darkness they did. Since that day of grim sacrifice and of the service of dark honor, none of my house has set foot in or clapped eyes upon that dear land of such precious memory, that kingdom—now almost legendary to my folk—which its last, rightful king willingly gave up so very much to preserve and protect."

"I am most glad, Prince Byruhn," said Bili slowly and gravely, "to know at long last the truth of the ending of that long-ago struggle. It always has been difficult for me—and

for many another—to credit sudden cowardice to a man who
had fought so bravely and so often before. Yet, that is just
what was then and has often since been declared in official
records and histories, that King Mahrtuhn suddenly turned
craven at the mere thought of facing the King of Harzburk
and his Iron Majesty's armies.

"I rejoice to learn, here, that King Mahrtuhn's supposed
flight was rather the very apex of bravery, for he must surely
have known what his enemies would say of that flight . . .
and of him. There are no words in any language sufficient to
praise or even to measure or plumb so deep and utterly
selfless an amount of courage and honor, my lord prince."

Byruhn inclined his head and said simply, but with clear
and intense feeling, "I thank you for those words, sir duke."

Bili went on, "But I would know more, Prince Byruhn. Elmuh, there, says that he is not a man. Then what, pray tell, is
he? Why do he and the others of his kind address me as
'champion,' and what is this Last Battle of which he has spoken?"

Byruhn tapped his pipe on his bootheel, then began to
work at the inside of the bowl with the rounded point of a
tiny jeweled dagger. "As to your initial question, at least, you
are telepathic and so is he, so let him tell you, mind to mind,
cousin. That way will take far less time than spoken words,
and it were wise we all were far away from this little
deathtrap of a valley. There is yet more apple spirit—will
not you and your lady again join me?"

"I *am* about half man, lord champion," Master Elmuh began, silently. "My father was a full-blood Kleesahk, but my
mother was a Ganik."

"*Ganik*, Master Elmuh?" The term was yet another new
one, to Bili and also to Rahksahnah.

"The folk you think of as 'shaggies,' lord, and you as
Muhkohee, lady. Not all of them are so small as those hereabouts; to west and north, near to my lord prince's stronghold,
dwell families of Ganiks who grow much larger, though still
smaller than pure Kleesahks. It has been with these few man-
families that my father's species have interbred over the
years. Most Kleesahk-Ganik hybrids have been sterile, for the
relationship of the two species is very distant; I often have
grieved that I, too, was not sterile, during all the long years
that poor little Buhbuh suffered so much and wrought such
evil out of that suffering. But now, lord champion, your kind
act has ended both his sufferings and mine own."

It was the first time Bili had ever been thanked—and very profusely and repeatedly thanked, at that—by a father for killing in battle that father's only son . . . and such thanks made him feel strange and not a little uneasy.

Still, he questioned on. "But whence came your father's kind, these Kleesahk? If he and they are not true men, then what matter of creature are they, Master Elmuh? If not true men, neither are they, from what little I've so far seen of them, true beasts."

"My father came from the mountains to the north, along with his own father and mother, his brothers and his sisters and a few other kin. Where my kind originated, I know not, nor did my father, wise as he truly was. We had dwelt in the mountains for scores, at least, of our generations, and we Kleesahk live longer than do most men, true men.

"Before ever the first true man set foot in the mountains, Kleesahk were there. As to exactly what we Kleesahk are, I do not know that, nor did my father or his fathers. In some few ways, we are like to true men, but in many other ways, we are more akin to beasts; although our shapes are roughly manlike, our minds are much more alike to your prairiecats."

Bili grinned and beamed, "I never knew of a prairiecat who could make me think he was a fifty-foot lizard when I looked at him; or any man, either, although it has been my honor to know and call friend both the Undying High Lord Milo and the Undying High Lady Aldora."

Elmuh replied, "Nor, lord champion, have I ever met a true man who could project such illusions, nor can a single Kleesahk do it with a believable reality of appearance. Depending on the number of man-minds we wish to cozen, it takes at least two of my kind to cause men to see that which we wish them to see, and, as you witnessed this day, if even one of those Kleesahk participating is forcefully distracted, the illusion vanishes completely. Far easier is it to cause men to *not* see that which truly exists before them."

"Not to see, Master Elmuh?" Bili beamed his bewilderment.

All at once, Bili's unusually keen sixth sense told him that something beyond the pale of normality was being woven. Then, with a smile, Elmuh beamed, "Look about you, please, lord champion."

Bili did . . . and gasped and started, despite himself, in his very real amazement. Not only had the prince and Rahksahnah and the two prairiecats suddenly disappeared, but the fire, the rude shelter, the piles of gear, everything! He sat alone, save for only the gigantic Elmuh, in a tiny forest glade. Yet a questing hand to either side told him indisputably that both Rahksahnah and Whitetip still sat beside him, and the heat beating on his face told him that the deep bed of coals still glowed in the shallow pit before him. But only for a bare second was it thus; then, as if a gust of wind had dispersed a blinding mist, all was again normal and as before.

"That, lord champion," attested Elmuh blandly, "is not seeing that which exists. It is both simple and easy . . . for Kleesahk and hybrids of our kind. Right often our young do it self-taught, with no formal training of any degree or description. But I have not yet been able to teach any true man to do it. That Kleesahk talent is how, over the millennia beyond reckoning, Kleesahk have concealed themselves from those of you savage, aggressive, murderous true men who penetrated the mountains and forests and wastes we have inhabited.

"You see, lord champion, we, unlike you true men, do not take enjoyment from causing hurt and pain and death; we kill beasts only for food and men only as a last resort, to save our own lives or those of our kin and loved ones.

"Observe." The half-Kleesahk gestured. "I wear no armor, nor do I carry sword or axe or even dirk. And even my simple hunter's knife is wrought of bronze, rather than of iron or steel."

"Yes, I noticed that when your hunters went out, earlier," Bili remarked silently. "Such of their hunting gear as was not of bronze was shod with bone or even with chipped stone. Why?"

Elmuh shook his massive, bone-crested head. "Not from any dearth of those metals, lord champion, but because for some reason that not I nor any one has ever been able to fathom—we Kleesahk experience but scant success in performing our illusions when in close proximity to aught of steel or iron, even a single knifeblade."

"Yet," Bili stated baldly, "that huge man—your son— whom I slew back on that plateau, just before the earthquake and the fires, rode in a full steel-plate panoply and swung the biggest steel sword I've ever seen."

Elmuh sighed and beamed in a mindspeak much overlaid with grief, "Yes, poor little Buhbuh could wear and bear steel, for there was but little of the Kleesahk in him, save only for his size and certain other purely physiological features. The blood of the pure Kleesahk is become thinned. In most respects, poor Buhbuh was a man, but a truly mad man. He led that huge band of pitiless outlaw raiders for scores of years—as I have previously informed you, Kleesahk live longer lives than do you true men, and in this trait too, Buhbuh was more like to me and my father than to his trueman antecedents—and, but for him and his savage marauders, long since would there have been real peace, rather than an armed and very uneasy truce, between my lord prince and the folk to the eastward—Ahrmehnee and Moon Maidens."

"You *want* peace, then, you Kleesahk and the Muhkohee . . . ahh, these Ganiks, was it, Master Elmuh?" This mindspoken query came from Rahksahnah.

"I crave real peace with all my being, my lady," Elmuh beamed forcefully and with much emotion. "So, too, does my dear lord and his royal father, King Kahl the Third. Brutish, bloodthirsty tribes press us all from north and west, you see. Within our unhappy land are renegades and large families of man-eaters—Ganiks who are become so interbred that most are half mad and some are wholly mad—more fierce and feral and deadly than the beasts whose skins they wear. The very last thing that my lord prince or any of the rest of us needs is additional enemies. Too, the Last Battle looms ever nearer and, even with you now among us, lord champion, we will need every aid we can raise up or borrow."

Rahksahnah beamed, half-questioningly. "Then, my Bili, perhaps we should send for the Ahrmehnee headmen now with us, Soormehlyuhn and . . ."

"No," Bili interrupted with his own powerful mindspeak. "There is enough time for that. There is still much that I would know.

"Master Elmuh, when first we met, this morning, you spoke certain cryptic words of my having come into these mountains as the fulfillment of some ancient prophecy. You spoke then, also, of a Last Battle, and you have just done so yet again. You continue to address me as champion. Champion of what, good master? What of this prophecy and this Last Battle?" He paused, then remembered the other thing he wanted answered.

"And, too, back there at the main camp, you said something as I recall of an 'Eyeless Wise One.' Is he one of your kind? The chief of you Kleesahks, perhaps?"

"No, my lord champion, the Eyeless Wise One was no *Teenéhdjook*—which is the proper name for my father's kind in their own, seldom-used, spoken language, 'Kleesahk' being their word for us hybrids. No, he was a man, a true, pure man, but very old, for a full man, perhaps ten scores of years old.

"He came into the mountains wherein my kin then dwelt some fifty years before I was born—nearly two hundred years ago, that is. He rode a small horse, with a score of other horses following him, and with him too were some dozens of those great, long-fanged cats, such as that one by your side.

"His horse had lost its footing on a narrow ledge and had slipped, falling down a steep, shaly slope and pinning beneath its weight the leg of the Eyeless Wise One. Although not really injured, the beast was terrified, and had his mind not been continually soothed by the mindspeak of the gathered cats, he would surely have struggled so violently that both he and his aged rider would have slid over the nearby edge and plunged to their deaths on the rocks far below.

"The cats did what little they could—soothing the horse and keeping the other horses back away from the dangerous area. But with only fangs and claws, neither of which could find purchase on smooth, hard stone, there was no way that any of them could get to or succor the old man. That was when my father and his two brothers chanced upon that site of impending tragedy.

"At once and instinctively, my father and uncles made to cloud the mind of the Eyeless Wise One, bid him see them not, for this is how the Teenéhdjook had traditionally protected themselves from true men; but the Eyeless Wise One, lacking eyes of his own, had learned to so mesh his mind with those of the great cats that he could see out of their eyes, and, as you are become aware, lord champion, our illusions are ineffective on the minds of beasts.

"Then did the Eyeless Wise One's powerful mind enter into that of my father. He sensed my father's inborn fear of him as a representative of a different, a savage and bloodthirsty species, and he bid my father not fear and asked, graciously, the help of the three Teenéhdjook to free him and the horse from out of their predicament.

"Now, my father and his kin had never before been mindspoken by a true man. Indeed, they had always thought that only the Teenéhdjook and certain of the other beasts could so communicate, and so he was truly fascinated that a man would so bespeak him. He sent his two brothers back to their cave to fetch strong ropes of braided strips of hide, and whilst they were gone he and the Wise Old One reassured the disturbed, protective cats that the Teenéhdjook meant not harm but rather salvation to the trapped man.

"Upon the return of my uncles with many coils of sturdy rope and three other Teenéhdjook, my father and another slid down the treacherous slope and secured the horse, then held it steady whilst my father lifted it enough that he might free the Eyeless Wise One and get him up onto the ledge from which he and the horse had plunged.

"That feat accomplished, my uncles drew the small horse back up as well, but so nervous were all the horses that no amount of mental soothing by the cats, the Teenéhdjook or the Eyeless Wise One could assure him a safe and uneventful ride if he should be placed upon one of the near-hysterical creatures. With his much-damaged leg, the Eyeless Wise One could not walk, so my father bore the eyeless man in his arms back to the commodious cavern which had for generations been the home of the Teenéhdjook.

"The Eyeless Wise One, perforce, wintered with my father, while his old bones slowly knitted, for we—my father and his kin—did not yet own the healing skills we now possess, which were, indeed, the generous guesting-gift of this highly uncommon true man.

"For vast knowledge of the mind had he, of men and of beasts, far and away more than even the wisest and most venerable of the Teenéhdjook then owned. Even though his man's mind was very different from those of my father and his kin, he soon proved able to explore Teenéhdjook minds, especially that of my father. He plumbed every depth of his host's mind, he rooted out hidden abilities and latent talents, and then did he show my father and the others how to do things they none of them had ever before done or even thought of doing.

"The healing of flesh and of bone was but one such new thing; he could not do it himself, for his mind did not own that potential, but he taught my father to do it when he discovered that blessed potential in his very different mind. Then, armed with his new and wonderful abilities, was my father able to help his guest in certain ways.

"They two became fast friends—the first such friendship between a true man and a Teenéhdjook as was ever before known to have existed, for as I have said the Teenéhdjook then both feared men with good cause and carefully avoided any contact with them. But before he departed westward in the spring with his horses and his cats, this man gifted my father, also, with glimpses he had in some way had of the future of him and his get and of the Teenéhdjook. Then he rode on toward the setting sun, bound, he said, for a place he called the Sea of Grass, where he had been born so many long years before. And that was the last that any Teenéhdjook ever saw of the Eyeless Wise One, who called himself Blind Hari of Krooguh and who had given them so very much."

Bili shivered all over, felt the hairs at the nape of his thick neck all aprickle. He had often heard of Blind Hari of Krooguh, as had all Kindred-born and bred. The name and the story of this hundred-and-fifty-year-old tribal bard who, with the Undying High Lord Milo of Morai, had led the first forty-odd clans on their twenty-year-long trek from the Sea of Grass to Kehnooryos Ehlas was a much-recounted part of any bard's repertoire—be that bard a clan bard or a traveling professional. But Bili, like most of the last few generations of Kindred, had always considered it to be mere legend.

But now, in the light of what Master Elmuh had just related, he recalled the last few verses of the *Saga of Blind Hari*, recalled how it was recounted that this ancient man had tired of the new and hateful life of the settled clansmen and, longing for the Sea of Grass and the life-style of the nomad, had returned west some decades after the conquest of the east.

Bili had often meant to ask Milo and the Undying High Lady Aldora—whose lover he had been for some months—if Blind Hari of Krooguh had ever actually existed, but he had always forgotten to do so in the press of events. Now, from the mind of this alien creature, he had at long last learned the truth.

"But what of this prophecy, Master Elmuh? What of this so-called Last Battle?"

However, Prince Byruhn chose that moment to speak. "Young cousin, I would hope that you have learned all that you would from our Elmuh. But, if not, your queries must be continued at another time, I fear me. We cannot march fast, what with my infantry and your wounded, so we must leave within the hour, are we to be certain of reaching the Safe Glen, ere nightfall."

The prince tucked his cold pipe into his belt purse and arose; so too did Bili. Boldly facing the older, bigger man across the firepit, he demanded, "Why should I and my force quit this vale? That still has not been explained to my satisfaction, Prince Byruhn. Furthermore, why—if leave we do—should we follow your banner? Why should we not simply ride eastward, back to the Ahrmehnee lands?"

The prince sighed gustily, "No, you did not learn much of present value from Elmuh, it seems. Very well, then I'll try to explain. Those raiders you fought and routed before the earthquake were but a scant third part of the outlaw horde who haunt these hills and vales all along the eastern border—which is why there are no villages and but few farms hereabouts, since the outlaws prey upon their own kin as relentlessly as upon the Ahrmehnee.

"Moreover, you may be dead certain that they know you are here and also know about how many you number, young cousin. That they have not already attacked you I can only attribute to the turmoil of the tremors and the fires, added to the great losses you and yours inflicted upon those in this area.

"But attack they will, eventually, and probably sooner than later, and in vast, overwhelming numbers. This position is untenable—surely you with your obvious war sense can see that. Your force is simply not large enough to adequately man the hills roundabout, and, even if it were, the slopes of those hills are a much steeper pitch within than without the vale. Nor could you hold here for any long time, in any case, with no supplies, scant graze and a near dearth of large game.

"As for riding back eastward, it would be sheer suicide! You'll be ambushed and bushwhacked and sniped at by bowmen and dartmen and slingers until your party is weak and sufficiently demoralized for an all-out attack. If you so choose to die, I'll regret your needless deaths, young cousin, but I'll not try to physically impede you.

"I'll say but one thing more, ere we two part, *Do not allow the outlaws to take any one of you alive.* Any kind of an honorable death, even by your own dirk, is preferable to the suffering of what those animals will do to your body."

"And if I, we, do follow your banner today," demanded Bili, "what is to be our status? Will my force and I be free to leave, to go back east, when we wish? Or must we, soon or late, fight our way from under your sway? What is to be the price you will exact for your aid to us today, Prince Byruhn?"

The tall prince smiled thinly. "Spoken bluntly and openly,

young cousin. Yes, I guessed rightly, you surely are my kind of a man. In answer no less blunt and honest, I would hope that when once you have been imparted all this night, you and yours would freely choose to enter my employ for some brief time. But, if not, if you choose otherwise, I shall do my utmost to see you all safely across the Ahrmehnee border. On that you have my Sword Oath." He gripped both his big hands about the wire-wound hilt of his battle sword, sincerity shining from his steady blue-green eyes.

CHAPTER X

The column did move slowly, it moved very slowly indeed, and over tracks and trails full many of which were but ill-suited to the easy passage of horse litters; but the prince drove them all hard, his face and manner a study in anxious concern. His obvious worry for his and their own safety served to take the bite out of his often harsh words. Thanks in no small part to the ceaseless prodding of that high-ranking nobleman, however, they did reach their goal—the so-called Safe Glen—with the slanting rays of the setting sun.

Price Byruhn's face and manner became more relaxed, though still wary, as craggy hills reared up to closely flank the winding track—which track showed man-made improvements here and there along its length. Farther along the track, shrewdly placed and built into the living rock, small but strong-looking stone towers reared up; armed men stood upon the parapets, the westering sun glinting on the polished steel of their weapons. From tall staffs set in the apex of each tower, large banners rippled in the wind, and upon them Bili could clearly note and recognize the Rampant Green Stallion of Kuhmbuhluhn. On shorter staffs, two smaller banners snapped—one bearing what at the distance looked like a red-brown dog or wolf on a blue-green field, the other being a black boar upon a field of silver-gray.

As the long column passed between these grim strongpoints, spears and bared blades were raised in salute and the voices from above lustily cheered their overlord. Prince Byruhn raised his sword hand in gracious greeting and acknowledgement of the homage.

Then the track began to wind through truly tortuous twists and turns, doubling back here and there and several times crossing rushing streams over well-built bridges wrought of squared timbers. Small but sturdy-looking squad keeps overlooked each bridge, others dotted the steep slopes between, and the visible portions of the hill crests were all fortified as well, natural saddles and low points being filled in with dressed stone and capped by expanses of crenellated defenses.

Bili thought, as he, Rahksahnah and other nobles followed the prince over yet another oil-soaked and pitch-smeared wooden bridge, that he would surely hate to have the task of leading a force of attackers against these multiple and most formidable fortifications. Surprise would be a true impossibility, for those atop the outer towers could see for long miles in all directions in daylight, and the terrain leading toward this narrow gap was so treacherous that a night march would be out of the question. Nor could he envisage manhandling siege engines to within range even of the outer works. It would all have to be done by unmounted men, and losses would be stupendous.

At long last, the head of the column negotiated a final hairpin turn to come to a halt before a massive, double-valved gate, which gave every appearance of having been crafted by and for the use of a race of giants. The weathered, metal-shod portals soared more than thirty feet up between the sheer walls of rock—gray granite which had been polished far smoother than nature often accomplished unaided. The tops of the gates were crowned with a hedge of long, down-pointing bladespikes, and above the gates, a broad arch of stone, set with merlons and another set of flagstaffs on which the same three banners snapped in the wind, spanned the gap; which gap was, at this point, only a bare score of feet in width.

At sight of Prince Byruhn's bared face, a half-armored man atop the fortified arch turned about and shouted something. At once there came the cracking of a whip and the bray of a mule, then, with a hideous, damned-soul screeching of pivots, the massive gates swung slowly open. Bili whistled softly through his teeth when he saw just how truly titanic those gates really were—the uprights at least two feet in thickness, battened with foot-thick timbers and clinched with iron spikes, the least of which was at least four feet long and as thick as a spear shaft.

As the van passed under the arch, the beam which had barred those portals became visible—the squared trunk of what had assuredly been the very grandfather of all oak trees, its tremendous weight lifted from niches cut in the living rock by a system of cables and pulleys.

Noting the direction of the young lowlander's gaze, the

prince chuckled. "How like you Count Sandee's door, young cousin? Think you it might withstand a few hard raps?"

Bili shook his helmeted head slowly and said gravely, "My lord prince, I've never seen or even heard tell of the like of such gates. Methinks the ram to crack them is yet to be wrought, and I would doubt that even the largest of the High Lord's stonethrowers could easily breach them, even were there a position within range on which to mount a large engine. But what of fire?"

The prince shrugged. "Well, wet green hides are hung, of course. But there's another defense against fire, and I'll show you it . . . when and if you decide to follow my banner."

The roadway proved level, though winding still, for a little distance beyond the gate. But then the pitch of the incline abruptly steepened until it became necessary for the riders all to dismount and lead their weary, dusty horses up the long flight of broad steps cut out of the stone of the mountain.

On the left hand reared the flank of another man-smoothed hill, while on the right, beyond a low wall of roughly dressed stones, icy water rushed in a white froth over an uneven bed of rounded rocks.

As the prince and Bili and Rahksahnah reached the wide crest, the last great blaze of the setting sun beamed over their shoulders to illumine the heart of this place that the prince and his men called the Safe Glen. But it was now obvious to the newcomers that they were within what was much more than a mere mountain glen.

A network of long, narrow vales let into each other, and finally several larger ones opened into the farther end of a central, open area which gently inclined on all sides toward the very middle, where lay a sheen of lake perhaps a hundred yards in diameter. From their perch, the van could see stubbled fields and winter-sere pasturelands in the flatter areas of all the vales visible; the upper and narrower parts appeared to be given over mostly to brushy expanses or to small stands of timber.

Neat stone cottages were scattered here and there, their architecture reminding Bili more of Ahrmehnee habitations than of anything else, their chimneys now uniformly smoking with the evening cookfires. Somewhere within that veritable maze of tiny and larger vales, a cow could be heard bawling loudly, while elsewhere a dog yapped insistently. Human figures, dim with the distance and the hurrying darkness, could be seen up beyond the glinting lake, chivvying sheep or goats into a stone pen or fold.

On the near side of the spreading lake, a huge and lofty tower soared up into the darkening sky, its battlements higher even than the tops of the mountains that ringed the Safe Glen. It reared up at least a hundred feet, Bili reckoned, maybe a third again more; and, high as it was, it still was no slender structure such as those Bili had seen in the Middle Kingdoms, rather was it squat and incredibly massive, some sixty feet or more on each of the two sides he could see.

Between his eyrie and that tower sprawled a commodious stone-and-timber palace. It could be called nothing else, being far and away too large to be designated house. Light was now commencing to pour from windows that looked to be glazed, and a host of figures were to be seen scurrying hither and yon between the main structure and its semi-connected outbuildings.

The prince waved down at the brightly lit building. "Sandee's Cot, young cousin, our destination. You and I, your lady, nobles and officers will bide there this night. The Teenéhdjook and your troopers, Ahrmehnee and common Moon Maidens will find comfort in yon tower, along with the bulk of my own men. Those few from here will be seeking out their own homes, of course."

As the prince told it on their slow walk down to the cot, the late Count Sandee had fallen in a battle against the outlaws a few months back. He had died without issue—legitimate or otherwise—and so his mark and county were being held for the crown by the grizzled old warrior who had been seneschal, Sir Steev Stanlee—severely, hideously scarred, missing most of his front teeth, all of the right and part of the left ear, as well as all or part of several thick fingers. The old fighter bustled about his multitudinous duties with a stiff-legged limp which told the experienced eye the tale of a once-smashed knee, but for all his old scars and maimings, he was friendly, jolly and virtually abrim with a hearty gallows humor which instantly attracted Bili.

The central chamber of Sandee's Cot was not so long as that of Morguhn Hall—Bili's birthplace and home in the Duchy of Morguhn, far to the east—nor so wide, nor were its furnishings and hangings so rich or so varied, but it was nonetheless at least comfortable, warmed and partially lit as it was by the wide and high fireplaces at either end.

Smoky tallow lamps were set in highly polished wall

sconces and in man-high standing holders the length and breadth of the room, imparting along with their dim and flaring light a persistent burned-meat odor. But on the dais which supported the high table, tapers of fine beeswax in candelabra of chiseled copper gave illumination for the prince, Bili, Rahksahnah, Vahrtaht Panosyuhn, Vahk Soormehlyuhn, *Vahrohneeskos* Gneedos Kahmruhn of Skaht, Senior Lieutenant of Freefighters Frehd Brakit and old Sir Steev.

Those at the high table commenced their meal with a clear meat broth, pungent with dried onions, garlic and herbs, then went on to succulent little fishes, each coated with meal and fried to crispness; fresh-baked breads and roasted potatoes and mounds of pickled cabbage, turnips and parsnips accompanied the roasted and boiled meats—mutton and pork for the lower tables, lamb and kid and larded venison for the high. Then they were served salty, double-baked breads and various cheeses, along with cellar-hung apples, strawbarrel pears and assorted nuts for the distinguished guests.

Cracking nuts for himself and Rahksahnah in his powerful hands, Bili felt that he had not dined so well since last he had left Morguhn Hall, months agone. When he had washed down the sweet nutmeats with a swallow of honey ale, he addressed himself to the prince.

"Prince Byruhn, your vassal sets a truly noble table. It has been long since I feasted so well and fully."

Byruhn chuckled good-naturedly. "Do not expect any better than that we all just enjoyed even at my father's court, Duke Bili. It ever is a great pleasure to me, being a man who admittedly takes an abiding joy in his victuals, to visit Sandee's Cot, for the meals if nothing else.

"The vales herein are rich and well watered, the black loam lies deep over the bones of the mountains, and Sandee's folk are consummate farmers and stockmen, fishponders and hunters. Were all my father's lands so productive and well tended . . ." He sighed, and a look of dark sadness crossed his face. "It be enough to make a strong man weep in pure frustration, noble cousin; for all or, at the least, full many of the vales and glens hereabouts could produce similarly, were we but able to at last extirpate these damned renegade outlaws, so that full-time farming and stockraising would be not only possible but worthwhile.

"As matters now lie in this part of the realm, the miserable folk outside the few safe glens, such as this one, are sore afeared of giving any appearance over that of bare subsistence, lest the damnable raiders come and strip bare their lands and barns and homes and fields. And I, alas, have never been able to number enough skilled fighters to smash these outlaws . . . ere now."

Bili wrinkled his brow in puzzlement. "Were our two positions reversed, my lord prince, I'd simply drum up the spear levy, put pikes in the hands of every man I owned between the ages of fifteen and forty-five, and set my retainers to drilling them. I'd use my mounted force to harry the outlaws, nip the bastards so shrewdly and so often that they'd have to finally come to me and stand at bay. Then I'd use my seasoned fighters to hold them in place, like a good pack of veteran boarhounds, until the levy could be force-marched up to butcher the scoundrels. My lord is a wise and war-canny man—I am much surprised that either he or his royal sire has not done such as I just detailed, long since."

Old Sir Steev snorted, his scarred face twisted in utter disgust. "Oh, aye, and in my lord duke's own lands, wherein I doubt me not that such a commoner levy would have manparts a-swinging betwixt their two legs, such a strategy would doubtless work . . . and often has, in times agone. But not here, my lord duke, assuredly not in these lands, and most assuredly not with these eternally cursed Ganiks!

"Not in a land mainly peopled by mealy-mouthed, addle-pated, god-haunted buggers who'll scream blue murder if they be raped or robbed and some few of our poor overworked garrison not be near about to prevent it or, at least, avenge it, but who'll not themselves raise a hand to aid themselves or even keep a steel dirk or a spear on their farms!"

With a heavy sigh, the prince responded to Bili's look of consternation. "If you are thinking, my young cousin, that such as Sir Steev has described be most unlike the breed of burkers, you be assuredly right, it is not. But then, outside the safe glens, very few of the landworkers be descended of Kuhmbuhluhners. Most of the folk over whom my house holds tenuous sway are an exceeding strange people who had drifted into this stretch of mountains only a few years earlier than did my forebears and their few thousands loyalist supporters.

"These non-Kuhmbuhluhners cannot be called a tribe, for they are not—they none of them recognize any central chief or any council of elders. Each family group is, rather, ruled by the eldest able-bodied male member. Few of these families are more than very distantly related, blood-wise, for they almost always cleave strictly to their own, all manner of incest being their way of life for generations if not centuries. Only their common religion, their most unusual customs and singular habits mark them as similar."

Bili sought through his recent memory for a moment, and at last he located that endless word used by the two Ahrmehnee headmen. "These, then, these non-Kuhmbuhluhners, would be what the Ahrmehnee call Orgahnikahnsehrvaishuhnee, lord prince?"

Prince Byruhn nodded. "Aye, that's one of their names for themselves, though in practice it's usually shortened to Ganik. They are a stiff-necked, self-righteous people who boldly claim direct descent from the very Earth Gods themselves. They prate on endlessly of the beauty and the purity of their bare, drab, deprived and religion-dominated life-style. They never cease to proselytize among any folk who are happier than they are, and they have even been heard to solemnly attest that had the Earth Gods, the folk who ruled these lands of old, adopted their own narrow and cheerless beliefs, the War of the Gods might never have occurred!"

Once more the prince sighed gustily. "We all, even our Elmuh and his gentle ilk, have come at last to the hard conclusion that the only sure way to rid these mountains of ours of these deliberately primitive, deliberately backward, fanatically hidebound and stubborn cannibals will be to extirpate them with steel and fire wherever and whenever we find them.

"There is no reasoning with the vast majority of them. My father and his father tried that tack for long, frustrating years. These Ganiks have no honor, sworn oaths mean nothing to them, and all are mentally unstable to one degree or another. Furthermore, without the replacement pool formed by these scattered but numerous families, the raider bands of outlaws soon could be wiped out—completely and for all time."

"The 'Ganeek' women and the children, too, you would slay, Prince Byruhn?" demanded Rahksahnah, the gaze of her black eyes burning intensely into his blue-green ones.

The big man shrugged. "Nits make lice, my lady. Those children are weaned on human flesh, you know; as for the Ganik womenfolk, they are even more vicious and fanatic than their menfolk. Those harpies it is who do the inhuman torturing of any helpless wight captured by the men; they are the ones who roast the quivering flesh of the living bodies of prisoners and then force the poor wretches to eat of themselves."

Bili noted that both *Vahrohneeskos* Gneedos and the hard-bitten Lieutenant Brakit looked a mite greenish, and he felt a trifle queasy himself; but the Ahrmehnee headmen and Rahksahnah just looked grim, with jaws firmly set and eyes hard—they had heard rumors of such horrors for all their lives.

After a long draft of the ale to settle his stomach, Bili asked bluntly, "And this is what you want me and my force for, Prince Byruhn? To help you to wipe out these Organikahnsehrvaishuhnee?"

Byruhn nodded shortly. "Partially, young sir, partially; but we'll not really need to kill too many of them. When once they know that we mean business and that we at last have sufficient force to carry out my will, they'll move on—move farther south or west, but out of my lands, at least. Their doleful songs tell of many such moves over the years; it would appear that no normal folk will tolerate their presence for any long time. Nor can anyone blame those who drive out or eject such a mad and maddening people, I trow!

"But there is a second reason, a reason far more important than helping to rid our lands of these Ganiks, cousin Bili. You and your disciplined, well-armed veterans are of immense value here in the southeast, but of even more in the northwest, round and about New Kuhmbuhluhnburk, where sits my father, in great jeopardy.

"Know you, young cousin, that we are gravely threatened in the northwest of the kingdom by a migrating tribe of folk from across the northern river, from the mountains of Ohyoh. Although suffering immense losses in so doing, they overran the northernmost of our safe glens some years agone, and now are they using it as an advance base against us, raiding deep and ever deeper into our lands. Their announced goal—or so say their heralds, for unlike these accursed Ganiks, they at least follow civilized modes of daily affairs and war—is to drive out my house and all our folk and to then take over for themselves all of our lands and places. They seem to know of the Ganiks of old, say that it was their own forebears who drove them south, and have solemnly promised to exterminate them this time around, then push on eastward and drive the Ahrmehnee, too, from their lands. They are a most martial and determined people; were they not so deadly a threat to me and mine, I could easily find much reason to admire them."

A deep, menacing growl rumbled from the two Ahrmehnee headmen, and Rahksahnah fingered her dagger hilt. But the prince seemed neither to hear nor see and continued on.

"If I could have drawn support from the cannibals—who are no less threatened by these invaders than are mine and me—or if I could have depended upon them and the raiders they breed and harbor to have not precipitated a border war or to have not laid siege to this or other safe glens, the northerners might have been thrown back before they were become so powerful. But with the ever constant need to guard my back with my slim forces, I dared not meet large bodies of them in open battle, and so I lost the initiative, and lands to boot.

"Further, there has been and still is much turmoil in the lands north of the Ohyoh, the lands whence these invaders came, so each six-month sees them reinforced with more fighters—good fighters, too."

The massive warrior brooded for a moment, rolling a ball of bread between his horny thumb and finger. Then he spoke again.

"A third reason for your value to us all, Cousin Bili, is the Prophecy of the Kleesahk—of the Teenéhdjook, rather, since they had it before they came south and began to breed with the northern Ganiks. It . . . but, wait, let Elmuh tell it, he can do it far better than can I."

In a booming voice which rose even above the hubbub from the lower tables, a voice that, indeed, shut off all noise in the hall as a driven bung halts the flow of wine from a pipe, he roared, "Elmuh! Come up here and tell these guests of the Prophecy given your race of old."

CHAPTER XI

Hari of Krooguh idly stroked the down-soft fur of the prairiecat cub snoozing in his lap. He sat on a flat-topped rock near the mouth of that same mountain cave which had sheltered him and his hosts throughout the long, bitter months of the winter just past.

Far, far below his perch, the tiny stream of autumn days was become a rushing, turbulent flood of snow-melt waters from off the higher elevations and mountains. Beyond that stream, on a small plateau, the horses grazed avidly on fresh, tender green shoots of grass, guarded from depredation of lean wolf or hungry bear or prowling treecat by several of the adult prairiecats, whose lounging gray or brownish forms Hari could see here and there.

He could see them. With his own pale-blue eyes could the old man see them, and he could but consider this fact to be a true miracle. Nearly two hundred years old—as true men reckon time—Hari of Krooguh had been stark blind for more than one hundred and fifty of those years. Yet slowly, during the long months that he had wintered here with these strange but gentle giants, these Teenéhdjook, his sight had returned to him.

Another cat cub wandered out, blinking in the splash of bright sunlight after the dimness of the cave's interior, and the "sleeping" cub in Hari's lap suddenly came to life and full wakefulness. He gathered his legs beneath his tense little body, his ears laid flat back against his neck and his foot-long tail twitching. When his unsuspecting littermate ambled within easy range, the sometime sleeper's hindquarters swayed rapidly from side to side once, twice, thrice; and then he launched himself onto and full-tilt into his sister, and the two cubs commenced to roll over and over on the sun-warmed ledge—snarling and spitting, growling and clawing and biting with their small, sharp teeth. The enraged growls the two

136

emitted seemed far deeper and more menacing than such small animals could possibly produce.

At last, the attacked female wrenched herself free of the tangle and stood for a moment—stiff-legged, broadside to her attacker, her own small ears laid back and the soft fur fluffed up high along the line of her spine, her tail swishing and her white fangs bared at the crouching male cub—before flinging herself back into the fray.

Hearing the joyful sounds of the combat, first one, then another of the prairiecat litter trotted bouncing out onto the ledge to lend their own weight, teeth, claws and abundant vitality to the ongoing fracas. Hari sat and watched, grinning and chuckling, until at last all four cubs lay panting or preening their ruffled fur in the sun.

The dark shadow of a gliding eagle swept over the ledge, its wide-spreading pinions momentarily blotting out the sunlight, and all four cubs crouched instinctively in alarm, snarling in sudden fear, their eyes staring up toward this danger. Hari too looked aloft at the avian predator, his sinewy old hand closing about a jagged lump of rock fallen from the mountain above, but the bird wheeled to the right and soared out of sight behind a peak, obviously searching for smaller, more vulnerable prey than prairiecat cubs large as adult bobcats.

Then, from out of the cave, came the Eldest, having to stoop almost double to negotiate the six-foot-high opening. The Eldest greeted Hari telepathically, as neither had been able to twist his tongue around the other's oral language to any great extent.

The Eldest numbered half again as many years as did Hari of Krooguh, yet he was neither stooped nor withered of body. Only a generous stippling of white among the coarse dark-brown hairs that covered all his huge body, saving only face, palms and the soles of his feet, announced him any whit different or more ancient than his sons and grandsons and their get.

As the Eldest came from beneath the rock overhang and out into the full sunlight, the cubs rushed up to gambol and cavort over and about his huge feet. Stooping again, he gathered up two of the playful young beastlets and cradled them in his massive arms, gently ruffling their fur with his long, black-nailed fingers, while rumbling smoothing contrabasso sounds of endearment to them.

Feeling once more safe and secure with this big twolegs

they had known for all of their young lives, one cub began to lick down the chest hair of the Eldest, while the other commenced to worry at the loose skin between the thumb and the forefinger of one gigantic hand with a set of sharp, sparkling-white teeth.

When his dark-green irises had contracted enough to give him optimum vision in the bright glare, the Eldest crossed the outer ledge to sink onto the rock beside Hari, the thick black callosities protecting his almost-fleshless buttocks and the bone beneath from the hard surface that his mighty weight pressed them against. When he had drawn up and crossed his short legs, the other two cubs clambered up to reexplore the familiar lap.

"You are unhappy, Hari of Krooguh," the Eldest beamed silently. "Why is this so?"

Hari's sigh was audible, but he replied just as silently. "Because the winter has fled and the spring marches closer with every passing day, dear friend. Because I have found here, with you and yours, great happiness and more peace than I have ever before known in a very long life. Because I long to live out the rest of my days here, but cannot."

The Eldest nodded sagely. "You feel responsibility to see the great cats back to the place of high grasses and no hills, them and the horses. But why can they not go on toward the setting sun along with each other, without you, friend Hari? Big as I am, I still would hate to have to fight even a single prairiecat, nor are any of your horses exactly gentle and defenseless. Remember those two wolves the stallion killed in the snow?"

Hari sighed again and shook his head of braided white hair. "Were wolves and treecats and bears, storms and rivers and rockslides the only dangers, I would not fear for any of them. But such is not the case, honored Eldest. These four-legged beasts all must get close enough for the cats and the horses to have at least a chance to give as much as or more than they receive. The most dangerous predator, however, moves upon two legs and can maim or slay at a distance.

"Since most men cannot communicate as can you and yours, I, and the folk of the Horseclans, they would look upon the cats as large, dangerous beasts and slay them to protect their livestock or hunt them down to death for their beautiful fur. The horses they would ride down and rope for a life of servitude, killing those that their cruelties could not bend to their will. The horses and the cats are my friends as you and your family are my friends, and I will not rest easy if I think that any of my friends are being hunted like wild beasts."

"No, it is not good to be hunted," the Eldest agreed. "My kind were so hunted by men, until we learned to so cloud the minds of those hunters that they saw us not. For hundreds of our generations has this skill served to protect us from your smaller but more vicious kind. It is not a difficult talent to develop; you have learned it and so have most of the adult cats, too, but I fear the horses never will learn it, their minds are just too . . . different."

Hari nodded again, resignedly. "So, you see, I must go."

"You will leave us soon?" questioned the Eldest sadly.

"Within eight more suns, at the most," Hari replied just as sadly. "Still ahead of me are many miles of mountains. I cannot move fast or far in any one day because the cats have not the endurance of the horses and so must either go slowly or rest often, and when again winter comes upon the land, I wish to be in milder surroundings than mountains."

"That would be most wise," stated the Eldest. "Such deep caves as this one are rare, and even if you found another and let the cats hunt for you, without a fire you would die, and who would there be to find and cut and fetch back wood for you? Perhaps I should send along a son or two to see to your welfare until . . . ?"

"No, honored Eldest, no. You and yours have already done far more for me than I ever can repay. Your brave sons saved my life at great risk to their own lives, then you sheltered and fed me for long months—me, an alien creature whose race has ever dealt yours only savagery and death, who long ago drove your kind to the wildest and most inaccessible portions of the lands. And yet you did still more for me, honored Eldest—you gave me back that which I had thought forever lost—my sight."

"I could not have helped your body to repair its eyes had not you shown my mind how to so heal the infirmities and injuries of others, friend Hari. Untold future generations of Teenéhdjook will bless you for that great gift, so speak you not of debts owed me and mine, for it is assuredly we who owe you. Therefore, it is settled, this matter; two of my sons will journey on with you as far as the foothills to the west. You will not need to push the cats too hard, for if you must winter once more in mountains, my sons will provide all needs for you and the horses."

Using wood and bone bound with sinew for the frames, the Teenéhdjook fashioned crude but effective saddles on which adult cats could crouch on the backs of the horses, with the hooked claws sunk into several thicknesses of rawhide coverings to steady them. With his own huge, skillful hands, the Eldest made a pair of hide panniers, that the cubs might relax and snooze in safety while journeying.

On the last night he was to abide with the Eldest in the now-familiar mountain cave, Hari of Krooguh imparted to his host what, with his rare and amazing abilities, he had seen of the future of these Teenéhdjook.

"Honored Eldest, before ten more winters have passed, you and yours will find it needful to leave this fine cave and move on. You will move south and west and into mountains in which dwell true-men of two differing races. Some few of your kind dwell with them already, and they have long since interbred with a subrace of true-men who are much larger than most true men, although still not so large as Teenéhdjook.

"The one of these southern races will respect you and will deal honorably and fairly with you and you will find that they can be trusted; the other race will fear you and they cannot ever be trusted by even those of their own blood.

"After long years, when both you and your sons are but old bones, one of your grandsons not yet born will be the eldest of the Teenéhdjook. His kind and the folk of the good true-men will be hard-pressed by the bad true-men and by another folk as well. For a while, it will seem that all will be lost, that it will be only a matter of time until evil will triumph totally over good and that to further combat the many minions of that evil would be but to postpone the inevitable.

"But then, from out of the eastern lands, will come riding a champion. He and his forces will help in driving the brutal, untrustworthy men from out your land, and because of him and those who love him, the Good will be victorious in the Last Battle with Evil.

"You will have passed all this knowledge on to your sons, and they to theirs. You also will have passed the signs by which this champion may be known. He will be big for a true-man, this champion, a proven warrior and leader of warriors; he will be a hereditary chief in his own lands and the eldest of either nine or eleven sons; he and his followers will ride through a wall of fire to reach you, and the champion will shed Teenéhdjook blood ere he mindspeaks your grandson and that grandson plumbs his mind to learn that the long-awaited champion is at last arrived."

"And so," said old Elmuh, speaking slowly and obviously having difficulty in voicing certain consonants, "this Eyeless Wise One, this Hari of Krooguh, rode on westward with the next dawning. My father and one of his brothers journeyed with their guest, the cats and the horses until, with the first snows, the western foothills were reached. Then did my father and my uncle begin their trek back into the high mountains. No Teenéhdjook ever saw him again, this Eyeless Wise true-man."

"So, you see, Cousin Bili," said Prince Byruhn, "this is why our Elmuh hailed you, back in that little vale where you all had camped, as the champion. After all, it might be said that you and your force rode through a wall of fire to reach my lands, and you did shed a measure of Teenéhdjook blood, when the haft of your thrown axe broke our Djehree's big nose. You are a proven warrior and a leader of warriors, as well as a duke and a chief, in your own holdings. Are you the eldest of nine or eleven brothers?"

"Both, really," answered Bili wonderingly. "My mothers bore my father eleven boy babes, but two died in or near infancy. There were nine of us until last year, then the next eldest to me, Djef Morguhn, was killed leading a sortie against the Ehleen rebels who were besieging my hall. Two others of my brothers were with me back on that plateau before the earthquake and the fires, but they are not with me now and I know not if they made it down safely or if they escaped the flaming forests."

"Steel grant that your brothers be safe," the prince said feelingly, then went on, "but back to the Prophecy, cousin. You see, everything about you was foretold long years ago, so how can you be aught else but this champion who will bring us victory over our foes?"

Bili was beginning to feel the jaws of some nebulous trap closing inexorably about him, so he demanded, "Just how much of the rest of these prophecies have really come to pass, Master Elmuh? When did your ancestors leave their cave home, and why did they leave? Simply because of the Prophecy?"

Elmuh mindspoke Bili, beaming in preface. "Please, Lord Champion, let us two converse silently; I am more than half

Teenéhdjook, and our mouths and throats were never truly made to speak the words of true-men.

"But, in answer to your question, a little more than seven years after Hari of Krooguh left it, the thunder and lightning of a summer storm precipitated a rockfall from above which partially buried the entrance of the cave and seriously weakened the ledge outside it. No sooner had the Teenéhdjook cleared enough of the blockage to get out onto the ledge than did the most of that ledge slide crashing down into the abyss, taking with it to their untimely deaths an adult male, a female of breeding age and two adolescents.

"Without the ledge and the path below it, access to the cave was made so difficult that the Eldest decided that he and his must leave and seek another dwelling place. Any direction would perhaps have been as good, but he and his sons recalled the predictions of Hari of Krooguh, so they set out to the southwest. Before the last of the leaves had fallen, they came into New Kuhmbuhluhn, wherein they found living a few pureblooded Teenéhdjook, some Kleesahk, a small group of very large true-men and many Kuhmbuhluhners, all ruled over by the grandfather of Prince Byruhn."

The Eldest and his family had heard and scented the men and horses and squeaking wagons of the approaching column long before it came into sight along the winding forest way. They had journeyed far since leaving the cave, now ruined, which had been their home for so many years, and they had been camped and resting near a bubbling little spring for a week—hunting, foraging and building weathertight shelters, since they intended to winter in the sheltered spot, for they had found hereabouts no recent traces of mankind, the ancient and pitiless enemy.

None of the shelters were at all visible from the track, even to the keen eyes of the Teenéhdjook. Nonetheless, the chary beings, all adult males and females, fanned out in a rough circle about the site and began to range out their beams, seeking the minds of true-men in order to cloud from them any notice of the huge nonhumans.

At last, after perhaps a quarter-hour, the head of the column came into sight and began to toil past the place where the Eldest stood partially concealed. Some of the true-men rode horses—about half of those horses bigger and beefier than had been the horses of Hari of Krooguh, the rest being domesticated mountain ponies—some were afoot and goading on spans of lowing oxen, the broad backs of these supporting coils of heavy iron chain and thick ropes, while yet another span drew a rough wain filled with axes, adzes, saws, and more ropes and chains.

But the men and various animals were not what suddenly drew and held the fascinated attention of the Eldest, what attracted his eyes was the three who walked behind the lumbering, creaking wain. Although clothed like the full-men in cloth and leather, the keen vision and keener nose of the Eldest assured him that the two smaller, less hirsute of them were at least related to his kind and that the third, who was almost as tall and as massive as he, could be nothing but an adult male Teenéhdjook!

"Correct, Old One," this strange Teenéhdjook who wore the coverings of a true-man beamed into the Eldest's wondering mind. "I am known as the Fowler, from my skill at downing birds in flight with my slingstones. These two runts here are my get by a true-woman, a Ganik—it's their dam's blood makes their pelts so thin and ratty. But they're good sons, all the same."

"You *live* with true-men, *breed* with them, and they do not seek to do you harm, Fowler?" Despite the words of the long-ago prophecy, avoidance of savage, cruel true-men was ingrained and made the Eldest dubious. "How can this be so? True-men have *always* hated and hunted Teenéhdjook."

"And most of them do still," the stranger agreed blandly. "But not these who call themselves Kuhmbuhluhners. We have lived in safety and peace among them since first they came to these mountains, fleeing enemies who had robbed them of their former homes and lands, somewhere to the north and east. They respect us for our great size and strength and our skills at hunting, and they protect us and the big Ganiks from the small Ganiks, most of whom hate and fear us.

"It is tiresome to hold the mind-cloud for long, Old One. Why do you not drop yours and I will introduce you to Duke Fillip, the short, thick man up there on the dark-red horse. He is a full brother of the king, Byruhn III of Kuhmbuhluhn, and both he and his royal brother are firm friends to all Teenéhdjook and Kleesahks. There have never been enough of us—of your kind and mine—here in the kingdom, and you will be made most welcome."

"No!" the Eldest stated firmly and unequivocally, his innate caution prevailing. "My family depend upon me, I cannot place them in jeopardy. Were you alone, Fowler, or with only a few true-men, it might be different, but . . ."

The Fowler became visibly—visibly to another Teenéhdjook—excited. "Your family, Old One? There are then more than the three males—you and two more—I can sense?"

"There are more," admitted the Eldest grudgingly, "but they are far away and well hidden, and my sons and I will slay many men before they can get near to the females and the young. How many of those men are willing to die this day?"

"No one of them, I would imagine," the Fowler replied dryly. "True-men value their own lives as highly as we do ours. But there is no need for threats and still less for a battle; so far, my two sons and I are the only beings who even know the nearness of you and the other two males . . . except for the horses and oxen, of course, but they can sense that you are not hunting them.

"I respect your caution, Old One, the wisdom of distrusting that with which you are unfamiliar, and so I will not tell the duke—and then, him only—of you and yours and this conversation until the party reach the place of big trees, where we all are bound this day. Then I will come back along this trail with one of my sons and the duke, for we must converse more upon these matters. The Kingdom of New Kuhmbuhluhn lies in dire need of the strength of you and your family, and—"

"I will meet with you and your son," agreed the Eldest. "But if you bring even the one true-man, none of you will ever see me or mine again."

"Oh, all right," said the Fowler a little peevishly. "My son and I will come back along this trail. When you are sure that we are indeed alone, with no true-men close behind, you can show yourself or bespeak me and we will come to you. Is that plan easeful to your mind, Old One?"

That first meeting had been just after dawn. It was almost noon before one of the sons of the Eldest beamed back that the stranger Teenéhdjook and his half-breed son were loping back along the trail, alone and followed by no creatures he could see or smell or sense the minds of. Nonetheless, the Eldest let the two proceed nearly a mile more before he stepped onto the trail before them, leaving a son and a grandson concealed in the fringes of the forest, each of them armed with several bone-tipped darts.

After that meeting, there were many others, some with the Fowler, alone, others with him and various of his brothers, sisters and their get, finally with a mixed group of the Teenéhdjook, Kleesahk and two of the big Ganik women who were either mates or mothers of the others of the party. This last group the Fowler persuaded the Eldest to conduct to his wellconcealed campsite. There were other group meetings after that one; Kuhmbuhluhner Teenéhdjook and Kleesahk went with the sons and grandsons of the Eldest to hunt, while the Ganik women foraged beside the females of the other species: then all sat or hunkered side by side to feast about the fires: then all slept through the frigid night, huddled together under the furs inside the snug shelters deep in the forest.

It was not until the first soft-green shoots were pushing up through the last remnants of the last snows of the dying winter that the Eldest finally consented to a meeting with trueman Kuhmbuhluhners. Two of these men came, accompanied by the Fowler, one of his brothers and two of his Kleesahk sons, all four now very familiar to the Eldest.

Cautious until the very end, the Eldest insisted that this momentous meeting take place many miles from the campsite, and although he appeared alone, he and those with whom he met were under constant observation by his sons and grandsons, all well armed with darts and ready slings.

The Eldest recognized one of the men who rode into the clearing as him who had led the tree-cutting party of which the Fowler had been a part on the late-autumn day they had first met and mindspoken. The short, broad Duke Fillip rode beside and a little behind his human companion—a man who looked and smelled much like him, though taller and even broader. Both men's bared heads were crowned with shocks of hair only a few shades lighter than the dark-red hide of the duke's big horse, both were of a weathered-ruddy complexion and both had bushy brows over blue-green eyes. The bigger man was, of course, Byruhn III, King of New Kuhmbuhluhn.

"Lord prince," said old Elmuh, "the lord champion now has heard all up to the first meeting of my grandfather with his highness King Byruhn III. Shall I continue?"

"No, Elmuh, thank you. I shall take up the tale. Return to your meal," the prince said and nodded graciously.

"Know you, Cousin Bili," Byruhn began, "that before the arrival of the family of Elmuh's grandsire, Teenéhdjook

owned far fewer powers than now they do. Before even the
Kuhmbuhluhners came down from the north, those early
Teenéhdjook and Kleesahk—for they had been interbreeding
with the big Ganiks for years—had aided the true-men to
massacre and drive out the great warparty of Ahrmehnee and
Moon Maidens who invaded from the east. But no sooner
was that crisis done than the savage small Ganiks turned on
their erstwhile allies so viciously and in such numbers that
these less warlike ones found it necessary to find and fortify a
glen much like this one. They were living there, under inter-
mittent siege, when my great-grandfather and his folk arrived
and, making common cause with them, used their superior
arms and war skills and bigger horses to drive the small
Ganiks back to whence they had come.

"King Mahrtuhn and his folk found the Teenéhdjook
priceless in the work of building. Each of them had the
strength of many full-grown men, of course, but more, they
were more agile than most men and had no slightest fear of
heights. Despite the seeming clumsiness of their huge hands
and thick fingers, they were capable of doing very delicate
work in wood or stone and many another medium, while their
differently structured eyes could easily see smaller things or
objects much farther away than could your average true-man.

"Also, this acute vision and their well-developed sense of
smell made them superlative hunters, even better when once
they were taught the use of the bow and the spear-throwing
stick. And they knew every edible wild plant in these mountains and glens. They it was who kept my forebears and the
other folk fed until land could be cleared and crops planted
and reaped.

"But the Teenéhdjook were a dying breed until the arrival
of Elmuh's grandfather's family, for those Teenéhdjook we
found here had but two pureblood females still living, and
one of them too old to breed. This was the original reason
why the Teenéhdjook males had bred with the big Ganik
women. But—as Elmuh earlier told you—such hybrids are almost always sterile, as mules are, and they uniformly lack the
full size and strength of a full Teenéhdjook, nor do they ever
live as long.

"King Mahrtuhn and his sons and retainers were quick to
recognize and appreciate the value of these large, strong, vastly talented, but inherently gentle and retiring creatures. Very
soon after the arrival of my forebears, all of these outsized
beings were placed under royal protection, they were honored

and privileged subjects, only required to perform such tasks or labors as it pleased them to do. They would have made fearsome fighters in the battle line, but as the most of them loathe warfare and will kill only for food or in final defense of themselves or their families, King Mahrtuhn exempted them from weapons training or war drills. The royal foresters it was who taught the big ones the use of bow and spear-thrower, and then only in the context of the hunting of game animals.

"Being what they are—in many ways, especially moral ones, they are far superior to most true-men—the Teenéhdjook and Kleesahk never tried to take unfair advantage of the great respect borne for them by King Mahrtuhn and the Kuhmbuhluhners; rather did they conceive a sincere love for these first humans of normal stature who had ever proffered them true friendship in a span of time known by the hills alone.

"Rather did they come to respect and revere these true-men who treated them as large but praiseworthy men like themselves, not as huge, potentially dangerous animals.

"Especially did they come to revere King Mahrtuhn. No one had realized the depth of their devotion and adoration of him until his death, when they all joined to give his husk a truly magnificent resting place—carving a tomb out of the living rock of what has since been called King's Rest Mountain.

"But with their grieving done, they did not hesitate to transfer the full measure of their love, allegiance and unswerving loyalty to his sons—King Byruhn III and Duke Fillip, his younger brother—both of whom were telepaths, as too is King Byruhn's only living son, my father, King Djahn. And the two royal brothers admired and respected their huge and mighty subjects in as full a measure as had their late father. So when the Fowler—who, being one of the very few fullblood Teenéhdjook still living in his group, was their Eldest or leader—notified the duke and the king of the presence of a large family of pure-strain Teenéhdjook camped in the northeastern reaches of New Kuhmbuhluhn, told of their natural terror of all true-men and suggested that, if granted time to patiently win them over, he could persuade them to settle permanently in the kingdom, my eager grandfather and great-uncle promptly pledged their full cooperation.

"Lumbering operations were shifted to another forest, and a string of watch posts linked by pony patrols was established to make certain that no true-men wandered into the designated area and alarmed the new family of Teenéhdjook. The Fowler was relieved of all other responsibilities for an indefinite time and given leave to choose whomever he wished whenever he wished to accompany him on his visits to the new group.

"Only when the Fowler felt the time was right was a meeting arranged between the Eldest of these new Teenéhdjook and the royal brothers of New Kuhmbuhluhn. As agreed, they came without escort, save for the Fowler and his sons; hunters they rode, rather than destriers, and they were completely unarmed save only for their swords and dirks, so great and deep was their knowledge of the honorable and gentle ways of those they sought.

"That meeting was a complete and unqualified success. The Eldest of the new-come Teenéhdjook was allowed free and full access to the innermost recesses of the minds of both men, that he might know from the outset that all he had been told by the Fowler and his kind had been unembellished truth and that he and his family were not being lured into any manner of trap or ambush.

"Thus, young cousin, did Elmuh's grandfather and his family take up open residence in, and become ever-loyal subjects of, the Kingdom of New Kuhmbuhluhn. But it was not until they had become settled and secure among the true-men—whose races had been their enemies and their very terror for uncounted ages—that the Eldest revealed to King Djahn the prophecies of the Eyeless Wise One which had directed them here."

At that juncture, Rahksahnah asked, "But Prince Byruhn, if continue a pure strain of these Teenéhdjook, wished your grandfather, why allow did he interbreedings with these Ganiks to go on? Master Elmuh stated did that both his mother and his mate Ganiks were. Horses or kine you would not so carelessly permit to breed . . . at least, would not any sane woman . . . or man."

"Aye, my lady," agreed Byruhn, nodding, "the breeding of domestic animals must be always controlled. But, my lady, the Teenéhdjook are not kine, nor any other type of beast. They are men, else there could never be any form of issue from their matings with Ganiks. Moreover, they are staunch and valuable subjects and, as such, are and should be free to take such mates as they fancy, within their own class, of course. Not all of the Teenéhdjook chose to mate with

Ganiks or Kleesahk, not at the onset, at least. But some did—our Elmuh's sire, among them. And we Kuhmbuhluhners were to later find ourselves glad that they had so done.

"Personally speaking, of course, I cannot imagine bedding a Ganik woman, ever; the small ones or the large, though the large Ganiks at least keep themselves cleaner than the small. Not only do most Ganiks attire themselves in ill-cured or even green hides, but because of one of their host of gods or devils—this one called Plooshuhn—they never bathe their filthy bodies from birth to death, and they all dress their hair with a foul concoction of rancid butter and their own or someone else's urine."

Recalling the unholy reek of that horde of shaggies he and his squadron had fought back on the plateau, Bili set his jaws solidly and fought to hold down his rising gorge. Such unnatural creatures as the prince was describing sounded to him more bestial than the very wild beasts themselves.

"My lord duke," asked Lieutenant Brakit diffidently, "has this officer his lord's permission to address his highness the prince?"

Despite his nausea, long self-discipline forced a smile to Bili's lips to accompany his reply. "Of course you do. You'd not be dining up here at this table were you not nobly born." Then he said to Byruhn, "My lord prince, Lieutenant of Freefighters Frehd Brakit is, as I mentioned earlier, a cadet of the House and County of Pruhzburk; as such, as you have just heard, he knows the proper forms, and he has a question, I would presume. Will my lord deign to hear him?"

"And good it falls on my ears, such decent, old-fashioned courtesy, sir duke. It is to your credit that you command and lead men of such noble antecedents and matchless manners." His words were solemn and formal, but the smile he then turned upon Brakit was warm. "What would you of me, my fine Pruhzburker?"

At Bili's brusque nod, the officer asked, "Possibly a foolish question, your highness. But, with such a total lack of personal hygiene, how do these Ganiks keep themselves free of parasites and maintain their health?"

"No foolish question that, young man," said the prince, "rather, one clearly spawned from out the mind of a veteran and innovative field officer. My sincere compliments, Frehd of Pruhzburk; your question and the manner in which it was couched have deepened still more my respect for you and your employer. When your contract with Duke Bili be done, you need seek no further than New Kuhmbuhluhn for an-other.

"In answer, They don't. You'll never find a still-living small Ganik not ahop with fleas and acrawl with lice, and with wormy guts, like as not, to boot. So few of their sickly children survive to adulthood that they were long since an ex-tinct race, did they not all breed like voles in a summer pas-ture, or maggots in a cow-pat.

"The big Ganiks, though far and away cleaner in their per-sons and their habits, still are unattractive to me and to most other true-men, with their long, horsy faces and their big, overprominent beaver teeth. The most petite of their women still will stand, barefoot, some foot taller than I; but they all—both men and women, if of full Ganik blood—are poorly proportioned, being thin and gangly, with big heads set upon narrow shoulders. Their arms are shorter and their skinny legs much longer, proportionately, than in normal folk, their hips are right often broader than any other part of them, and the dugs of the women are but flopping, pendulous sacks."

"Ugh!" Bili wrinkled his lips in distaste. "Why then are the Teenéhdjook males so fond of these big Ganiks?"

The prince shrugged. "In the beginning, I suppose that a good deal of the attraction was novelty; you see, the big Ganiks are almost hairless—that is, they have far less body hair than even true-men and true-women, much less Teenéhdjook—and a male Teenéhdjook can be every bit as randy as any man-at-arms you ever saw, although I'll say in their defense that these Teenéhdjook and the Kleesahk, most of them, habitually control themselves better than many true-men. Later on, they had no choice but to breed with the big Ganiks.

"You see, some years after Elmuh's forebears settled here among us Kuhmbuhluhners, a deadly and most mysterious plague struck, affecting only the pure-strain Teenéhdjook, not either the Ganiks or the Kleesahk. This disease did to death the oldest and the youngest, mainly, but also all the gravid fe-males . . . and unfortunately, all of the Teenéhdjook females of breeding age were carrying, at that time. Now there are no pure-blood Teenéhdjook that I know of in all of New Kuhmbuhluhn, alas. Some few who claim to be, have the size to be, are at the very best at least a quarter Ganik, probably more, in truth."

The prince had a long draft from his goblet, then said,

"Cousin Bili, I'll now be as blunt with you as you were with me this morning. You've heard, by now, about all that there is to know of my House, lands and peoples and the great and deadly problems that beset us all, but you have yet to set my mind to rest on certain facts concerning you and your rather heterogeneous following. So now you must tell me. Just how does a Confederation *thoheeks* come to be captaining a band composed of not only Ehleenee, Horseclansmen and burker Freefighters, but Ahrmehnee tribesmen and Moon Maidens, as well?"

CHAPTER XII

"Last spring," Bili began, "I was summoned down from Harzburk, because my sire, *Thoheeks* Hwahruhn, had been taken quite ill and was feared to be near death; and die he did, very shortly after I had arrived in Morguhn. But, at the same time, I and most of my nobles were faced with a rebellion of certain disloyal nobles, bemused peasants and city commoners and a gaggle of blood thirsty priests and monks of the Ehleen Church.

"They sought to trap me and my loyalists in my capital city, Morguhnpolis, but with the timely assistance of some score and a half of Freefighter city guardsmen, we all managed to hack our way out and gain to my country seat, Morguhn Hall. This they shortly invested, of course, but it was a mere armed rabble they commanded, no army, and a single nighttime sortie so agitated and alarmed them that they began to hack each other in the dark and most had fled by a little after dawn.

"With all save a couple of my noblemen, a few score Freefighters and the warriors of a small clan new-come from the Sea of Grass, the Undying High Lord Milo and I hotly pursued the rebel bastards, rode the cowardly scum down and slew some hundreds of them on the road to Morguhnpolis.

"Halfway to my capital, my scratch force was augmented by several troops of Confederation light cavalry, lancers, mostly, and then we all rode on. But we found Morguhnpolis deserted. The rebel leaders had, realizing apparently that they could not hold the city, driven all the commoners out the west gate, then rebarred that gate and affected their own escape by way of a secret tunnel that led from a subcellar of the city palace to an old quarry some half a mile outside the walls. And while we took up pursuit of the mob of commoners along the west road, the mounted leaders together with a large contingent of rebels from the neighboring Duchy of Vawn—wherein the risings had succeeded—rode north into the Duchy of Skaht, then angled west into the Ahrmehnee lands before turning south and so gaining to Vawn. The Ahrmehnee warriors, Sacred Sun bless them, killed at least a third of the rebel *poosteesee* before they were done. Too bad they didn't get them all . . . especially their leader, *Vahrohneeskos* Drehkos Daiviz of Morguhn!

"With the rebels holed up in or mustering around Vawnpolis, a large proportion of the Confederation Regulars quartered on the inhabitants of the trade city of the Duchy of Morguhn—Kehnooryos Deskahti, which had been firmly rebel and had had to be stormed by High Lord Milo's infantry—and with me, the High Lady Aldora, my nobles and Freefighters and some hundreds of Confederation cavalry going through Morguhn like a dose of salts and scotching rebels wherever we found the bastards, the High Lord began to assemble the noblemen of the entire archduchy with their retainers and a vast horde of unemployed Freefighters in and around Morguhnpolis.

"When all had rallied, he left strong garrisons in both Kehnooryos Deskahti and Morguhnpolis, brought in a few specialist officers from the Confederation capital, marched the bulk of the regular foot over to Morguhnpolis, then set our column on the road to Vawnpolis. It should've been a short, easy advance, but thanks to that same bastard, Drehkos Daiviz of Morguhn, it was anything but! With a partly mounted force of rebels from Vawnpolis, the old devil harried us near every step of the way—raiding supply and reinforcement columns, picking off vanguards and flankers and stragglers whenever the opportunity presented itself, felling trees to block the trade road, polluting the water, sniping at the columns and at camp sentries. Finally, he and his full force ambushed the head of the column one afternoon. Although we beat off the boy-buggers, we took heavy losses.

"He struck us only one other time in force, when, a few days after that ambush, his entire strength first arrow-rained a camp we were departing, then charged the rear guards and camp strikers, heavily armed and ahorse. Again, our losses were great—both in men and in material—but so many men did the rebels lose that morning that they never again could mount the strength for raids in force against us. And so, after we had reorganized and resupplied, we marched on to Vawnpolis virtually unopposed."

"For all your probably justified hatred and loathing of this Baronet Drehkos, Cousin Bili," remarked the prince, "he strikes me as a rare and precious breed of great captain. In his salad days, he must have been a renowned warrior. He'd served as a professional, perhaps?"

Bili shook his shaven head vehemently. "On the contrary, lord prince, aside from the usual arms training received by the sound sons of any nobleman, he had never gone armed for any purpose other than the hunt . . . until this hell-spawned rebellion. He had been a city lordling, held title to no land save his city house, and had been a sort of gentle joke to and among the other nobility of the duchy—known only for drinking, feasting and spending vast sums of his wealthy wife's inheritance on hare-brained schemes of one sort or other."

"Hmmph," the prince remarked again. "Then the man must've been of that even rarer breed—the born military genius, whose mighty talents never surface until and if the need for them arises. King Buk I—known as the Headsplitter—the first king of the Old Dynasty of Pitzburk, was said to have been one such unheralded genius of defensive warfare, if you'll recall."

Bili grimaced. "Yes, I do recall, and King Buk Headsplitter was one of the defenders we had to fight at the siege of Vawnpolis."

One side of Byruhn's bushy eyebrow went up. "Young cousin, have you had too much of the drink? King Buk died a good three hundred years agone."

Bili smiled grimly. "No, lord prince, I'm not befuddled with wine or spirits. One of the accomplishments of the traitorous Baronet Drehkos was the ability to read Old Mehrikan, both Old and Modern Ehleeneekos and even those strange curlicues that the Zahrtohgahns call writing. In the Vawnpolis citadel, he chanced across some collection of ancient books on various aspects of warfare, assembled and stored there by a long-dead *Thoheeks* Vawn. One of them was supposedly penned or at least dictated by old King Buk I of Pitzburk, and the back-stabbing baronet used that book and the others well, very well indeed.

"At the outset, Vawnpolis had been little stronger and no more able to withstand serious attack or prolonged siege than my own capital city, Morguhnpolis, especially since it held no real professional soldiers and relatively few men trained to arms. When we arrived under the walls of Vawnpolis, we numbered nearly forty thousand men, the largest numbers of them Confederation Regulars, and equipped with a complete and modern siege train. We had with us old Sir Ehd Gahth-wahlt, a justly famous expert at the reduction of cities and burks, and so we all expected a quick and relatively painless victory.

"What we got, however, was very different from what we had anticipated at the start. We reduced a pair of salients with the intent of using them as forward emplacements for engines, only to find to our cost and consternation that both were but devilishly conceived and constructed traps.

"Although our engines bombarded the works and walls and the city within them almost continuously, still each well-planned and well-executed assault bought us nothing save more hundreds of casualties. Finally, the High Lady Aldora and Sir Ehd and I, who then were sharing the overall command in the High Lord's absence, set ourselves to starving the city out, swallowing our frustration as best we could."

"This High Lady Aldora willingly shared her authority over the warriors with both you and another man?" asked Rahksahnah. "She must be a very powerful and self-assured woman, and of a most generous and forbearing nature, Bili."

"She is, all those things, and more, Rahksahnah," Bili quickly agreed. But he thought it just as well not to mention that he and Aldora had, before and during and after the times which he was discussing, been most passionate lovers. He added, "The High Lady Aldora is a fine strategist and a very gifted cavalry tactician; she it was who wrote one of those books that Baronet Drehkos found and used so disastrously against us.

"And this final strategy into which we had found ourselves forced might have succeeded in the end, for the city had never been well or even adequately supplied and was in pitiable condition but then the decision was taken out of our hands.

"The High Lord Milo had, while still fighting the rebellion in my duchy, captured two supposed kooreeooee—leaders of the Ehleen Church for the duchies of Morguhn and of Vawn—who were in actuality witchmen, agents of the Witch Kingdom, far to the south; he had earlier captured another of these human monsters who had headed an earlier, similar rebellion in a duchy farther south, and the answers wrung out of the first had helped him to partially head off affairs in Morguhn.

"Leaving the army at Vawnpolis, he had personally escorted these two new captives up to the Confederation capital at

Kehnooryos Atheenahs and had them put to the same severe degrees of question as the first. The answers they two were at long last persuaded to reveal so alarmed the High Lord that he returned posthaste to the camps under the still-embattled walls of Vawnpolis and insisted—over the vehement objections of Aldora, me, Sir Ehd and every other commander— that the city be granted terms of honorable surrender, despite their many and hideous crimes and treacheries and their long and costly resistance to rightful authority. He is, after all, the Undying High Lord, and so his will was done.

"What he had learned that had so agitated him was that other agents of the Witch Kingdom were, even then, in the Ahrmehnee *Stahn,* persuading the Ahrmehnee tribes and the Moon Maidens to arise and set aflame the entire border shared with the Confederation. Most of the tribes had already sent their warriors to camp around the village of their *nahkhahrah* and the time was worn exceedingly thin, was widespread warfare to be kept out of the duchies of the western borders.

"While the High Lord with all his infantry and quite a few rearmed former rebels, marched directly up the trade road, through the Frainyuhn lands, clearly bound for the main gathering of Ahrmehnee at the largest village of the Taishyuhns, operations against the virtually defenseless Ahrmehnee tribal lands to north and south were also commenced.

"The High Lady Aldora, with most of the Regular cavalry, a few Kindred noblemen and their retainers and Baronet Drehkos commanding what remained of his mobile force of rebels, circled around to strike from the north. I, along with all of the mounted Freefighters and most of the Kindred nobles, circled to strike upward from the south. The High Lord correctly thought that, did enough Ahrmehnee refugees—dispossessed, terrified, wounded and maimed, and starving—pour into the war camps with blood-curdling tales of burnings, butcheries, rapes and pillagings, the warriors would decide that they were needed in their home lands, and so would delay or forget the projected invasion of the Confederation.

"I trust that the High Lady's force did a thorough job, for as I have said, she is a master tactician of cavalry operations. For my own part, the Freefighters and I soon taught the Kindred among us the proper way to put the fear of Steel into peasants—we looted, we drove off livestock and slew where we could not capture. Rapine was encouraged, but we only killed folk when they forced us to it. We burned every structure that would take fire and tried to knock down the few that wouldn't, and the fanned-out squadrons pushed on steadily toward the north, driving the surviving villagers before us."

Prince Byruhn noted that the expressions of both of the Ahrmehnee headmen—Vahrtahn Panosyuhn and Vahk Soormehlyuhn—and of the lovely Rahksahnah had become hard and grim and flushed with a degree of anger as Bili recounted the planned and executed depredations of the Ahrmehnee lands.

"Assuming that, sooner or later, a sufficiently large number of Ahrmehnee warriors would come down from the north to offer serious opposition, I had been following a day or so behind the front-line squadrons with a reserve force and the trains. Then, when we were about halfway through our assigned territory, the High Lord farspoke me, ordering a cessation of hostile acts against the Ahrmehnee and a general withdrawal of most of my forces to the south, and thence back into Confederation lands.

"He went on to inform me that the *nahkhahrah* Kokh Taishyuhn had indicated to him a desire to merge the Ahrmehnee *Stahn* with the Confederation, and that Aldora, too, was being recalled.

"Then he gave me another mission. I was to take the best of each of the then existing squadrons—the best units, men, horses and weapons—combine them into a single squadron and head them due west, collecting support as I passed the areas of the various squadrons. I was warned to be on the lookout for several troops of Moon Maidens and was advised to render them any needed assistance in tracking down and eliminating a column of witchfolk and pack mules, headed south.

"As matters turned out, we none of us ever saw hide nor hair of that column, but we did find the Moon Maidens and a force of Ahrmehnee warriors, to boot. They were on that plateau, backed at bay against the wall of a cliff and hopelessly battling two to three thousand shaggies—your small Ganiks—who were being led by Elmuh's son, Buhbuh.

"I detached my bowmasters and sent them to range along the top of that cliff, and when next the shaggies charged, they quilled as many as they could to soften them up for the kill. It was a steep slope from my position down to the shaggies,

but not too steep, it developed; I led the rest of the squadron
down it and full into the shaggies, taking them on the flank.

"Precious few of those shaggies were astride full horses,
and those little mountain ponies are no match at all for an
ordinary horse of decent size, much less war-trained destriers,
so the initial impact was less fighting than striving to keep
one's seat and helping one's mount to stay on its feet while
bowling over ponies like ninepins.

"But real fighting came soon enough. For all that few of
the shaggies had decent weapons and fewer still had any
form of armor, they still outnumbered us by at least six to
one, and that crashing charge gradually lost its impetus. I
fought my way clear on the other side of the press and was
shortly joined by a young knight of rare bravery, Sir Geros
Lahvoheetos of Morguhn, who had been riding guard on my
Red Eagle Banner and had himself taken it when the banner-
man was slain.

"With me lifting and waving the banner while his incredibly clear tenor voice rose even above the stupefying din of
the battle, we rallied a good two thirds of the squadron
around me and were just set to compound the damage to the
shaggies with another full charge, when the bowmasters came
riding down out of a steep gap to our left, shortly followed
by Rahksahnah and her Moon Maidens and these two brave
Ahrmehnee here at the head of some scores of their warriors.

"That second charge broke the shaggies, thoroughly routed
the stinking bastards, and we pursued them all the way to the
far-western edge of that plateau. It was while we were all
coming back from the pursuit that the earthquake struck. Just
before that happened, I had an exceedingly strong presentiment of terrible danger, though I knew not of what kind the
danger was. But when I saw a vast assortment of wild
beasts—large and small, predators and prey, all together—
racing to get off that plateau as fast as they could run, hop or
scuttle, I began to understand, and when the first tremor
struck, I knew that were we to survive, we had better follow
the game off the plateau.

"I never again want to undertake another such ride, putting terrified horses down a steep track hardly wide enough
for a small deer, but most of us made it safely down before
the entire plateau rippled like roiled water and poured down
upon itself. And then, huge rocks started to pour down out of
the skies, each of them so hot that they set fires almost every-
where they struck; it was in attempts to evade those fires that

my force became split and separated. I can only hope, and pray Sun, Wind and Steel that those now missing—my two brothers, Count Hari, Sir Geros, and the rest—are safely to the east, in Ahrmehnee lands."

The prince leaned forward to look down the board at the two Ahrmehnee men. "Your Ahrmehnee are good warriors and not easily cozened, so how did you allow yourselves to be trapped by so large a body of the outlaws?" Then he glanced, smiling, at Rahksahnah. "And how was it that my lady and her Moon Maidens came to be fighting alongside males?"

As Vahrtahn Panosyuhn began to speak, Bili listened attentively. He, too, had wondered just how the situation on the plateau had come about, but in the press of so many events and wearing the weighty mantle of overall leadership, he had simply had no time to inquire into the matter.

"When the terrible tidings were brought up to the village of the *nahkhahrah* that not only were the lands and villages of the five northern tribes being put to fire and sword but the portions of the *stahn* owned by the six southern and western tribes seemed destined to endure like savageries, armed we did, and all our men, and rode for home.

"But when still we were in Kehrkohryuhn lands, crossed we did the track of ten hundred or more of Muhkohee, so we our force did split—half riding southeast to oppose and slow the lowlanders, half on the track of the Muhkohee setting out. And not hard was that sorry track to follow, *Der* Byruhn, for the smoke of burning farms and villages marked it well for us—from Kehrkohryuhn, through the full width of Panosyuhn and into Soormehlyuhn it led.

"By the time we near the western verge of Soormehlyuhn were got, however, the satanic raiders had learned that on their bloody trail we were and, rightly fearing us in our righteous rage, increased they their progress, not bothering to fire the last three or four villages where they butchered or even to steal much except fresh ponies and weapons and food.

"Just before onto the Tongue of Soormehlyuhn—that which Dook Bili a 'plateau' calls—we found a place where those we pursued joined had with another force almost as large, so most glad we all were to shortly overtaken be by the *brahbehrnuh* and her Maidens, for not ten hundreds we were without them.

"When to the very last village we came, close to the dirty Muhkohee we knew we were, for steam still from their ponies' dung did rise up and from the pitiful bodies of the women and old folk and little children the barbaric pigs had slain and mutilated, blood still ran.

"The honored Vahk of a secret way spoke he then, a steep but shorter pass and also a cave that might place our fighters where the Muhkohee stand and fight us must on our own grounds. To trap them, we sought, you see. *Der* Byruhn. But trapped were we!

"Those of us who led through the caverns by the honored Vahk were had to dismount and our horses and ponies lead, for the way was low-ceilinged, so they who through the pass went earlier reached the plain before the cliff where was the cave mouth. Those few of that force surviving said that, as the Muhkohee seemed to be fleeing down the Tongue, assuredly bound for their own lands, decided did they all to attack at once, not waiting for us coming through the cave, as had been planned and agreed, earlier.

"But no sooner had they charged out of hiding in the pass and engaged the raiders than did near twice as many more of the Muhkohee, led by the huge one on the Northorse, come from the little forest and from folds of ground and rock that had hidden them. That battle still raging was when we from out the cave's mouth did come.

"Although there tens of hundreds appeared to be, allow them to butcher those of our ancient race we could not, not without our own swords adding to the balance. Into that fight would every Ahrmehnee have ridden as soon as he saw it and his pony could mount upon, but the *brahbehrnuh* insisted that we not go piecemeal but rather wait until all together were and so spur out as one body. And this we did.

"But just too many of the thrice-damned Muhkohee there were, *Der* Byruhn. Mighty and matchless warriors are our men of the Ahrmehnee *Stahn*, fearsome are the Maidens of the Silver Lady, and scores of Mahkohee did we all slay, but seemed it that for every savage we hacked down, three rose up to take his place, and human flesh and bone can but so much endure.

"Surrounded we all were, but to keep us all together did this serve, and together did we hew our way out of the press of our enemies and back to the cave mouth withdraw, fighting every step of the way. Then, for one whole day and the part of another did we defend that cave mouth, attack after attack by the savages beating off. Three messengers to alert the *stahn* sent we out—not for aid sent we them, for we knew that our last battle were we all fighting, help from the *nahkhahrah* never in time to save our lives could have reached us there. One, my nephew, Moorahd, was a brave lad. I know not if any of them even off the Tongue of Soormehlyuhn safely rode."

"One of them, at least, was a Moon Maiden," said Bili; it was statement, not question.

"Yes," answered Rahksahnah, "Zehlahna was our best rider and on our fastest, strongest mare. But how knew you, Bili?"

"She reached the vanguard of my column when still I was some distance from the plateau, my dear. The horse was full spent, the best it could manage was a stumbling walk, but the woman was making the best time that she could, for all that she was herself near death from a terrible wound in her throat. She had great difficulty in speaking, so I entered her mind and received your message just before she breathed her last. Then we backtracked her to the plateau."

Vahrtahn again took up his tale. "And so we all fought on. Fortunately, two springs there were in the cave, so lack for water we did not; and, as the Soormehlyuhns had considered it to be a place of final refuge and an emergency citadel, weapons and food and horse fodder stored there were. But by the third attack of the second day, all our darts and arrows gone were and reduced to throwing chunks of rock and spare axes we all were.

"The next attack was delayed while the Muhkohee vainly for the upper entrance to the cave did search. That time we used to add to the low wall we had built across the mouth of the cave ... and to slay all of the seriously wounded of us, that the fiendish Muhkohee might not them alive take." A tic began to jerk in the Ahrmehnee's cheek, and his two hands were clenched so tightly together that the big knuckles stood out as white as virgin snow.

"Then did the monstrous leader and his search party from the upper areas come back, and shortly the Muhkohee began to mill about and shout and wave their weapons as always they just before attacking us had done. And then they charged. And we awaiting our certain deaths, stood with our arms to hand.

"But then, when still the barbarians were more than five score yards distant, ponies began to go down and men as well, many, many of them, for no apparent reason. Not until the mob had rolled closer did we, could we, see a drizzle of

black-shafted arrows was falling among our foes, seemingly
from out of the clear skies—not enough to halt the Muhkohee, by any means, but enough to slow and confuse them.

"Next, on that day of miracles, hundreds of steel-sheathed
men on big lowlander horses came charging down the eastern
flank of the cliff line and slammed full-tilt into the damned
savages! What a splendid sight that was for us all to see, *Der*
Byruhn! Near ten hundreds of the sons of filth went down, it
seemed, when first the Lowlanders struck.

"We wanted to join the fight at once, but decided did we
that longer would it take to open our wall enough to get out
the horses than would it take to go back up and out the back
entrance, then circle around through the open pass. Atop the
cliff, we found the lowlander archers, with all their shafts
spent; they were preparing to go back to whence they had
come and thence down that steep, shaley slope to join the
battle, below. But we persuaded them to come with us the
longer but safer way.

"On the plain we arrived just as Dook Bili rallying his
fighters was for another charge and with him we joined our
own swords and spears and axes. What a day that was, *Der*
Byruhn! The murderous pack broke at the second charge and
chased and slew we did them for far and far until off the
Tongue of Soormehlyuhn they fled, those who could still, and
Dook Bili halted us did. Coming back we were when the
earth shook."

"Thank you, *Dehrehbeh* Vahrtahn," said the prince,
gravely.

"*Der* Byruhn," the Ahrmehnee protested, "I am not a
dehrehbeh, only a simple village headman. The *dehrehbeh* of
the Panosyuhn Tribe is—"

The prince shook his head forcefully. "If you lead and
speak for those Ahrmehnee warriors here present, you're a
dehrehbeh, as far as I'm concerned, young man, but I'll call
you whatever you wish.

"So, then, *Pahrohn* Vahrtahn, how many of these accursed
Ganik outlaws would you say were slain in all—by both your
force over the full period and by Duke Bili's at the end?"

The swarthy young man scratched his head and squinted
for a moment. "If not twenty hundreds, *Der* Byruhn, close
on it."

The prince turned back to Bili. "And you, young cousin,
would you concur with that figure?"

Bili nodded once. "There were some hundreds of dead

shaggies all around the mouth of that cave, my lord, and more of them scattered on the plain. The first charge I led was devastatingly effective—though the horses counted for more than us men in that particular instance, that and the impetus of coming down that almost-sheer slope. I'd put the total shaggy casualties of all the actions at more in the neighborhood of twenty-five hundred."

Smiling like a winter wolf, Byruhn said, "Coming off the plateau where they did, the bastards would've almost surely had to come through the eastern forest to reach their base by the quickest route. That would mean that the earthquake and, more important, the fires would have caught them there. And that's one of the better pieces of news I've heard in years.

"Buhbuh led about six thousand outlaws, total. If your estimate is correct, cousin, and if as few as five hundred more were lost when the forest burned, that strength will be halved, anyway. With so many men of fighting age lost—and I'm not even thinking about those too badly wounded to offer resistance, mind you—such forces as only I command here in the southerly reaches of the kingdom might be able to . . . ahhh . . . persuade the small Ganiks hereabouts to move on and harass somebody else's stretch of mountains.

"But with your fine force here to help us . . . you do intend to join with us for the duration of our campaign, do you not, cousin Bili? My poor old father needs every sword he can raise in the north, and I can spare not a one of these in the south until the devilspawn Ganiks be driven out."

"My lord prince," Bili answered slowly, carefully choosing his words, "I—we all—greatly appreciate your kind aid and this lavish hospitality to utter strangers, trespassing armed on your lands. But what you now ask is not my decision to make—not to make alone, that is. Before I can answer yea or nay, I must council with my captains, my lady and my allies, for their lives and well-being will be as much in jeopardy as mine own in these actions you contemplate. You will have my answer when I have heard and weighed the views of all."

"Spoken honestly and openly," said Byruhn. "So be it."

CHAPTER XIII

When once the prince had completed his ablutions, Bili and Rahksahnah made use of the welcome bath house, which occupied one end of the outbuilding housing the kitchens for Sandee's Cot and was warmed by its fires and ovens. The dust and dirt and dried sweat of the long, wearisome day laved away, they then made their way back into the main building and the bedchamber they had been assigned, wrapped against the chill air of the mountain night in yards of unbleached and scratchy woolen cloth, carrying their clothing and weapons.

At the door of the bedchamber, Gy Ynstyn and Meeree waited to take the boots and other leather gear for cleaning and burnishing. Just before following Rahksahnah into the small room, Bili gave Gy an order to transmit: All hale members of the mixed force were to assemble around the foot of the lofty tower keep in the third hour after tomorrow's dawning.

In the chamber, Bili found Meeree talking softly to Rahksahnah in Ahrmehnee, but the woman broke off when he entered, cast him a long, hard look and stalked from the room, with a rattling of spur chains and saber sheath.

"Poor Meeree," said Rahksahnah, sadly, while Bili was arranging his bared sword and cased dirk within easy reach of the feather bed, "she knows that the Will of the Lady it is, but still cannot reconcile herself that the ways of the Hold dead are, in fact. Your man, Gy Furface, she chose as battle companion that she might remain near to me; but if refuses she does to change, to adapt to this strange, new order of living, better it would have been if another man she taken had, I fear."

Bili chuckled. "Yes, I know, she had the brass to . . . shall we say, threaten me, this morning, when I was on my way to you. But don't worry about her, dear. I don't."

Rahksahnah, however, still looked deeply troubled, and

164

there was much concern in her voice. "Underestimate Meeree do not, my Bili. Stronger she is than she appears, and quick as a snake with blade or spear, nor so proficient are most with thrown knife or axe or dart."

"Which only means," said Bili good-naturedly, "'that she is a fine trooper for this mixed squadron of mine. And no matter if she still loves you, she must be doing right by Gy, for I cannot recall ever seeing him smile so much. Besides, with the two of us now to care for and see to, Gy would've needed help anyway. Now, come to bed, my dear, there is much we must discuss before the morning."

But serious as were the matters pressing upon Bili's mind, they did not talk at once. For both were young—Bili almost nineteen and Rahksahnah some few months his junior—they had found and shared their first blissful pleasure earlier in the past day and, although their minds were aroil with other, more worldly concerns, their vibrant young bodies, pressed closely together for warmth, speedily aroused insistent demands for fresh delights.

Firm with purpose, Bili strove mightily to master these demands of his flesh, to reaffirm that iron self-discipline with which he always had ordered his life, only to find his oft-vaunted self-control leaking away like so much water from a sundered pot; and when his tentatively probing mindspeak found the surface of Rahksahnah's consciousness seething with equal passion, he gave up the struggle, tightened his strong arms about her body and covered her mouth with his own.

That first kiss lengthened, deepened, as tongue found seeking, maddening tongue in a flurry of impassioned activity. Still crushing her firm, pliant warmth hard against his own body with his left arm, her hardening nipples branding desire deep within him, he stroked his callused right palm down the length of her back to cup one flat buttock—tenderly, at the first, then harder, his fingers digging into the elastic flesh as his passions mounted.

Somewhere, in the far recesses of her mind, Rahksahnah knew that she should feel guilt for so quickly forsaking even the memory of Meeree, the love and the years they had shared, but never once in all those years had Meeree's touch, Meeree's kiss, aroused her one half so much as did the touches, the kisses, the mere close proximity of the huge and different and now-dear lowlander man, this Bili of Morguhn.

"Perhaps," she thought without thinking, really, her con-

sciousness fully involved in the unbearable pleasure that the
massive man was inflicting upon her more than willing flesh,
"perhaps it is the Lady's doing; perhaps She has willed that
my mind cast out memories of the past, of the old ways of
the Hold, that I may more easily accept this man I have
chosen as a true equal, in all ways. If this be true, I pray that
She do the like for poor, suffering Meeree, that she may soon
find real happiness with her bearded man, Gy, and forget the
old, dead ways. And I must ask my Bili why this one man has
a bushy beard when none of the others, save the Ahrmehnee,
do. . . ."

And then even that last stronghold of coherent thought was
submerged, drowned in the relentless tide of passion sweeping
through every fiber of her being. Rahksahnah surrendered to
it, utterly and without pause, let it carry her, unresisting, to
the inevitable heights of bliss.

Neither Rahksahnah nor Bili had any way of knowing that
Meeree, full-armed, stood in the darkened hallway just beyond the door, having chosen the first watch of the night as
her lot, leaving the other three watches to Bili's Freefighter
bodyguards.

For all the thickness of the stone walls and the stout, iron-
bound portal, Meeree's keen ears still could clearly hear the
sounds of lovemaking emanating from the chamber she
guarded—the sighs, the gasps, the moans, the wet-slithering-
slapping sounds. When the mattress ropes and the bedframe
commenced a rhythmic squeaking-creaking, Meeree's even
white teeth met in the flesh of her lower lip.

So hard did her hands grip the spear haft and the hilt of
her sheathed saber that her two arms trembled and ached
with the strain. But that pain was no more noticed than was
the sharper one from her tooth-torn lip; the only pain that
she could truly feel was from deep within her, and it
would, she knew, never be assuaged until . . . unless the
brahbehrnuh again became hers, body and soul, as before,
as was right and proper and ordained. But, no, it no longer
was ordained by Her, the Silver Goddess.

Through the dense fabric of the oaken door came the
high-pitched, breathless cry of ultimate pleasure, rising above
the deep-throated—and, to Meeree, hideous—love groan of
the man, to be followed by gasps and pantings and low mur-
murs.

Letting go the spear with her right hand to let the left take
over its support, Meeree dug furiously under her shirt and

breastplate until she found that for which she sought. Her sinewy fingers, hardened by long years of gripping hilt and haft, easily snapped the fine silver chain. Then she withdrew her hand to cast both chain and crescent pendant forcefully down the pitch-black hallway to tinkle first against the wall stones, then clank onto the hardwood floor.

Alone, there in the full-darkness, where none could see, Meeree did that which she had not done since early childhood. She swallowed the sobs, but allowed the tears of frustration and rage and loss to flow freely down her callused cheeks, to drip from her chin.

The watcher outside heard no further sounds from the bedchamber, for Bili and Rahksahnah, their passions temporarily slaked, were communicating by mindspeak.

"What think you, love?" asked Bili. "Should I . . . we . . . do that which Prince Byruhn wants us to do? Should we help him to drive these Ganiks from out his lands, then, for all we now know, get ourselves embroiled in his war with these invaders from the north? It is not a decision to be made lightly or by me alone, as I told Lord Byruhn earlier. You and your force, the Ahrmehnee, the Freefighters and my Confederation nobles all must have a part in the choice, are they to lay their lives on the line at the behest of me and the prince."

"These Ganiks, Bili, have long been a sore menace to us and to the Ahrmehnee, so I feel certain that both of the headmen and all of their warriors will want to take a part in their extirpation or expulsion from lands so near to their own. As for the Moon Maidens, they will go where I lead . . . and I go wherever you go.

"But most of the war band is Freefighters, my Bili. What think you they will choose to do?"

Bili shrugged his broad shoulders. "They'll do whatever I and their officers tell them to do. Rahksahnah. They're all professional soldiers, and one fight is as much as another to them; they fight for loot, not glory, and they'll freely follow any strong captain who has a name for victories, as do I.

"Now, the Confederation noblemen are something entirely different. They all have homes and lands to go back to and so have little reason to seek out a fight that really is none of their affair. They were with me in the Ahrmehnee lands only by reason of the orders of him who is overlord of us all—the High Lord Milo of Morai.

"Here and now, I cannot say that I speak for the High

Lord, and I truly have no idea just what he would either do or advise doing in this situation. For all his reiterated longings for peace within and along his borders, this Byruhn could be lying in his teeth, and an internally secure New Kumbuhluhn could pose a serious threat to the Ahrmehnee *Stahn* and to the Confederation lands, beyond. Nor does his house, from what he has told us, have any reason to love our Confederation, the Kindred or the Ehleenee.

"I would like to know him better and to know much more of his aspirations and goals, but I think he has told and had us told all he intends for us to know until and unless we swear our oaths and our swords to his service."

Immediately the prince had given the diners leave to depart the hall of Sandee's Cot, Master Elmuh and the other Kleesahk had made for the tarn-side tower. After he had seen to the wounded, rebandaged where necessary and reinforced the mental instructions for the knitting of bones and muscles and flesh, he clouded out pain from their consciousnesses that they might sink easily into restful, healing sleep throughout the coming night. Then he and his two Kleesahk assistants returned to the ground level of the towering keep.

Soon, all ten of the huge humanoids were stretched out on their low beds and, draped in quilted coverlets of gigantic proportions, seemingly asleep. But the appearance was deceiving. No one of them slept, not yet, for they all had had their instructions from the prince, passed on to them by Pah-El-muh.

Therefore, the powerful minds of the ten Kleesahk were meshed, as they all lay supine, first willing all true-men and true-women within the upper levels of the tower to sleep a deep sleep, then implanting within all those human minds the thoughts and beliefs that were necessary to prepare them for the coming day.

While Bili and Rahksahnah lay abed, while Meeree wept in the darkness, while the faithful Kleesahk joined minds to weave their invisible web of what some there would have called wizardry, the prince and old Sir Steev sat closeted together within a small, secure office just off the great hall of Sandee's Cot. An ewer of brandied wine sat between them on the small, sturdy table, and a brass goblet was before each of them. The two men's pipes and the thick tallow taper had combined to thicken the atmosphere in the windowless room, but neither seemed to notice.

Sir Steev's lined and scarred face looked worried, and the same disquietude was clear in his voice. "Lord prince, you have given me leave to speak freely, so I'll say this: whatall you are doing with these lowlanders may not be truly wrong, but it's not right, either, not by a long shot. Count Sandee would not've—"

"Pah!" Prince Byruhn waved a hand through the smoke he had just expelled. "Old Sandee was a senile, doddering fool, and he's well dead, so far as the kingdom's interests are concerned.

"And that, old friend, is all that should be of importance to either of us, just now—the good of the kingdom. You know and I know that my father *must* have more troops, a stronger force in the north . . . and *soon*. Yet there is, or has been, no way that we could strip the garrisons from the safe glens here in the south.

"Oh, not because of fear for our own; the damned Ganiks know better than to try to take one of the glens. But without patrols to sting them now and again, those damned outlaws and their 'peaceable' kin would long since have so incited the Ahrmehnee that we would've found ourselves with an invasion from the southeast as well as from the northwest, and in such a sorry pass, you could kiss the kingdom goodbye. New Kuhmbuhluhn would be ground between the two like grist, and the only sure winners would likely be these contemptible Ganiks.

"What I am doing, what I am having the Kleesahk do for me—for us, all of us, really—is eminently practical and vitally necessary . . . but it is clearly not honorable, and no doubt my overactive conscience will see to it that I suffer long and hard for it, in times to come.

"But for the nonce, old friend, I can see naught else I can do, am I to see the kingdom preserved for my nephew and his sons and theirs. I'll see to it that all of these strangers are amply rewarded for those services they render the kingdom—land, if they want it, gold, if they prefer. Could anything be fairer than that, I ask?"

"Yes," said Sir Steev, "although you'd prefer not to hear it. The fair thing would be to allow them to choose freely, their minds unobscured by the craft of the Kleesahk."

The prince sighed. "Another blunt, honest nobleman today.

And I agree with you . . . up to a point. But what you counsel is the one thing that I cannot afford to chance.

"Don't you see, Steev, with these two-hundred-odd new troops to take command of this glen, I can take two thirds of the present garrison north, along with a good half of the other two garrisons. Not truly large numbers of troops, true, but perhaps enough to tip the balance at a crucial moment . . . and I feel that ultimate test looming closer with every fiber of my body.

"Then, when the outlaws are broken and the man-eating Ganiks have been started moving south, out of our lands and our hair, it will be another matter. Then we will be able to offer free choice to the strangers—either leave unopposed for their own homelands, bearing our sincere thanks and a bit of specie, or take their full oaths to me or to my father and receive lands and possibly a title, if they be gentleborn."

Sir Steev just shook his head. "I can see why my lord prince feels that he must do as he is doing, of course, but still I like it not. It smacks of treachery, to me, and no good ever came from such underhandedness. But I am your man, as you well know, so I will do as I be bid."

Prince Byruhn nodded. "I know, Steev, and I appreciate both your honesty and your loyalty. Here is what I want done. As soon as Duke Bili and his folk are on the hip, you are to form up all of the men who don't have close family ties in this glen. I've figured it closely; that will leave some hundred and fifty men of fighting age to aid and be guides for the strangers, with the young'uns and the gaffers manning the gate and the outer defenses; it's worked before and it will work again, I doubt me not, and it won't be for long, in any case. I don't think that even the hard-core outlaws will try to stand against so many armored professionals on those big horses, not they, who are afraid to stand and fight Ahrmehnee even, unless they outnumber them on an order of ten to one."

Sir Steev frowned. "But the Ganiks are all past-master bushwhackers, and these strangers don't know the country, for all their skills and equipage and fine horseflesh."

"Which is why," Byruhn went on patiently, "every unit of them that rides out of here for whatever purpose will have guides from this glen—men who *do* know the lay of the land hereabouts. Duke Bili himself is extraordinarily gifted with telepathic abilities and certain other rare mental talents that Pah-Elmuh has recognized and noted, and he also has those two prairiecats, so there'll be no bushwhacking of him and his immediate party by Ganiks or anyone else.

"As regards the others, well, our Elmuh desires to stay, ostensibly to see the wounded strangers healthy again, but I think his real reason is his desire to stay near to Duke Bili, and I am inclined to agree. I'll only take four Kleesahk with me, leaving Elmuh and five others here; one or two accompanying each party should preclude any ambushers scoring on them."

"And what of me, lord prince?" inquired Sir Steev. "Do I ride north with my lord or do I remain in Sandee's Cot?"

Rather than answering directly, Byruhn asked, but gently, knowing beforehand that it was a sore point with the late middle-aged warrior. "Steev, are you not the only surviving son of the late Count Sandee?"

"Aye," Sir Steev snapped, his eyes hard and his lips become a thin, straight line. "But never so acknowledged in the count's lifetime, my lord, not even after your grace knighted me and the old man's sons got on the right side of the blanket were all slain."

"Nonetheless, Steev, you know and I know and my father and a goodly number of other folk, as well. Therefore, as you are widely known to be the last living son of Count Sandee, my father and I both agree that it were senseless to allow the title to remain vacant. Before I leave this glen, I intend to publicly invest you, old friend, and you will remain here as the kingdom's Count of the South and, as such, in overall command of the three safe glens, their garrisons and the mobile units between. Is that answer enough to your original question, Count Sandee?" The prince paused, but when no answer was forthcoming, he snapped, "Well, man?"

Poor old Sir Steev gave every appearance of having been clubbed near senseless. He shook his head slowly from side to side and, although his lips moved ceaselessly, no sounds came from between them. At last, he managed to stutteringly mumble, "No . . . but I . . . no, your grace is . . . no, I'm . . . not worthy of such honor . . ."

"Poppycock!" snorted Byruhn. "If I say you're worthy, if my father, the king, says you're worthy, who are you to disagree, eh? And we *do* so say, Count Steev. By fire and Steel, man, you've served the kingdom the most of your life, and served well, too, else you'd not be a knight, gentle blood or no."

The old knight had recovered a little, enough at least to

speak more coherently. "But . . . but only my sire was gentle-born, your grace, and he never once granted me any kind of . . . and my mother was the daughter of a Ganik slave, got by a common man-at-arms, and . . ."

"And no one of us ever got the chance to choose our mothers . . . or our fathers, either, for that matter," stated Byruhn baldly, "and the asinine beliefs of these half-mad Ganiks be damned; we have no choice but to play the cards that fickle fortune deals us, be the total hand good or foul. Agreed?"

When no reply was immediately forthcoming, Byruhn clenched his big right hand and slammed the side of the fist onto the tabletop to get his companion's attention. He did.

"Well, do you agree with your overlord or not, Count Sandee?"

"Oh, my dear lord prince," said Sir Steev, desperation in his voice, "I be but a simple knight-castellan, as your grace must know full well. And I . . ."

"And now I suppose you are going to try to convince me, all else having failed," chuckled Byruhn, again good-natured, "that you have not the wit and experience to manage properly the holdings of a count. Right? Oh, Steev, Steev, old comrade, we are not fools up in New Kuhmbuhluhnburk, you know. We were aware just who was ordering affairs for the County of the South while old Sandee slipped further and further from reality in his senile dotage. Steev, you've been Count of the South for years, in all save name, and it's high time that you bore the title as well as the responsibility, enjoyed the privileges as well as did the work.

"Now, enough of this argument. You have but a bit ago affirmed yourself to be my man and also affirmed your total willingness to obey my orders, whether you agreed with them or not. All right, it is my will that you be invested with the titles and lands of your late father, that you become and remain for life the kingdom's Count of the South.

"Do you obey my dictates, Count Sandee? Or do you brand yourself foresworn and your earlier promises all lies?"

Old Sir Steev slipped from his chair to kneel before his prince, his scarred head hung in silent submission.

Byruhn patted the head affectionately. "Good. Now let's to bed. Tomorrow, we'll two closet with Duke Bili and his captains and start planning our campaign against the Ganiks."

At the appointed hour, Bili and Rahksahnah—who, with

their strikers and bodyguards, had been the only newcomers quartered at the hall, all the rest of the men and women having slept in the tower—strode across the minuscule plain to where the squadron had gathered to await them. Bili noted that all of them appeared fit and well rested and that even a few of the wounded stood among them.

When he had greeted his officers and the two Ahrmehnee headmen, Rahksahnah's lieutenant, Kahndoot, and the two cats, they but recently returned from night-hunting in the country beyond the surrounding crags of the safe glen, he summoned his followers to knot closely around him and addressed them.

He told them of the origins of New Kuhmbuhluhn and of the current problems besetting the realm—alien invaders from the north, outlaw rebels here in the south—and then he told them of the prince's desire that he and they serve him through the worst of the present crisis as a condotta, its principal mission to be that of smashing the outlaws, then harrying the cannibal Ganiks so severely that they would flee their holdings and leave the Kingdom.

He had told Prince Byruhn that he would leave the final decision to his followers, and he intended to do just so. Therefore, he made no attempt to persuade them one way or the other, simply stating facts, but drawing no personal conclusions from those facts, not that he imparted to them, at least. For he privately faced the fact that the suspicions of the duplicity of the prince he had mindspoken to Rahksahnah last night could be groundless and completely unwarranted. They could simply be bred of his long sojourn in the court and army of a king whom even his staunchest supporters—he had no friends—freely admitted was as devious as a viper. Perhaps he was wrong to ascribe to this Prince Byruhn the amorality of the Iron King.

As he spoke to his followers, he noted concern on many faces. Studying especially the Kindred and Ehleen nobility from the lands of the Confederation, he found what he surmised was anger at being detained and impatience to start back to the border and their homes.

Toward the end of his oration, the deep notes of an infantry bugle sounded from the direction of the main gate to the glen; the call sounded to him much like the one used in Harzburk to mark the change of the guard. But with the sounding of that mundane call, a visible stir seemed to pass quickly through those gathered about him, and before he could even finish that which he meant to say, he was deferentially interrupted by Lieutenant Brakit.

"My lord, if you please . . . ?"

"Yes, Brakit, you have a question?" asked Bili impatiently, anxious to finish his statements as soon as possible.

"No, my lord," answered the officer. "It is just that, with my lord's kind leave, I would serve the prince and New Kuhmbuhluhn. Only peace awaits now in the Ahrmehnee *Stahn* or in the Confederation, and peace offers no loot and precious little income for a professional soldier."

A chorus of nods and grunts of agreement and approval came from the other Freefighters. But Bili had fully expected such, and had he been in their places would probably have felt and acted the same. For why ride the hundreds of long, dusty miles up to the Middle Kingdoms to find employment when a small war existed right here where they now stood?

But then Vahrtahn Panosyuhn spoke, saying, "Dook Bili, we Ahrmehnee, too, would stand with, ride with, fight with this Prince Byruhn, for these accursed Muhkohee . . . er, Ganiks, are our ancient foes, too. It would be a very good thing for our *stahn*, the driving of them south and west and away from our borders."

The Moon Maiden, Lieutenant Kahdoot, put in, "I know not how feels in this matter the *brahbehrnuh*, but she and all the Maidens recall should that slay and drive mad many of our ancestors did these Ganiks. More they slay did back on the Tongue of Soormehlyuhn. And for vengeance these many blood debts now cry. Under the banner of this kingdom, exact the last drop of that vengeance we can."

So far, it had all gone about as Bili had expected it to go, although far sooner and without the arguments he had anticipated. But now he got the unmitigated shock of his life.

"My lord *thoheeks?*" Bili recognized the man pushing his way through to the front of the throng as Mikos of Eeahnospolis, a *kath-ahrohs*—pure-blooded, or at least reasonably pure-blooded—Ehleen who had remained loyal to the Confederation in the late rebellion and had fought for almost a year against his own kin and co-religionists.

The stocky young nobleman—he was some two or three years older than Bili—was as darkly handsome as any Ahrmehnee, and the new, purplish scars—one down his cheek from within his straight hair to the knob of muscle at the angle of his jaw, the other across his square chin—served to impart a rakish, dangerous appearance. Bili recalled that he was the one who had flatly refused to charge the "monster" yesterday morning, but also recalled that his valor could not be questioned on full many another occasion. One of those livid scars came from the second attack of the rebel cavalry during the march into Vawn. Mikos had been one of those valiant few score led by old *Thoheeks* Kehn Kahr, who had died in that furious melee along with many another. Bili had seen the other scar inflicted, while Mikos was taking part in one of the last assaults against the walls of Vawnpolis.

He raised a hand in greeting. "The doughty heir of Eeahnospolis. I suppose you're fairly itching to get back home, eh, Mikos? I can't say that I blame you much; it's probably full spring down that way, now."

Mikos nodded. "Aye, lord *thoheeks*, I long to see my home again, and yesterday this time I would've spoken firmly against the Freefighters and Ahrmehnee and Maidens. But I thought hard on the matter in the night, and now I feel some different.

"These Ganiks are a terrible folk; they give new depth and meaning to the word 'barbarian.' Such vile creatures should not be allowed to live . . . at least, not anywhere in proximity to decent people. And also, we all owe Prince Byruhn a debt.

"We all would likely be dead or worse by now, had he not come out and brought us back to this safe place, something he had no obligation to do, but did anyway. Nor can many of us forget the miraculous things that his Master Elmuh did and has continued to do for our wounded.

"Why, Lord Vlahkos Kamruhn of Skaht, *Vahrohneeskos* Gneedos's younger brother, though still weak, stands in this very throng today, when we all had thought this time yesterday that we were wise to start gathering wood for his pyre. Nor is he the only one; Captain of Freefighters Tyluh, though not really conscious yet, swallowed some thin broth for Master Elmuh this morning.

"And," Mikos then asked, "did my lord *thoheeks* not tell us all when we joined him on his dash westward that the High Lord informed him that the Ahrmehnee *Stahn* will be joining this Confederation of ours?"

All Bili said was, "Yes, Lord Mikos."

"Then," asserted Mikos, "what sort of allies would they think us Ehleenee and Kindred to be if we proved more interested in getting quickly back home than in helping them to drive an old and serious menace from their border?"

Then the crowning shock came to Bili of Morguhn. Another chorus—this one all of Confederation nobility, every man jack of them!—of vocalized agreement and quite a few mindspeak beamings from Kindred confirming full assent to the words of Mikos Eeahnospolis smote ears and mind alike.

Never before, in all of his dealings with them, had he experienced or even heard of any aggregation of the hot-blooded, fractious, often-brawling Confederation noblemen agreeing on anything, not if given time and leave to "discuss" the issue. Even in the deadly serious meetings of the war council of the High Lord during the march upon Vawnpolis and the subsequent siege, it had often been all that the High Lord, the High Lady, Sir Ehd Gahthwahlt, the *ahrkeetho-heeks* and Bili could do to keep steel from being drawn and used by the proud, stubborn and temperamental *thoheeksee* of western Karaleenos. What had just occurred here, this morning, was completely unnatural!

CHAPTER XIV

Despite the incense smoldering atop the coals in the many braziers, the room already stank of death to any with senses unclouded by drugs, but the big old man on the big wide bed still lived, though only the movements of his chest and the occasional flutter of an eyelid gave such notice.

But Bili of Morguhn was not presently in that ancient, injured dying husk on the bed. He was in the young, strong, healthy and vibrant body of the country nobleman he once had been: Bili, *Thoheeks* and chief of Clan Morguhn, who had fought through the whole of the Great Rebellion with the High Lord Milo and the High Lady Aldora, and had gone on into the bitter campaign in the Ahrmehnee Mountains . . . and then even farther west into uncharted lands and dangers.

What had brought him back to this weak and dying hulk of aged flesh and brittle bones? He had been happy back there, back then, reliving again the prologue to the most exciting period of his long career, those months of bitter sweet memory, nearly seventy years ago. Then something, someone, had called him back to the present, summoned him back into the wreck that old age and injury had made of that once-mighty body, now slowly sliding into death.

Then it came once more, a tentative, questing mental probe. It was familiar, or once had been so; if only his mind were clear . . .

"Bili? Bili of Morguhn? My dear love, do still you live?"

He forced open his veined and sticky eyelids. He could discern little in the smoky dimness of the bedchamber, but could still see well enough to feel certain that no one had joined him here in this room of imminent death. A ghost, perhaps? Piffle! Even with his great and most unusual extrasensory abilities, he never had detected any such thing and was of the firm opinion that ghosts—if they existed at all—existed in the minds of the living. In the mind . . . *mindspeak!*

"Who calls Bili of Morguhn?" he beamed with a power still undiminished by his physical debility.

"You do still live then, my dear, dear, old love." There was relief in the dimly perceived beaming. "I . . . I had feared that . . . that I had waited too long, my Bili."

"My lady . . . ?"

"Yes, love, it's me, Aldora."

"Please forgive me for worrying you, my lady. It's the drugs of the Zahrtohgahn, they ease pain but also serve to cloud the other senses, to greater or lesser degrees. And, too, I . . . my mind was a-journeying far back in time, to the time just after the Great Rebellion, when . . ."

"Oh, yes, my dearest one, I think that those were the last truly happy years of my long, long life. Those precious years when you and your little children lived with me in Kehnooryos Atheenahs."

"I had not relived so far yet, my lady. I was still in New Kuhmbuhluhn with Prince Byruhn, the Kleesahk and . . . and my Rahksahnah."

"Yeeesss . . . ?" Acid dripped from her beaming. "It is interesting that the near-final thoughts of a man I—Aldora Linsze Treeah-Pohtohmas-Pahpahs, the Undying High Lady of the Confederation and the Sea Isles—honored with my love and favor for most of his life, should be of a man-hating, half-Ahrmehnee slut he knew but for . . . how short a time was it, Prince Morguhn?"

"My lady, my lady," Bili tiredly remonstrated, as often before in the long, long ago, "even when I told her of you, of what you and I had together shared, Rahksahnah never resented you, nor did she ever speak ill of you. Why then do you still so resent and vilify a long-dead woman whom you never even met during her lifetime? Why, my lady?"

There was a note of repentance, of regret, in her next beaming. "Why, Bili? Do you not know why? You should, if great age truly imparts great wisdom . . . which old saw I tend to doubt, and on far better grounds than most could produce.

"Because I love you, Bili. Because frustrated women become bitchy, and I have nurtured my love and harbored my frustration for more than three score years. Because that nasty mixture of love and frustration, that unbearable turgidity that my soul became when I finally faced the fact that soon or late I would lose, would be forever denied him that I so loved . . . so love, even now . . . seems to find and enjoy

its fullest release by striking hurtfully at my very love
through one that I know he loved, then lost.

"Dear, sweet Bili, I truly, truly am sorry for what I said. I
do not—have never done so—hate your Rahksahnah or
resent her. May Wind grant her repose in His Home. . . . I
right often wish truly that I might soon be vouchsafed the
sweet blessing of death, that we three—I and you and your
Rahksahnah, too—might ride the endless plains of the Home
of Wind. I could even share you, my Bili, did I but know
that we would never be parted, that the one could never outlive the other for the rest of eternity.

"And when I dream again those happy, hopeless dreams, I
think that the old Ehleen blackrobes were right, even more
right than they could have imagined. We Undying are
cursed—really and truly cursed, though not in the way those
vultures meant the term—to live endless years without one to
love, that is the curse, Bili, to be fearful of allowing oneself
to bestow love as Nature intended it be bestowed, that is both
foul curse and eternal damnation.

"Within bare weeks of our first meeting, Bili, I had come
to love you far more deeply than ever before I had loved any
man—and I was older than you now are, even then. Milo
saw it, knew it for the soul-deep love that it was and tried to
warn me of the certain agonies it would surely breed; and I
knew deep within me that he was right, too, but who ever
could argue an effective case against so powerful an emotion
as love?

"When I could not raise your mind, could not farspeak
you for so long a time, while you were in New
Kuhmbuhluhn, I was forced to reluctantly agree with the majority opinion, that you were dead; and, although my grief
was almost insupportable, I could still not help feeling in a
way relieved, relieved that your untimely death had thus
ended something harmful to me that I would not have been
able to muster the courage, the resolution, to end finally and
for all time while still you lived.

"But then, love, when I had almost recovered and had already set about seducing Drehkos, one of my own, cursed
kind, you reappeared; riding your big, black horse out of the
unknown and back into my life. That Bili was not the same
as he who rode into those unmapped lands; the Bili who rode
out was far older and wiser than his years, aged and altered
by care and suffering. But that love that I so prized and so
feared did not recognize or care, rather did it spring in a bare

moment into full and vibrant blossom, like some lovely, magical, but dreaded flower.

"And that old, old flower is in full blossom still, my dearest, although its cruel thorns have raked and torn my heart each day and night of the forty years since last I saw you, touched you . . . kissed you. Oh, dear Bili, did you not ever wonder why I have mindspoken you occasionally, yet never have come near to you, have indeed so arranged my travels that we two never would be in the same place at the same time?"

"I knew, my lady, I knew why," Bili answered gently. "The Lady Mara once tried to tell me why, so too did Tim and Gil, but they could sense in my mind that there was no reason, that I knew . . . and understood, for I have never ceased to love you, my lady, or to miss your dear self beside me, by day and by night, and I too have often wished that we might grow old together and, finally, go to Wind together. But wishing will not, cannot make it come to pass.

"Yes, my lady, life and the forces that serve to shape it have treated us two and the love we shared most cruelly. But then that is the way of life and our world, Aldora. It is rare that they treat love or lovers kindly, be those lovers Undying or mortals.

"But, my love, you must not speak of, think of, ending your life prematurely, for this great Confederation of ours, its tens of thousands of folk, depend in many ways upon you and your countless talents."

"But . . . but, Bili, you are . . . are dying, they all say. It has been hard enough to bear when you were but a day's ride distant, when I could, if I wished, mindspeak with you. Oh, my dear love, how can I live on the endless, empty years with you gone forever?"

"You will live one day after the other, Aldora, and someday, somehow, somewhere, Nature will compensate your loss—though you may not immediately recognize that compensation for what it really is. This is fact, not speculation, my love, I know of my own experiences. You are being robbed of but one love, Aldora, but think you back—I have been denied every woman I ever loved, by death or by unalterable circumstance.

"I, too, have suffered, Aldora, for the most part of what has been a very long life . . . for a mortal man. Suicide would have been easy for me, for I do not fear death. Right often over the years have I contemplated or even fondled some dirk or dagger of mine, absently weighing the slight and fleeting bite of the steel against the long, dull suffering it would so quickly assuage, erase forever.

"But then, always, have I recalled my duties, my many responsibilities to my overlords and the Confederation, to the folk I rule and administer, to my clan and house. So I always have sheathed the bright, sharp steel and forgotten it in the press of everyday affairs. So must you put aside your disloyal, selfish thoughts, Aldora, remembering instead your duties and all those—many of them still unborn—who depend and will depend upon you."

Then he asked, "Are you here, love, in my palace?"

There was infinite sadness and a touch of shame in her beaming. "No, my Bili, no. I am far north and west, with the army, in the southerly reaches of what used to be the Kingdom of Ohyoh, years back. I . . . I could not force myself to come to your . . . your death, Bili. I would . . . I must remember you as . . . as you were when last we met . . . and loved. So I sent Tim, instead; he might even be there by now, if he was blessed with dry roads and no delays."

"Then, are we to converse more while still we can, Aldora, you must range me again in a few hours. The pain is returning, stronger this time. I must mindcall the physician, and you will not be able to get through to my mind while his drugs are in full effect. I regret this necessity, my dear, but this pain is more than I can endure."

"So, you see, Tim," said Milo, "although it will probably mean I'll have to take your place with the army in the field, for however long it takes us to find and groom a new prince, it is imperative that Karaleenos in particular remain under a firm, strong hand after Bili's death. Aldora is a superlative tactician, especially of cavalry, but she had never been a talented strategist, as you are by now aware. Drehkos is much like her in that respect. Also, I don't know how this Confederation of ours would get along without him administering its affairs from Theesispolis.

"Mara is a good fighter, as too are Gil and Neeka, but none of them has ever shown any military command potential. So you must stay here, in Karaleenos, for a while and I must go back into active campaigning, in the west, for the same amount of time. That's just the way the stick floats, Tim."

"And what of me?" demanded Gil. "Can I stay here, with Tim, or must I go back up to Theesispolis?"

Milo smiled. "Do whichever you wish, Gil. Neeka goes west with me, but I'm certain Drehkos and Mara can fumble along without the two of you for a while. If they should need help for some reason or other, you're not very far from the capital, here. Besides, if you're here with him, there'll certainly be a bit less fast and frequent traffic on the roads between here and Theesispolis."

Tim and Gil, sitting each with an arm about the well-loved other and hands clasped tightly, looked and radiated their pleasure at the arrangement. But Neeka's sloe-black eyes regarded Milo with a look compounded of trouble, unease and hurt.

A little later, when Tim and Gil had departed the tower chamber that Tim might bathe, sleep and restore himself after his long, hard journey, Neeka asked, softly. "Why are you taking me west with you, Milo? Is it because you truly want me near to you? Or is it really because you still distrust me?"

Milo drank from his silver goblet, regarding the saturnine beauty over the chased rim, with a look of mockery and mirth.

"Distrust you?" he mindspoke, on a level which very few anywhere in the Confederation could have intercepted. "Of course not, girl, you're being silly. I did at one time, twenty years or so back, and with good cause, you must admit. But when once we'd delved the furthest corners of your mind, gotten to and first explored, then thwarted or prepared for our own use all of those subconscious guides and instructions that those devilish Witchmen had implanted, there was no longer any slightest reason to distrust you.

"No, pet, I'm taking you with me for the simplest and the most basic of reasons: still, after nearly a half century, do I lust after that fine, ripe body of yours. Campaigning in those mountains is no fun, especially for a commander. Aldora is certain to have chosen herself a lover or five from among her officers, for as rank hath its responsibilities, rank also hath its privileges. Moon Maidens are just not to my rather discriminating tastes—too skinny and muscular and flat-chested, most of them. So why not take along a woman who does suit my fancy, eh?"

Neeka treated him to a sidelong gaze and a quick half-smile, which fleeted across her full, dark-red lips, then was gone. Picking absorbedly at the gold-thread embroidery of her garments, she mindspoke on the same vastly advanced level. Of all the Undying—Milo, Mara, Aldora, Drehkos, Tim and Gil—only Neeka, Aldora, Milo and one mortal man, who now lay dying in this very palace, had ever been able to attain the use of that level of communication.

"Naturally, I'm flattered, Milo. What seventy-odd-year-old woman wouldn't be? And while I know I would be very happy there, with *you*, still I think it best that I stay in the capital, or at least somewhere here in the east."

His brows elevated sharply. "Why, Neeka? Have you, then, tired of this exceedingly ancient one as a lover?"

She flushed, then smiled. "I'll make a note to remind you of that question whenever we two get a chance to bed together again. No, that's not it at all, and if I thought your doubt serious, I'd feel deeply hurt, Milo.

"No, rather it's that damned Aldora; she hates me, always has, and makes no secret of it in any company or none. I feel certain that she would prefer to see me dead, did she think she could get away with it."

"You fear her, then, Neeka?" asked Milo.

"Not really, no. I used to, but not anymore. It's just that I know that if I go with you, she will make us both miserable until I come back here; just as she did Tim and Gil, until Gil stopped campaigning with Tim. It seems she hates Gil, too."

Milo sighed and set down his goblet. "Neeka, Aldora hates any woman who seems happy, not just you and Gil and Mara, but mortal women, too. Although she is extremely promiscuous—openly and deliberately—she has never loved deeply but three times in all her years. One of those men was her adoptive father, the chief who led Clan Linszee to Ehlai when the Horseclans came to Kehnooryos Ehlas, and he has been dead over a century; the other mortal she loved is this same Prince Bili, who now lies dying, downstairs; the third is me, but I never have reciprocated her passion, and she has long since given up trying to arouse any in me.

"But she still craves, must have, my approval, it seems. When I threatened to have her forcibly ejected from the Confederation proper, threatened to force her to either live on the Pirate Archipelago or leave this part of the world altogether, after she made a nearly successful attempt to drown Mara, some sixty-odd years back, she and I came to an understanding of sorts. That understanding still holds between me and Aldora, Neeka.

"So if we—you and I—campaign together, Aldora will be the very proper co-commander. Not that she'll desist of her hate and her envy of you; that would be just too much to ask of her. But she'll not make open display of it, for she fears to anger me. She knows that her soul needs my support, even if it can never have my love."

One of Milo's bodyguards knocked, then entered at the summons. "Lord Milo, Lady Neeka, the Zahrtohgahn, Master Ahkmehd, craves audience; he waits beyond the door."

The slight, deeply wrinkled, dark-brown man who entered the portal held open for him by the bodyguard knew both Milo and Neeka of old. He had served several years in Theesispolis before becoming Prince Bili's personal physician and trusted friend nearly forty years before. Milo arose to clasp the pink-palmed hand warmly, then assisted the aged Zahrtohgahn to a seat on one of the couches.

Then the High Lord said, "I'm afraid that there's nothing to drink here that your religion will allow you, master."

The dark-skinned old man showed worn yellow teeth in a hint of a smile. "Thank you, my lord, it does not matter; I drink little save herb teas, anyway, these last few years. Nor do most foods any longer attract me. I only eat because I know that my body requires the sustenance.

"I come to you because you wished to know of aught of an unusual nature concerning poor old Bili . . . the prince, that is. I have but just come from him."

"And . . . ?" inquired Milo.

"I have been using a combination of drugs and hypnotism to relieve him of his agonies, while my apprentice and I seek and search and experiment in thus-far-vain attempts to come up with something, some combination, that might possibly halt these hideous infections and possibly grant my old friend down there a few more years of life.

"Because of the hypnosis, I have been able to graduate the levels of the drugs slowly, thus keeping him comfortable without endangering his life with the drugs themselves—some of them are deadly poisons, you know, in the proper combinations or proportions.

"I had dosed him again and reinforced the hypnosis a bit after dawn, which should have kept him in comfort through the most of this day. But someone, someone with a very high level of mindspeak ability, intruded into his mind and dispelled the soothing web I had woven there. In his pain, he mind-called me, and I have just had to redo my work. Worse, I have had to administer more drugs.

"Can my lord see to it that this happens not again? I say not, with any certainty, that any decoction Ohmahr and I may devise will or can save Lord Bili's life, but while still he lives there is at least the bare chance."

Milo fiercely cracked his knuckles, cold anger on his face and in his voice. "You're damned right I'll see that it happens not again, Master Ahkmehd! Did you . . . were you able to get from Bili the name of the person responsible this time?"

The elderly man sighed and spread his hands—withered, in appearance like the rest of his body, but still as strong and as sure as those of the apprentice who was nearly fifty years his junior. "There were two names tumbling over and over in his mind and his speech, Lord Milo. Rahksahnah—that was one of them."

The High Lord shook his head. "No, that was the name of Bili's first wife. She's long dead. What was the other?"

"Aldora, my lord. I presume he meant the High Lady . . . but she is not here, in the palace, not that I know of, anyway. One of the High Lord Tim's guards mentioned to someone that the Illustrious Lady Aldora was far and far to the north, with the Army of the Confederation. Has she the power to do so much at such a distance, Lord Milo?"

Milo grimaced. "That much and more, master. But I'll warn her off, never fear. When you leave, tell my guards to send the prairiecats that came with me up here to me; with the aid of their minds, I can range Aldora. She has no right to kill Bili with her selfishness.

"I know what she must be suffering, for she has loved him—deeply and truly—for more than seventy years. But she is not the only one put out by this tragedy. Bili the Axe was a most unusual man, we'll all miss him sorely, and I doubt that we'll ever find again such a man to hold Karaleenos for us, for the Confederation."

ABOUT THE AUTHOR

ROBERT ADAMS lives in Seminole County, Florida. Like the characters in his books, he is partial to fencing and fancy swordplay, hunting and riding, good food and drink. At one time Robert could be found slaving over a hot forge, making a new sword or busily reconstructing a historically accurate military costume, but, unfortunately, he no longer has time for this as he's far too busy writing.